THE THRONE OF THORNATA

THE THRONE OF THORNATA

PETE BIEHL

First hardcover edition May 2022

Cover Art by Joseph Gruber
Map by Joseph Gruber

The Throne of Thornata

ISBN 978-1-7365286-3-1 (hardcover)
ISBN 978-1-7365286-4-8 (paperback)
ISBN 978-1-7365286-5-5 (ebook)

www.petebiehl.com

For Dad,
Gone but not forgotten.

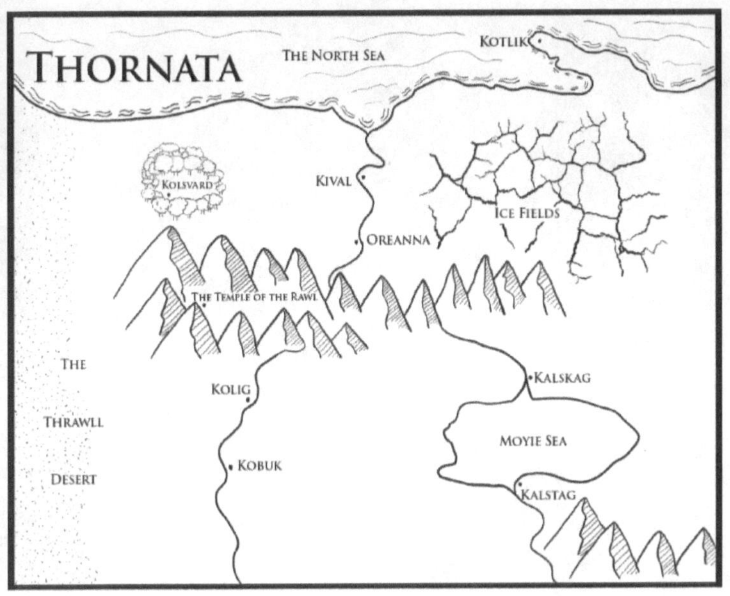

THORNATA
THE NORTH SEA
KOTLIK
KOLSVARD
KIVAL
ICE FIELDS
OREANNA
THE TEMPLE OF THE RAWL
THE
THRAWLL
DESERT
KOLIG
KALSKAG
MOYIE SEA
KOBUK
KALSTAG

Chapter One

Idanox had never been a man who found himself easily disturbed. Still, while listening to the mage Srenpe lay out everything he would need for the task at hand, he had felt the slightest touch of a chill run down the length of his spine. The outcast mage had been evasive over the past few weeks about what exactly his allegedly brilliant plan entailed. The more information his men reported to him on Srenpe's activities and demands, the more Idanox began to fear he should have demanded more details before paying the mage half of his fee up front. It had come as a surprise when Srenpe had come to the Hoyt leader the night before and informed him he would soon be ready to put his plans into motion. Per the mage's earlier estimates, Idanox had expected it to be another week or two before the project was prepared to execute.

Second thoughts had crept into Idanox's mind ever since forging a partnership with this dark mage. Each time, he had forced such doubts into the back of his mind, telling himself the ends would justify the means. The fact of the matter was that he needed the young Rawl wielder disposed of, and he had no better options available. His own men had proven incapable, and the mage had the type of nasty reputation Idanox felt would be helpful. He had led the Hoyt to the verge of total victory before the boy's interference. It could not be allowed to continue. However, there was no denying that Srenpe was a dangerous man, and an alliance with him could prove to be equally dangerous. He was already planning contingencies, methods of breaking the partnership in a less than ceremonial manner if necessary. It would've been unwise to enter an alliance with such an unpredictable man without a means in place of ending it violently if needed.

But there was no point in dwelling on his doubts now. The partnership had been forged despite Idanox's various misgivings, and mulling over his qualms about it did him no good. His only option now was to hope it would produce the results he desperately needed. Winter would begin to break in a matter of weeks, and he needed the Rawl wielder dead and gone as soon as possible. He had already lost far more men than he could afford.

Allowing the boy to continue running around the province and disrupting his plans at every turn was out of the question. For the time being, an alliance with Srenpe was the lesser of two evils.

One of his lieutenants had entered the room he had been using as an office since his arrival in Kolsvard in late autumn. Idanox guessed his purpose before the man could open his mouth. Srenpe was ready to begin whatever it was he was going to do. His men had spent the last three days preparing everything Srenpe had requested of them. None of them had been able to relay to their leader what the mage's plans entailed. Each had been trusted with a few specific tasks and given no explanations. All they had been able to relay was that Srenpe insisted every detail be prepared precisely as he requested. Whatever the mage was planning, he wanted it to be a surprise for everyone else.

The chill in his spine intensified, a chill which had nothing to do with the bitterly cold Thornatan winter night. To what madness had he committed himself with this mage? Telling himself for what felt like the thousandth time that this was a necessity, he rose to his feet, wrapping his black cloak around his shoulders. There was no reason to delay; the sooner he got this over with, the sooner he could be rid of the Rawl wielder and Srenpe. If the Hoyt did not return to their planned business soon, another year would pass before he could seize control of the province. The brutal climate of the far northern province proved to be a hindrance as often as a boon. He followed his lieutenant down the corridor into the large wide-open room Srenpe had requested for his work.

"Good evening, Idanox. What a lovely evening, is it not? Are you ready to begin?" Srenpe said as soon as he stepped through the door.

The Hoyt leader looked around, hoping to glean some idea of what the mage was planning. To his surprise, he found the vast room relatively empty. When Srenpe had requested a large room for his work, Idanox had expected to find a much more elaborate arrangement. Srenpe had requested so many items in preparation that he had expected to find the room full of various materials and odd contraptions. As usual, Srenpe was dressed all in robes of crimson, and his staff was lying on a table at his side. There was an odd assortment of herbs and powders that he had requested along with it. Idanox noted that the most unusual of his requests had not been brought into the chamber yet.

I hope for your sake you are not wasting my time, mage.

"I am ready, but do you plan on explaining this grand scheme of yours first, Srenpe?" Idanox asked, making a concerted effort not to let any hint of a tremble creep into his voice. In every encounter, he had worked carefully to display an image of utmost confidence to Srenpe. This dark mage was not a man who Idanox wanted to sense weakness at any time.

"Of course I will explain, my dear friend. But it would be for the best if I begin and then explain as I go.

Things will be so much easier to understand if I do. There is not much point in me standing here and giving you a long-winded explanation now. You will find this is a matter you will understand much better with a visual aid," Srenpe replied, a sly smile twisting across his face.

Resisting the urge to remind the mage of the fact they were not friends in any sense of the word, Idanox contented himself with giving a curt nod. Srenpe turned to the Hoyt men Idanox had assigned to work for him and began murmuring instructions, careful to keep his face averted from Idanox.

Secretive to the last, Idanox thought to himself, irritated once more by the mage's deceptive nature. The assistants were moving to a door at the far end of the chamber. They returned within moments, along with the most curious of Srenpe's requests.

The Thornatan soldier was shackled at the wrists and ankles, shuffling awkwardly along the floor of the long dark room until he was directly in front of the mage. The Hoyt men he had tasked with this job had done well; he perfectly fit the request. He was quite a large man, well over six feet tall and muscular. Srenpe had stressed to no end the need for the man to be as large as possible, again offering no explanation.

As he stepped into the light at the center of the chamber, only the soldier's eyes showed the slightest hint of uncertainty; the rest of his face remaining defiant in the face of his captors. Idanox had to admire his ability to conceal his fear. The man must've realized this night would not have a happy ending for him.

"Welcome, my friend. Thank you for joining us here tonight. My name is Srenpe. May I ask yours?" Srenpe greeted the soldier as though he were welcoming an old friend into his home for supper.

"Kill me and be done with it, Hoyt scum. There is no need to waste your time with these benign pleasantries." The soldier's voice was hollow and empty, as though he was already resigned to his fate. There was not a quiver in his tone despite his impending doom. Once again, Idanox could not help but admire the man's courage in the face of certain death.

"Oh no, my dear man, I'm afraid you are terribly mistaken. It's quite understandable, of course, considering the circumstances of your arrival here. Please, rest assured, I am no Hoyt. I am a mage in service to the Order of Mages. I merely asked for the assistance of the Hoyt in bringing you here. I have absolutely no intention of killing you. I apologize profusely if that is the impression you have been operating under this evening. You have my word." Srenpe's smile was quite disarming, and his voice sounded as though he were trying to soothe a nervous kitten. Idanox shifted uneasily, disturbed by how Srenpe was able to make himself appear so kind and feeble. Was there already some sort of magic at work in the mage's words?

"My name is Quentin," the soldier replied, his stance softening ever so slightly. Idanox's respect for the soldier fell somewhat. What type of fool would buy Srenpe's act, no matter how convincing? No doubt, the man wanted to cling to any shred of hope he could find. Desperation had never been an excuse for ignorance in Idanox's mind.

"It's my pleasure to meet you, Quentin. I have brought you here because I am hoping you will agree to help me with an experiment I wish to conduct. I am a professor for the Order of Mages, you see, and I travel across the Empire seeking answers to the great questions of life. I have come to this place to study the various herbs growing in this region. Thornata is a remarkable place, with a climate the like of which cannot be found elsewhere in the Empire," the mage explained, gesturing toward the assortment of herbs and powders on the table, the reassuring smile never leaving his face. "The pine forests surrounding this city, in particular, are an ideal environment for certain herbs I have been studying."

"I know nothing about herbs. What help can I possibly be?" Quentin was obviously skeptical.

That makes two of us, Idanox thought to himself, growing more impatient with Srenpe's little game by the second.

"You have not eaten today, have you, Quentin? I can only assume my Hoyt helpers have not been particularly hospitable to you. Once again, I must apologize most profusely. If there were gentler helpers available to me in this city, I would have requested their assistance.

Sometimes we need to have partnerships with those we deem unsavory in the name of the greater good. I have their assurance they will set you free once you have assisted me."

Idanox scowled at this statement; he had made no such assurance.

"It is fortunate for you that I am studying the effects of one herb in particular. I believe when mixed with water, this herb can relieve the pangs of hunger! Such an incredible discovery if true, is it not? Can you imagine the implications such a discovery would wield? We could put an end to poor children dying of starvation in the streets!"

Idanox was growing impatient with this spectacle. He could not possibly care any less if this soldier's belly was empty, and he would not be releasing him, no matter what promises Srenpe was making. He was beginning to suspect this mage was making a fool of him, and if he was correct, Srenpe would also not be leaving this room alive. Still, he had gone along with this farce so far. What harm could come from letting the mage finish his asinine little game? If Srenpe wanted to continue to dig his grave deeper, that was his business.

"That would be quite impressive, Professor Srenpe. But I'm afraid I still don't understand why you needed to kidnap me for this experiment," Quentin said.

"A fair question, my good man. As I'm sure you realize, Quentin, these outlaws you find yourself surrounded with have taken their share of losses lately,"

Srenpe said, enraging the Hoyt leader even further. "As such, it is hard for them to feed all of their men, so they asked me to find a solution. We have a business partnership, you see. They protect me while I am in the wild doing my studies, and I do what I can to assist them with feeding and healing their fighters. The sacrifices we make in the name of the greater good can be rather unpleasant at times, as I'm sure you understand. However, they are quite stubborn, and none of them wish to be my test subjects. They have no such qualms about experimenting on you. I'm sure you would expect nothing less from such men. As I said, it is a partnership born out of need. I bear no more love for the Hoyt than you do."

"I have your word I will be allowed to leave if I help you with this experiment?" the soldier asked.

"You have my word, Quentin. These men have given me theirs as well, and they have never disappointed me, at least not when it comes to keeping a promise."

Idanox could not help but begrudgingly admire the mage's acting skills. Whatever else he may be, Srenpe was a master manipulator, a trait the Hoyt leader admired. Idanox could see shades of himself in the mage's lies, though he was far superior at the art of deception.

"Very well then. Let's get on with it."

"Wonderful! Thank you, my friend! You are making a real difference today, and if this works as I think it will, we could end hunger and starvation across the Empire! Men, women, and children in poverty will owe you a debt forevermore, Quentin!" Srenpe cried out, flourishing his arms dramatically for effect. "If I have it my way, there will be an Imperial holiday named in your honor!"

Beaming ear to ear, Srenpe turned back to the tables and began crushing herbs and powders together. He was taking great care that the soldier could not see any of what he was doing as he poured the mixture into a vial of water and began to shake the ingredients together. Within moments he had produced a dark green liquid, which he spun with great enthusiasm to display to the captive soldier.

"That did not take long at all, did it, Quentin? Such a simple formula. Imagine the possibilities! Please drink up, my friend. I am sure you are famished," Srenpe urged, beaming as widely as ever.

Quentin took the vile in his shackled hands, holding it close to his face to examine it. The green liquid did not look particularly appealing to the increasingly impatient Idanox, but the hungry soldier seemed hopeful. His eyes darted from the mage's encouraging smile to the vial before he finally moved it to his lips and began to drink. Once he had finished, he returned the flask to the still-beaming Srenpe.

"How are you feeling, Quentin? Can you feel the hunger fading away? Please describe everything you are experiencing after drinking the concoction; no detail is too small for my research," the mage said eagerly.

"I think so, but it's a strange feeling. It feels like a warmth spreading through my entire body. I can feel it everywhere—in my fingers, in my toes. It does not feel normal, though it doesn't hurt," Quentin replied, an uncertain look on his face.

"Excellent. That is precisely what I was hoping to hear! Such things do take some getting used to after all," Srenpe exclaimed.

Furious, Idanox stepped forward, ready to signal his men to put an end to both of these fools for having the audacity to waste his time. But without warning, Srenpe snatched his staff from the table and thrust it toward the captive Quentin. A loud crack emitted from the staff as though a lightning bolt had struck the inside of the building. The sound froze Idanox in his tracks. A brilliant purple light began to emanate from the staff, completely enveloping the soldier, whose face had lost all illusion of composure. The horrified screaming began, though it would prove to be short-lived as the soldier started to change.

His size was the first change. His large frame expanded, growing even taller and broader. The horrific grinding sound his bones made as they stretched and expanded was one Idanox suspected he would never forget. Quentin was larger than an ogre by the time the growing stopped, yet the changes to his body had only just begun. His facial features, already contorted in an expression of sheer agony, began to twist further, becoming beast-like, as though a human had been crossed with a wild bear. His nose stretched from his face like a snout, and though it was hard to be sure in the blinding purple light, Idanox thought his teeth were becoming sharper.

Srenpe's spell was having an impact on the man's skin as well; it was hardening like a rock, and soon the color began to change. As the purple light began to dissipate, Idanox moved in for a closer look at the man's face. Had he not witnessed what had happened, he would not have believed the creature standing before him had been a human moments earlier.

The monstrous creature stood remarkably still. Its only movement was the occasional blink of feral eyes that no longer showed any trace of the man who had stood in its place moments before. They were no longer the eyes of a human but those of a feral predator. Srenpe was conducting an exam of his own, circling the beast, taking in every inch of its features. He would occasionally touch it or prod at it with his staff while muttering to himself. When he seemed satisfied, he turned back to Idanox, beaming.

"Magnificent creature, isn't it, Idanox? I think this will serve your needs quite well. Don't you agree?" Srenpe said, turning toward Idanox at last.

"Is he still alive? Can he hear us?" Idanox asked, observing the creature, his emotions a mix of awe and disgust. He took a tentative step closer, taking care to stay out of reach of the enormous monster.

"Valid questions. The answer to both is yes, however, not in the sense you are thinking. The man known as

Quentin is no more. I could not restore him even if I wanted to, though I do not see what value there would be in doing so. His mind has effectively been removed, replaced with pure, savage instinct. However, his body is still here and quite improved, ready to serve you," Srenpe explained.

"It can follow commands?"

"Beast, break your shackles!" Srenpe snapped at the creature.

Without hesitation, the beast flung its arms wide, effortlessly snapping the iron shackles that had held its hands in place. The chains around its ankles met the same fate a moment later. Srenpe had moved away and was now returning with two large battle-axes, yet another of the requests he had made for his preparation. The axes were massive; any ordinary man would need both hands to wield one effectively, yet this beast took one in each hand as though each weighed no more than a pigeon egg.

"It will follow any order you give. It does not feel pain. It does not feel fear. It will not question any command you issue, for it is incapable of reason or regret. Once given a task, it will complete it at all costs. If you order it to kill the boy and the pet ogre tries to interfere, the pet ogre will die as well. Much more effective than an ordinary man with nuisances such as emotions and logic to hold him back. Watch this. Beast, cut off your left hand."

Without the slightest moment of hesitation, the beast raised the axe in its right hand and brought it down swiftly. Idanox jumped slightly at the deafening sound of its left hand and the battle-axe in it clattering to the floor in the otherwise silent room. To his amazement, almost immediately, a new hand began to form where the old had been severed seconds earlier. He guessed the appendage would fully regrow within minutes. Idanox scrutinized the beast's face. It was challenging to discern emotion on such an inhuman visage, yet he could not detect the faintest trace of pain.

"Amazing, isn't it, Idanox? Please go and fetch the men who have encountered the boy," Srenpe asked of the men Idanox had assigned to assist him.

It took about ten minutes for the men to return, by which time the severed hand had fully regrown and re-trieved the fallen battle-axe from the floor. Along with the men Srenpe has dispatched, there were four additional Hoyt fighters. The four newcomers made their way toward Srenpe and Idanox, yet their eyes were entirely occupied by the massive beast at their side. Once again, the deceptively charming smile darted across Srenpe's face.

"Welcome, gentlemen! I see you have noticed our large friend here. Please, allow me to explain. This magnif-icent creature is going to hunt down that troublesome Rawl wielder who has caused you so much grief. The last thing it needs is a scent, and it is my understanding that the four of you have encountered this boy," Srenpe said.

"Yes, that's right. We were the only survivors on the Moyie River after the first encounter. We were lucky enough to be close to shore when he destroyed our boats. All of our companions were washed away by the tidal wave," replied one of the men, finally tearing his eyes away from the great beast.

"It is fortunate that you have experienced his power firsthand; it will help our friend here get a better scent. Could you please hold still and allow him to pick up the scent? It should not take him long at all. The Rawl is a rather unusual and distinctive power after all. You do not need to do anything," Srenpe said, still smiling reassuringly.

The men shared darting glances between themselves and in the direction of Idanox before reluctantly nodding their consent. Srenpe muttered something to the beast, and it began to circle the four men like a wolf might its wounded prey. After two rotations, it came to a halt and waited for further instruction.

"Excellent. Our friend seems to have the scent. I need one more favor if you would be so kind as to oblige me. Gentlemen, could you draw your weapons, please?" Srenpe asked. They did so hesitantly, exchanging uncertain glances. "In thanks for your faithful service, you get the honor of being the first test of our new friend's abilities. Good luck to you!" Srenpe crowed before turning to the beast and pointing at the four unfortunate Hoyt warriors. "Kill them."

The first man never had a chance; one of the massive axes crushed his collarbone before he could process what was happening. The second had a split second longer, ducking as the second axe came racing for him, but he wasn't quick enough. The axe caught him in the head rather than the chest. The blows struck the men with such force that their bodies were barely recognizable as they crumpled to the floor in bloody heaps.

The last two men moved away from the beast defensively, one wielding a sword, the other a spear. They had wisely moved apart, obviously hoping this would keep the creature from attacking them both at once. The beast chose to go for the man with the spear first. The man thrust in self-defense and struck the creature in the gut. For a moment, he appeared to think he might survive. The triumphant expression flashing across his face betrayed the fact that he thought the blow might drop the mighty beast. But the monster kept coming, walking straight through the spear, driving it deeper into its own body as it pursued its victim. As the axe came down on the unfortunate man's head, his last remaining companion thought to take advantage of the distraction. He charged from behind and swung his sword with all his might at the great beast's leg.

The blow cut deep, yet the beast's thick skin kept it from penetrating too deeply. Such a powerful swing would have taken a normal man's limb clean off, yet here was this poor soul desperately attempting to wrench his sword free from the beast's rocklike skin. He was unable to free the blade before the beast swung one of its axes one last time, snuffing the man's life out with devastating power and precision. It had taken the creature a matter of seconds to dispose of all four men. Idanox could do nothing but look on in disgust.

"What do you think, Idanox? Quite effective in action, isn't he? I think he will do the job nicely." Srenpe was bursting with joy.

"I don't recall giving you permission to slaughter my men!" Idanox snapped back, seething in rage.

"I am sorry about that, but I thought a live example would be the best possible way to show you this incredible potential. I did not think you would agree to my experiment if I'd asked you in advance. As I said, visual aids are sometimes required. If I have upset you, my friend, I can leave," Srenpe replied, shooting Idanox the same innocent smile he had used with Quentin and the Hoyt fighters.

"Do you honestly think I will let you walk out of here after what you just did?" Idanox hissed, his nails digging into his palms as he clenched his fists. Several of his men moved in closer behind him, their hands reaching for their weapons.

"Do you honestly believe you can stop me?"

A deathly quiet fell over the room, and Idanox was forced to come to terms with a harsh reality. He did not like one bit what this mage had just done to his men. He could feel the eyes of his remaining men on him, expecting justice for this outrage. Yet there was nothing he could do, not after what he had witnessed this creature do. The beast could kill every single one of them where they stood if they tried to raise a hand against its master. No, it was best to let the mage stay, and the sooner the beast was dispatched on its hunt, the better.

"I understand your reasoning, Srenpe," Idanox replied, calming his tone, the diplomat in him going to work. "I simply wish you had given me a warning first. You have done incredible work, and I do not doubt this creature is exactly what we need. Even a Rawl wielder will be unable to stand against such a magnificent creation."

"No harm done, Idanox. No harm done at all," Srenpe replied, the same sneering smile still present. Idanox could not wait for the day he could wipe that smile off the mage's smug, arrogant face.

"Find the Rawl wielder and kill him at all costs. If anybody tries to stop you, kill them too. Bring the head back to Idanox here. I'm sure he will want confirmation," Srenpe instructed his beast. "Do not worry, Idanox. It will find you no matter where you go. It will not stop until it has achieved its directive."

The beast began walking at once, straight across the cavernous room and out the door. Idanox watched it go with a sense of apprehension. At the same time, he was also assured the boy would be dead soon. After the demonstration he had just witnessed, no other outcome was imaginable to him. By all accounts, the boy was formidable, but he could not possibly stand a chance against such a foe. Happy though he would be to see the end of the Rawl wielder, he still felt a building sense of foreboding in the back of his mind. What sort of monstrosity had he unleashed upon the world?

Chapter Two

General McLeod's voice was little more than a whisper, forcing the rest of the company to lean in close to make out his words. Any louder and the entire mission could've been jeopardized. The group huddled close together, struggling to listen to him over the whistle of the harsh winter wind.

"Is everybody ready? Does everybody know their assignment? Very well, Adel. Get us started when you are ready," General McLeod whispered, fog rising from his mouth into the crisp winter air.

The log cabin had three doors, three main entry points. It would take focus to breach all of them at once, but it was crucial the young man do it correctly. A few short months ago, he would never have attempted such a feat. But the confidence of an entire winter of practice was flowing through him, and he knew beyond any doubt that he would succeed. Adel drew his sword and nodded to the others, signaling to them that he was about to get things underway.

The cabin was large, standing alone in a small patch of forest southwest of the city of Kalskag, not far for the shore of the Moyie Sea. According to General McLeod, it served as a summer retreat for one of Kalskag's wealthy industry moguls but typically sat vacant during the winter months. However, word had reached the general that the man, an Idanox sympathizer, had loaned the building to Hoyt fighters to ride out the winter. Once they were done here, McLeod would begin the process of having the man charged with the crime of harboring the fugitives. McLeod had privately told Adel that he harbored little hope for justice. A few gold coins slid into the right hands could make almost any problem disappear for a rich man. Such secrets made Idanox's rise to power far less baffling.

The wind gusts came from all three directions at once, smashing into the three doors with pinpoint timing and precision. They struck with enough force to rip them from their hinges completely, splintering the bars the Hoyt had used to secure them. In unison, the teams of soldiers rushed through their assigned entrances within moments of the entryways being cleared. The Hoyt fighters inside were caught entirely off guard, most of them sleeping at this late hour. They had only posted two sentries outside, apparently feeling this safe house was a well-kept secret. Alsea had dispatched the sentries silently upon their arrival, leaving their companions entirely without warning of the impending attack. They never stood a chance.

Within moments, soldiers began to reemerge from the house, some leading shackled Hoyt fighters back toward the tree line. Adel waited back in the shadow of the trees, doing his best to stay out of sight. The Thornatan soldiers had matters inside the house under control just fine without his assistance. His job was to slow down any Hoyt who managed to get out of the house. Anybody who tried to make a run for it would get an unpleasant surprise before they got far. He had one opportunity, a lone Hoyt fighter sprinting from the nearest door and racing straight toward him. One swift wind blast directed at his knees sent the man tumbling to the ground, where a pair of soldiers apprehended him without issue.

The entire operation lasted less than ten minutes. In the end, they rounded up nine Hoyt fighters and killed three others who'd refused to be taken alive. The journey back to the city of Kalskag would not take long, though it would be far from pleasant. Every step was a struggle to pull from the soggy earth, and a thick fog emanated from Adel with each breath he took. After a mile, Adel's lungs were struggling to keep working in the bitterly cold night air. Winter was beginning to break, but it was not going without a fight. As the group made their way back toward Kalskag with their prisoners in tow, General McLeod fell back to walk alongside Adel.

"Another successful raid. That's four in the last fortnight. I am quite happy you decided to join us, my lad. If it weren't for you and your powers, I wouldn't be able to conduct these raids without putting my men in far more jeopardy. The Thornatan army owes you quite a debt, Adel."

"Have any of the prisoners we have already taken had anything useful to say? Particularly about the whereabouts of their dear leader?" Adel asked, suspecting he already knew the answer. They had conducted several successful raids since the weather had begun to warm up, but Idanox proved to be as elusive as ever. They wouldn't be able to stamp out the Hoyt for good until they got their hands on the outlaw gang's leader.

"No, they are loyal; I'll give them that much. I don't know what that smarmy bastard does to inspire such faith. I don't know the man well, but he always struck me as a pretentious ass, not a leader. But these raids still have value. We are hurting their ability to operate in this area of the province. The less mobility they have, the less dangerous they are to us. Every finger we cut off of the Hoyt makes Idanox's hand that much less lethal. Winter is nearing an end, and we will be able to push farther north soon enough. He can't hide from us forever," General McLeod replied before moving away to oversee the prisoners' transport.

Shortly after General McLeod had moved ahead to coordinate the prisoner movement with his men, Alsea appeared at Adel's side. She and Ola had been assigned with patrolling a wide perimeter around the safe house to ensure any nearby Hoyt forces could not flank their group. Ever since the trap the Hoyt had laid in the warehouse, General McLeod had taken no chances of a repeat ambush. Thus far, none had been attempted against them, but none of them wished to test their luck.

She gave him a playful shove as she approached, eliciting a smile from Adel as she fell into step beside him. She was a far cry from the distant young woman who had thought of him as a burden in the not-so-distant past. The winter spent together had brought them closer, and Adel now considered her as dear a friend as Ola.

"It's been a productive evening. It looks like you boys caught some real ugly fish tonight," she said, making sure her voice was loud enough to reach their prisoners.

"They let us reel them in without too much of a struggle. I wish we could net Idanox just as easily. I assume Ola is still covering our flank?" Adel asked, glancing around for a sign of his ogre friend. Ola rarely marched with the bulk of the group, preferring to hang back to ensure they were not followed.

"Oh, you know how he is, always paranoid we are going to be attacked from behind. I tried to tell him there aren't enough of these fools left in this part of the province to try to attack a group this size. But as you would suspect, he wouldn't hear it," Alsea said.

"Can you imagine trying to sneak up on us and running into him, with that massive sword of his? We would only have to follow the yellow trails they would leave in the snow as they ran away," Adel exclaimed, causing Alsea to snort with laughter.

They reached Kalskag as the sun was beginning to show itself on the eastern horizon. Adel and Alsea split off from the general and his men after they entered the city. The soldiers would see the prisoners safely to the city prison to await questioning and trial. Adel and Alsea wound their way through the city streets toward the small nondescript inn where they had rented a group of rooms for the past few weeks they had spent in the city. General McLeod felt it best they not stay at the army barracks with the rest of the soldiers. He trusted his men, but they all knew Idanox would pay a hefty price for Adel's head. It wasn't worth the risk to have him sleep near so many poorly paid soldiers. It would take one man a moment of weakness to cause problems. It was better if Adel and his companions stayed elsewhere. Only McLeod himself knew which inn they were staying in, for their own safety.

They made their way down a narrow hallway to the dining room of the inn and ordered breakfast from the innkeeper, a short chubby fellow who had treated them well during their stay. Ola arrived as the innkeeper was laying the food down on their table. It was still early enough that they were the only people in the room, which suited them just fine. Ola had a way of drawing the attention of the other diners. Ogres were quite uncommon in Thornata, and Ola's blue skin and massive stature stood out like a sore thumb.

"I saw no sign of anyone following us," Ola declared between heaping bites of smoked ham.

"I'm guessing most of their forces are still snowed in up north. General McLeod seems to think we have eradicated most of their outposts in this area," Adel replied.

"I hope that's the case. But General McLeod was also certain Idanox was in a warehouse in Kalstag. How many men died because of his bad information? Don't get me wrong, McLeod is a good man, but he is not immune to mistakes. I trust him, but I trust my own eyes and ears more," Ola said.

Ola has a point, Adel thought to himself. While the general's intelligence was usually accurate, the warehouse raid was a night none of them would soon forget. He supposed he should consider himself fortunate; at least he was able to relive the events of that awful night. Many men had not been so lucky. The ambush still returned to him in nightmares frequently. Adel suspected it would happen once again when he tried to fall asleep after breakfast, now that it was fresh in his mind once more.

"Well, I am confident of one thing," Alsea declared. "Wherever that rat Idanox is hiding, I don't think it's anywhere near here. If I had to guess, he is holed up in one of the northern cities, waiting out the winter. He knows even if we did find his location, it would be nigh impossible to move a force against him in the winter snows. But those will be melted soon enough, and then there won't be anyplace left for him to run where we can't get to him. His days are numbered, and he will realize it soon enough."

She was probably right; she usually was. With winter already breaking in the southern reaches of Thornata, the northern snows would soon begin to melt as well. Idanox was a coward, no doubt about it, but he was also an ambitious man with lofty goals. He would not be content to hide forever, and when he did finally show himself, they would make a quick end of him. With Idanox removed, Adel was confident the Hoyt would be disorganized enough that picking off the remaining fighters would be a much easier feat. The outlaw band was like a serpent. If they could cut off the head, the body may continue to writhe briefly, but it would prove to be relatively harmless without its brain.

The trio finished their breakfast in relative silence, all of them quite exhausted from their long night out in the cold. They rose from their table before any other guests of the inn had appeared and made their way toward a quiet corner on the topmost floor. Three rooms close to one another were their accommodations, and the innkeeper had taken care not to put any other guests near them. He had been quite accommodating for them, and General McLeod paid him well for his generous hospitality. This way it would be easier for them to hear possible attackers coming for them. To this point, there had been no such attack, but one could never be too cautious. They were outside their rooms when Ola stopped them.

"Adel, do you still wish to train today?"

The innkeeper had been allowing them to use a small courtyard behind the inn as a place to continue with Adel's sword training. The winter of lessons in bitterly cold temperatures had not been a particularly pleasant affair. Still, there was no denying the significant impact they had made on Adel's abilities. He was more confident than ever in his combat prowess. He suspected the bitter cold temperatures were hardening his body even further. After such a long night, the idea of training was not thrilling to him, but he knew the constant practice was making him better.

"Yes, Ola, we can train. But maybe a little later than usual today. It's been a long night. Would shortly before dusk be suitable? I really need to get some sleep today," he said, hoping Ola would agree to the later time. Adel had found his ogre friend to be a creature of habit, but fortunately, no protest was coming.

"As you wish. Good night to both of you," Ola replied, stepping into his room and closing his door.

"I don't think we can call it night anymore. I'm sick of going to bed while the sun is shining!" Alsea called after him. "I don't think he sleeps. I think he sits awake all night and day, sharpening that enormous sword of his and listening for assassins trying to creep up on us."

"I heard that," Ola called from inside the room. The pair chuckled. The ogre might as well have been a rabbit with his acute hearing.

"Note he did not deny it. Take no offense, Ola; I feel much safer having you and those ears of yours nearby. I'll see you downstairs for supper?" Alsea asked, to which Adel nodded. "Good, get some sleep. Good work last night."

She gave him a quick hug before disappearing into her room as well. The hugs were becoming a more regular occurrence, and they were not one Adel minded in the slightest. He stepped into his room, latching the door behind him and feeling quite pleased him himself. After washing his face in the basin, he headed to bed. As he had feared, memories of that night in the warehouse were waiting for him in his sleep.

It felt as though his head had just touched the pillow when a loud banging on his door shook him awake. Adel rose in his bed, finding himself covered in sweat. In his dream, the lightning bolt had struck the roof of the warehouse just as the pounding had come at his door. He realized he was breathing more heavily than usual and fought to bring it under control as he climbed to his feet. Retrieving his sword, he stumbled to the latch and released it, opening the door cautiously to find Alsea waiting for him. She also looked as though she had been woken suddenly and appeared none too pleased about it.

"General McLeod is here. He says he needs to speak with us, and it's urgent enough that it could not wait until we had more sleep. I told him he better not be exaggerating," she said, her tone of voice perfectly matching the annoyed expression on her face.

She led the way down the hall to a small sitting room. General McLeod was waiting with Ola, who looked as though he had never been more well rested in his life. Though irritated, Adel knew the general would not have disturbed them so soon if it were not necessary. For a moment, he allowed himself to hope that perhaps they had finally found Idanox, though he suspected this was not the case.

"I'm sorry to disturb you all, but I've received a report from Kolig. The snows are finally melting to a point where we can get messages across the province east and west again," General McLeod said, looking genuinely sorry for disturbing them.

"Idanox?" Adel asked, hoping he was right while dreading he was not. If they had found the elusive leader of the Hoyt, it would be worth the loss of sleep.

"No such luck, I'm afraid. Unfortunately, I did not come here to bring happy news. There is a small village about twenty miles east of Kolig, mostly potato farmers from my understanding. It seems some Hoyt survivors of the Battle of Kolig took up refuge there for the winter.

They've been holding the farmers and their families hostage all winter, stealing their gold and eating their food. That's what we know about anyway. I don't want to imagine what else they have done to those poor people," the general replied.

"Disgusting cowards," Adel spat. "Is the army moving against them?"

"That's the problem. The garrison at Kolig was badly diminished by the Hoyt attack last year, and most of the forces the duke sent to liberate the city headed home before the snows fell. They don't have the manpower to go after the Hoyt and protect Kolig at the same time. We can't take the risk of pulling too many men away from the city in case this is another clever ruse to draw us out. They have asked our team to go and free the hostages and deal with the Hoyt. I came to ask if the three of you would join us once more."

A forced march across miles of terrain that was still cold and partially covered by snow and ice did not sound like a pleasant journey to Adel. But he could not turn his back on these innocent people who needed their help. The Hoyt were especially brutal in their treatment of hostages; Alsea had seen that firsthand in Kolig after the fall of the city. They had to do something about it, no matter how hard the journey. A glance to Alsea confirmed her agreement, and a nod from Ola signaled his as well. All these months together, and he still struggled to interpret the ogre's face without gestures to help him.

"We are with you, General McLeod. When do we leave?" Adel asked.

"Pack your things and meet us outside the western gates just after dawn. We need to get moving right away. Those poor people have lived in fear long enough; let's not keep them waiting any longer. I figure it will take us at least a week to make the march in these conditions, maybe more, and that's if we push ourselves hard. It won't be a pleasant journey, but we don't have much choice. The terrain is flat at least, but I think we are in for a muddy march," General McLeod said.

After the general left, the three companions returned to their rooms to try to find what rest they could for the journey ahead. Adel knew the slow wait of winter was finally over. They would likely be continually moving from this point on until the Hoyt were defeated. Struggling to return to sleep, he hoped he was up to the challenge ahead. A winter of training may have helped his confidence grow, but the memories of the night in the warehouse were always lingering in the back of his mind. He could only hope there would be no repeat of that fateful night.

Chapter Three

Six days later, Adel's body was exhausted to an extent which he had rarely experienced before. They had nearly completed their desperate march toward the captive village, and each day had been more exhausting than the one before. They began their journey each morning long before the sun rose and did not stop until there were no traces on daylight left hanging in the sky. The first day had mainly been spent trudging through knee-high snow, but the burning rays of the spring sun had reduced the snow to slush. The melting had continued, and at this point they were hiking through a rather unpleasant mixture of water and mud. While the warmer days were appreciated, each step was a struggle to pull from the soggy earth, and Adel's muscles groaned in protest. They soon found themselves appreciating the early morning hours, when the ground was solid from the hard freeze that came every night.

Still, Adel knew the arduous march was a minor inconvenience compared to the nightmare these poor villagers had been enduring all winter long. Each time he caught himself becoming irritated at their tiresome journey, he reminded himself why it was so essential. Now on the sixth day, their advance scouts reported they would reach the village by nightfall, and Adel was looking forward to liberating the hostages from their brutal captors. Soon, there would be far fewer Hoyt scum to wreak havoc on the people of Thornata. General McLeod had made that much clear. He was taking no chances with the safety of the villagers. Any Hoyt found in the village would be killed on sight if they did not immediately throw down their weapons and surrender. The exhausting march would be worth it once this mission was over.

One troubling bit of news the scouts had brought back was that far more Hoyt fighters had hunkered down in this village than they had previously believed. General McLeod's initial report had indicated there were around twenty fighters, but the scouts reported seeing roughly twice that number. With their own numbers equaling twenty-eight total, the Hoyt would significantly outnumber them, a fact which was quite concerning. Still, McLeod assured them a solid plan could overcome the disparity in numbers easily enough.

No concrete plan had been set yet on how they would go about attacking the Hoyt. General McLeod would assess the situation once they had arrived at the village. He had made it clear in a private discussion with Adel that they would need his abilities to even the odds against them. There was also the matter of the hostages. The reports indicated the Hoyt had them spread throughout the village. If they weren't careful, they could end up getting many of these innocent people killed, a prospect Adel did not care to dwell on. As he usually did, he turned to Alsea for reassurance.

"What do you think about all of this?" he asked. "Will we be able to pull this off? I hate the idea that we could end up getting some of these people killed if we don't do this perfectly."

"Not doubting us already, are you? Or are you just doubting yourself, as usual? You've spent all winter in those inns, training with a sword and practicing using the Rawl. You're more prepared for this than you've ever been, Adel. Remember the green boy who wiped out an entire company of these Hoyt cowards in Kolig not so long ago? That kid would stand no chance against you!" Her laugh always had a way of relaxing him. "Look, I can't promise nothing will go wrong, Adel. But I can guarantee you the person you are today is the Adel who is the best equipped to face what lies ahead. We are going to go in there and do everything we can to help these people because nobody is better equipped to do so than us."

By nightfall, they were drawing near to the outskirts of the village. The general called a halt to their march before they were too close. McLeod did not want to risk an attack at night when they were unfamiliar with the area. Adel agreed it was best to let the scouts get the lay of the land overnight and then move in the next day. Alsea volunteered her services as well and vanished like a shadow in the direction of the village. Adel took a seat next to Ola in the frigid camp; they could not risk a fire with the Hoyt close by.

"I hope we can do this without any villagers getting hurt," he said.

His chat with Alsea earlier in the day had helped his confidence, but the closer they had drawn to the village, the more his anxiety had grown. Images of the night in the warehouse continued to dance through his mind. Many soldiers had died that night, and he had been unable to do anything to save them. That had been horrible enough, but this was far more intimidating. Those villagers were not soldiers; they had not voluntarily placed themselves in harm's way. They were innocent bystanders unfortunate enough to be caught up in a conflict that had nothing to do with them. What if the Hoyt found a way to neutralize his power again? What if they were walking into another cleverly laid trap?

"I feel better with Alsea out scouting; no offense to the general or his men," Ola said. "She will find all their locations. They can't hide from her. Once we know where they are, we will be able to set a plan to keep the villagers safe. Have faith, Adel. This group will be able to handle anything the Hoyt throw our way."

"You are right; she will find them all. I just wish she wouldn't insist on going out there on her own," Adel responded, and what appeared to be a smirk crossed Ola's face.

"We are both far too loud and clumsy to be of any assistance. We would only get in her way. Besides, you know she can handle herself, probably better than either of us if we're being completely honest with ourselves," Ola said.

Ola knew what he was talking about, and Alsea returned within the hour to make her report. They all gathered close to listen to what she had discovered. She spoke in hushed tones while they all continually looked over their shoulders, fearing Hoyt scouts may come upon them at any moment.

"They're keeping the villagers in three different places, all barns. Two of the barns are on the southwest edge of the village, and the third is on the east edge, not far from where we are now. It appears the Hoyt have split them up; the men are in the eastern barn, and the women and children are in the others. Most of the Hoyt are scattered throughout the village, living quite comfortably in these villagers' homes. They take shifts guarding the villagers; I got close enough to hear a few of them discussing it. They're hoping to use them as leverage to barter their way out of here if the army comes after them. Each barn has at least six guards," she said, using a stick to draw a crude diagram in some nearby slush. "The total number of Hoyt is hard to be sure of, but I counted at least thirty total. I'd be shocked if there weren't at least a few more than that. The good news for us is that apart from the guards at the barns, the rest of them are scattered throughout the village. They are all either alone or in small groups. We can pick them off easily enough once we free the hostages."

"Would it be possible to hit the eastern barn first and then the other two at once? Do you think we could keep it quiet enough?" General McLeod asked.

"I wouldn't risk it. With so many Hoyt at large in the village, it would just take one man coming down the road at the wrong moment to sound the alarm. If they get wind of us, the hostages we don't go after first will end up dead before we can get to them. If we are going to do this while keeping them all safe, I think we have to hit all three barns at once," Alsea replied.

They set about planning to attack all three barns at the same time. Adel, Alsea, and Ola would go with the group assigned to rescue the women and children, while General McLeod would lead a separate attack against the barn with the male prisoners. Adel would force the barn doors open and attempt to neutralize any Hoyt fighters outside, while Ola and a group of soldiers rushed in to dispatch any fighters inside. Alsea would help Adel cover the outside with her bow to ensure no Hoyt fled with any hostages. It was a sound plan, at least as sound as they could hope to form under such challenging conditions. There was no time to wait for a better solution to present itself. Every hour spent here increased their chances of being discovered.

When morning fell, the two groups wished each other luck and split off to their respective targets. The village was not large, yet it took Adel's group a long time to reach their destination. With no tree cover directly around the farming village's perimeter, they were forced to creep stealthily between houses to reach their barns. Alsea led the way, moving catlike at the front of the group, checking around every corner for potential threats. Each time they crept out from behind cover, Adel held his breath, praying they would not hear any shouts.

The two barns were situated beside each other in a relatively wide-open space, making them an even more challenging target to approach without being spotted. Alsea led them toward a small farmhouse positioned several hundred feet from the two barns. They would enter this house and initiate their attack from there. This would allow them to approach the barns unseen until they were within a few hundred feet. They reached the front door of the house without any cries of discovery, and Ola forced the door open.

The bulk of the group waited in the entryway while Ola took two of the Thornatan soldiers and thoroughly checked all the rooms to ensure they were alone. Once they had cleared the house, they made their way into the kitchen, which had a small window facing the two barns. Adel would operate from this spot, while Alsea would head to a room directly above the kitchen to have a vantage point with her bow. Any Hoyt who tried to flee with hostages would not get far. Ola and the eleven soldiers who had accompanied them would attack the barns on foot.

Adel threw the kitchen window open as the rest of the company departed. He was able to watch as Ola and the soldiers made their way silently across the field toward the doors of the two barns, six for each one. He heard a faint tap above his head and knew Alsea was signaling to let him know she was in position. He returned the tap and fixed his gaze on the barns, waiting for the first sign of trouble to show itself.

Ola and the soldiers were within fifty feet of the barn doors. Adel was beginning to breathe easier, becoming more confident with each step that this was going to work. It was nothing short of a miracle that they had come this far without the Hoyt discovering them. The guards inside the barn must've been too confident from a winter of no resistance; they felt no need to have a sentry looking out. He readied himself to call on the Rawl. He was to smash open the doors when the party was within a few feet. Then came the ear-shattering blast of a horn from the other end of the village, from the direction of the barn General McLeod and his men were attempting to take control of at the same time. Almost immediately, the barn doors flew open in response, and all hell broke loose.

"We're under attack! Grab the hostages!" cried the first Hoyt to step outside as he immediately spotted Ola and the soldiers creeping toward them. He attempted to shout something more but was interrupted by the crack of Alsea's bowstring and the arrow that buried itself in his head, dropping him to the ground in an instant. Another horn blasted, this one from one of the barns directly in front of them.

Everything was going wrong. Ola and the soldiers were charging full speed toward the barns now, and Adel was standing at the window with no help to give them.

"Adel! Adel! We have to protect their backs!" Alsea shouted from above. "More Hoyt will come from the village!"

She was right. With the horn blast, additional Hoyt fighters would be there within moments. But he couldn't see anyone approaching from this window; his view was too narrow. He could see nothing but the two barns directly in front of him. Throwing caution to the wind, Adel climbed onto the counter and shoved himself out the window and into the heart of the chaos. He drew his sword as soon as he was clear of the house. Alsea was shouting something at him, but he couldn't hear her over the cries coming from within the barns. She was most likely screaming for him to get back into cover, but there was little he could accomplish from there.

Turning toward the village, he saw trouble in the form of seven Hoyt fighters rushing toward them, armed with swords and axes. He focused on them, preparing to launch an attack with the Rawl, but something smashed into him from the side. Simultaneously spinning and launching into an attack, he was able to stop his sword a split second before cutting into a young child. The boy must have run from one of the barns. Had his instinctive counterattack landed, the boy would have been dead before he hit the ground.

Adel turned back toward the village. The Hoyt fighters were drawing close, too close for him to try to launch his planned wind attack against them. He sent a quick gust blasting toward them, trying to stall them for a few seconds. He seized the young boy by his shirt and tossed him into the window he had leaped through moments before. He did not like to handle the boy roughly, but there was no time to be gentler. If the boy were fortunate enough to survive this, he would be grateful for the rough treatment.

"Get down and stay there! Keep out of sight!" he shouted to the boy, hoping he would listen while knowing he could not watch to make sure he did.

The Hoyt were almost on top of him now. Alsea's bow twanged again, and one of them dropped to the ground. She had a poor angle; she was having the same problem that had forced Adel out of the house. She couldn't fire on the rest of them, as the jutting farmhouse wall obscured her view. It was up to Adel to hold them off. Setting everything else out of his mind, he focused on his attackers and braced himself.

The first man to arrive swung at him with a heavy axe. It was a hard swing, but Adel was used to parrying attacks from Ola and was able to deflect it without much difficulty. He struck back with a vicious counterattack, his swing aimed right at the Hoyt's head. The Hoyt stepped back to avoid it but in doing so gave Alsea all the opening she needed to plant an arrow through his back. He fell to the ground, mortally wounded, no longer a threat to Adel.

The five remaining Hoyt reached Adel at nearly the same moment, sending him into a frenzy of parries and counterattacks. He was able to defend himself well enough to avoid harm, but the attacks were coming so quickly that he immediately knew he would not be able to attack any of them successfully. They forced him into a steady retreat, driving him closer to the house, trying to put his back against a wall so they could finish him off. This strategy would prove to be a miscalculation on their part. Just as they backed him toward the wall, Alsea leaped from her window above. She came straight down on two of the Hoyt attackers, her long knives already in hand.

The distraction gave Adel a chance to slip the guard of one of his attackers, driving his sword straight between the man's ribs. It was now only two against one, allowing

Adel to counter more aggressively, forcing the Hoyt away from the house. They backpedaled away from his attack, moving toward the barns. They never saw Ola emerge from the barn behind them, his greatsword hacking one of them down before they even knew he was there. Adel finished the other with a thrust to the chest. He spun around, remembering Alsea had tackled two of his attackers, and was relieved to find her walking toward him, two bodies slumped on the ground behind her. She shot him a wink as she sheathed one of her long knives.

"Ola, what happened in the barns?" Adel cried, fearing this mission had gone as poorly as the raid on the warehouse.

"Relax, Adel. We managed to kill all the Hoyt inside before they could do anything rash. None of the villagers were hurt. The Hoyt here weren't much in the way of fighters; they were cowards who fled from Kolig because they didn't want to fight. This small village was no doubt an enticing target for them, the filthy cowards," Ola replied, grabbing Adel's arm to steady him.

Remembering the young boy he had tossed inside the house, he spun around to see him staring at them through the window. Relieved to find the boy had followed his instructions and stayed inside, he hurried over to help him back through the window. The boy did not seem upset with Adel. Instead, he seemed quite intrigued by Ola, staring at the massive blue-skinned ogre with pure astonishment etched across his face. The soldiers were beginning to lead the women and children out of the barns, and one woman ran to the boy, crying. Adel handed him back to his mother as she cried out in tearful thanks.

"General McLeod should be here by now," Ola reminded them, filling Adel with a feeling of great foreboding once again, his mind already formulating an expedition to the other barn.

Whatever had happened there, the Hoyt had been able to sound a horn before McLeod and his men had eliminated them. The Hoyt reinforcement to these barns had not been too severe, leading Adel to believe McLeod's group had borne the brunt of the counterassault. They needed to think of a route to reach the other barn. He was already trying to calculate how many soldiers should be left behind to guard the women and children they had just set free.

This would prove to be unnecessary, as the general arrived a few minutes later with the remaining soldiers and several male villagers in tow. A quick count told Adel two soldiers were missing, and the pained expression on the general's face told him they would not be coming back. Still, Adel could not help but feel joyful while watching the male villagers reunite with their wives and children. General McLeod motioned for them to give the villagers some space.

"Well done, everybody. We did an excellent thing here today. I want two teams of six men to sweep every building in this village and make sure all those bastards are dead. We aren't leaving until we are certain these people can safely get back to their normal lives. If a few more could find a nice spot to dig graves for Harold and Kylan, I would appreciate it. They served their people well today, and they deserve a nice place to rest," the general said.

Adel and his companions took seats in the grass, not far from the spot where the villagers were reuniting. They were unified in wanting to watch over them until they were confident the village was safe from the threat of the Hoyt. General McLeod joined them after a few minutes, sighing heavily as he knelt beside them. Adel knew the loss of two of his men pained the seasoned general more than he would ever show them.

"We got unlucky during our attack. A Hoyt was coming out to relieve himself as we were approaching, and he raised the alarm. Quite a few reinforcements came from the village. It's lucky we only lost two men. These people have been through a bad ordeal. I spoke with some of those men after we freed them from the barn. The Hoyt are nothing more than vicious animals, and they need to be put down like rabid dogs. The things the Hoyt have put them through are even worse than we feared. I am thankful to the three of you for coming with us. If you hadn't, I shudder to think how badly this operation could have gone," he said.

The two teams of soldiers returned within the hour. They confirmed the village was clear of Hoyt fighters, and the two fallen men were laid to rest. It was decided they would head to Kolig to regroup and hopefully gather intelligence on Idanox and his whereabouts. The villagers had gathered around them in a circle to thank them for their assistance. Adel once again felt a swell of pride, the doubts he had been racked with before the attack long since forgotten. In all his conflicts with the Hoyt, he had never felt so confident that he had made a meaningful difference. He was still dwelling on this happy thought when one of the villagers interrupted.

"General, is that one of your men over there?"

They turned as one to spot a figure approaching from a field to the north, heading straight for them. They could not make out any of the man's features from this distance, but he was undoubtedly coming right toward them.

Odd, Adel thought, glancing around. *All of our people are right here.* Yet this man was walking straight to them with a clear purpose, and it appeared he was wearing Thornatan army gear. A messenger from the garrison in Kolig, perhaps? The closer he got, it became clear this was a huge man. Adel suspected he might be as large as Ola or even bigger. As he drew closer still, it became apparent that something was very wrong indeed.

Chapter Four

The man, if that was indeed what was approaching, was advancing on them rapidly. He was not running but instead walking at a slightly quickened pace, his long strides carrying him rapidly across the field. He came straight toward them with no hesitation, no deviation in his route. He seemed to have a particular goal in mind. He held something in each hand, and as he drew ever closer, it became apparent that they were battle-axes—enormous battle-axes, which should not have been possible to hold with one hand. Adel doubted even the mighty Ola could wield such a weapon effectively in a lone hand. He did not know the man's intentions, but with those two axes in hand, he doubted they were pleasant. Still, what was he hoping to accomplish against so many of them? Monstrous strength notwithstanding, the man was vastly outnumbered.

The man was making no effort to slow down or speak to them as he approached. Adel placed his hand on the pommel of his sword. His suspicions that anybody approaching in such a manner could not possibly have good intentions were intensifying by the second. Searching the faces of his friends and the Thornatan soldiers, he could see he was not alone in this line of thinking. Alsea had already pulled her bow from her back and set an arrow to the string. Ola was drawing his sword, his eyes never leaving the approaching figure.

"Good day, friend! Do you have some business in this village?" General McLeod called out, obviously hoping to glean some hint at the man's purpose.

If the man had heard the general's question, he did not show any indication of it, continuing to advance without delay. He was within a hundred feet of them now, and Adel could make out more of his appearance. His clothing was similar to the everyday black attire the Thornatan soldiers wore under their armor, but it was strangely distorted. It bore an appearance of having been stretched out and torn as if somebody far too large had tried to force the garments onto his body. Now the man was within fifty feet, and Adel could clearly see his face. What he saw did not bring him any comfort.

It resembled a beast more than a man, the dark gray skin resembling the bark of an old tree. The eyes looked like it may have been a man at one point but now shone with a feral wolflike glow. The nose stretched from the face like the snout of a predator, designed to sniff out prey. It was now clear this creature was taller even than Ola, a sight Adel had never thought to see. This was not a man traveling the countryside at leisure. This was a predator on the hunt for prey. Based on the way it continued straight toward them, Adel suspected he knew what it was hunting.

"Form a line. I don't know what this thing is, but we need to keep it away from the villagers! A few men need to gather the villagers back inside one of the barns for their own safety!" General McLeod shouted, seeming to have reached the same conclusion as Adel.

The soldiers rushed to comply, roughly twenty men forming a line in front of the group with spears extended toward the approaching creature. Adel drew his sword, while Alsea pulled back slightly on her bowstring, raising the weapon and taking aim. Ola's sword was already drawn, the ogre crouched in a defensive stance. If any of this daunted the mysterious beast in the slightest, it did not show it, now drawing within ten feet, its pace never slowing. Adel took a deep breath. No matter what, he would not allow this creature to inflict more pain on these innocent villagers.

"Halt! Halt and identify yourself now!" the general cried.

The creature did not halt and did not identify itself. It continued walking straight into the line of waiting spears, apparently without a second thought. One massive axe swept wide with incredible force, tearing most of the weapons from the hands of the men holding them. The second axe came down in a vicious vertical strike, smashing into one of the men in front of it with incredible impact. The unfortunate soldier crumpled immediately to the ground with a sickening crunch. His armor had done him no good; the creature had struck him with inhuman power, shattering his body despite the iron protection.

The soldiers valiantly attempted to regroup, struggling to get their spears back in line to strike at the beast. But once again, it attacked, this time with a speed that defied its enormous size. The axes slashed out in both directions and dropped two more soldiers with grievous wounds. It swung the massive axes with a speed that should've been impossible for anything human. Each of the weapons must've weighed close to seventy pounds, yet the monster might as well have been swinging twigs. The crack of a bowstring split the air, and Alsea's arrow found its mark, striking the beast square in the chest.

Any hopes the arrow would stop or even slow the attack were quickly dashed. The only reaction from the beast was a primal scream of rage as it renewed its attack on the unfortunate soldiers in its path. Adel noticed the arrow had not sunk in as deeply as Alsea's shots usually did. The beast's skin must've been every bit as hard and thick as it looked. It lunged forward, this time moving straight toward Adel and his friends.

Ola seized Adel by the arm, shoving him back and away from the creature, moving forward to face it himself. The axes slashed out, but Ola was the most skilled fighter Adel had ever seen and had the strength to match his skill. Adel watched in amazement as Ola deflected every attack successfully. Still, he had never seen anyone able to fight the massive ogre on even footing. While Ola was able to defend himself, the creature was advancing continually, stifling any hope of a counterattack. Ola was in the position he so often forced his opponents into: a steady retreat against a stronger opponent. He was as strong as anyone Adel had ever seen, but this creature was stronger.

Adel knew he had to do something. He struck at the beast with a wind gust, blasting it several feet away from Ola and allowing several soldiers to launch an attack. They lunged forward, driving their spears deep into the thick hide of the beast. Again, if this pained the creature in any way, it did not show it, lashing out once more with its axes. It caught several more soldiers with devastating blows before launching itself straight at Adel, paying no mind to the several spears still protruding from its body.

Pure instinct saved him from the beast's rush, sending the power of the Rawl into the ground, immediately softening the hard dirt into soggy mud. The defensive maneuver was successful, and the creature sunk like a rock until the mud was up to its waist. Still, it struggled to continue forward like a rabid animal, another scream of rage blasting from its throat as Alsea buried another arrow in its chest and then a second in its neck. Still, it thrashed and struggled to free itself from the mud, seemingly unaware of the arrows or of the sword and spear thrusts that soon joined them as the general's men rushed in to attack the beast at close range. Adel stared in shock and disgust as the creature struggled to free itself from the mud, fighting through a dozen injuries, any one of which would have killed a normal man. Despite the resemblance, he could not believe this creature had ever been human. What sort of evil had borne this monster?

"Move back, create distance, and then reform the line!" General McLeod shouted, desperate to get his men out of the reach of the monster's enormous axes.

They all hurried to comply, General McLeod himself bringing up the rear. The beast sprung from the mud at last and once again rushed them as they were reforming the line of spears, barreling straight into the general and sending him tumbling to the dirt. The soldiers surged forward as one to come to their general's defense, striking at the beast with their spears and scoring several significant strikes—or strikes that should have been significant. This monstrous creature shrugged them aside as if they were nothing, renewing its furious assault with the axes.

Adel could only watch in horror as the beast hacked and hammered at the soldiers with the battle-axes. He could not attack with the Rawl without risk of harming the men himself. For a moment, he searched for an opening to attack with his sword, but the futility of the soldiers' attacks held him back. Several of the Thornatan soldiers died in the struggle, and several others were wounded so severely they had no choice but to retreat, hoping their comrades could shield them. All the while, the beast continued its relentless attack, impervious to any wounds they managed to deal it in return, including an arrow Alsea managed to plant perfectly in its eye socket.

How was this possible? Adel could not comprehend how such a creature could exist; nothing should've been able to absorb this much punishment. He doubted even the giant Klaweck would be able to fight through this amount of damage. But still, this monster fought on as though it were not wounded at all. Adel had to act before it was too late. He had to find a way to put a stop to this. If he didn't, this beast would kill every single one of them, along with the villagers they had just fought to save from such a fate. Perhaps a lighting blast could put an end to this beast, but it would kill everybody in its vicinity as well. The mud had slowed it down, but it had fought its way through quicker than should have been possible. Then an idea occurred to him, but he would need to hurry.

He spun in every direction, searching desperately for what he needed, and found it near one of the barns: a trough of water used for pigs to drink. He summoned his power once more, lifting the water from the trough and spinning it into a ball, much as he had the water from the river outside of Kolig. Then he sent it spinning through the air, straight at the head of the great beast. The water wrapped around the beast's head, swirling in continual motion, latched on to the creature's face like an amoeba.

The attack seemed to have the desired effect; the beast stopped lashing out at the men around it, instead frantically trying to swat the water away from its head. In its mindless rage, it seemed to think the water was another opponent, one that could be killed like any other. It dropped one of the axes, its hand scrabbling clawlike across its face, struggling to rid itself of this new attacker. Seeing an opportunity in the beast's distraction, Ola screamed for the soldiers to get away from the creature. Then, raising his massive greatsword, he charged the monster at full speed, swinging one last time with all his might. The blade caught the beast above the waist, cleanly severing both of its legs and sending it tumbling to the ground in two pieces.

Adel maintained his attack until the arms of the great beast finally stopped thrashing, then released the ball of water into the soil. There were a few moments of tense disbelief; nobody could seem to accept the fact that the seemingly unstoppable monster was dead.

What in the name of hell was that thing? Everybody seemed to shake out of the trance at once. They rushed to tend to the wounded, though none of them were in any hurry to get too close to the carcass of the great beast. Adel rushed to General McLeod's side, who had not moved since being knocked to the ground. He was relieved to find the general breathing and alert.

"I'm fine, lad, though I think I may have a few broken ribs. I took one hell of a hit. Guess I'm not as durable as I used to be. How are the men? How many did we lose?" he asked.

The answer to General McLeod's question was devastating. Over half of the men who had left Kalskag on this mission were dead. Many of those who remained had suffered severe injuries, some which could potentially kill them if they did not reach a healer in Kolig soon. Whatever that creature had been, it had done far more damage to them than the Hoyt they had come here to fight. Adel looked down at its body in disbelief, still unable to wrap his head around the fact that such a creature existed. Even in death, the mere sight of it was terrifying to behold.

Some of the villagers had begun to emerge from the barn, and they immediately began tending to the soldiers' wounds as best they could. Several just stared at the body of the great beast in shocked disbelief. Adel stood beside them, now noticing that despite the severity of the wound that had felled it, the creature had hardly bled at all. What type of animal was this? Were this a human, the ground beneath it would've been saturated with blood by now. It didn't make any sense. The agonized cry of a wounded soldier brought him out of his trance. He waved off a woman asking if he was injured, hurrying over to Ola and Alsea. His fascination with the beast was irrelevant, and there were no answers to be found by staring at it. He had been lucky enough to emerge from the battle unscathed. These men needed his help, or many of them would not survive.

"Some of these men won't last two days with their injuries. We have to get them to Kolig, and we have to do it now. These villagers aren't equipped to handle wounds this severe. They need trained healers, and they can't afford any delays," Adel said. Alsea nodded in agreement, but Ola was staring at the beast as well and did not seem convinced.

"We need to burn this thing's body," he exclaimed, pointing toward the carcass.

"Ola, these men will die without help that we cannot give them. Even the general is wounded. We must regroup. If we don't get to Kolig as soon as possible, most of these men will die. We need your help, Ola. Ask the villagers to burn the body if you insist, but we have to move fast," Adel urged.

To Adel's surprise, Ola did not argue the point; he merely nodded and moved over to instruct a group of villagers. Adel and Alsea hurriedly began binding what wounds they could and gathering the soldiers in a group for departure. Some would need to be carried on makeshift stretchers, which would slow them down even further.

Within the hour, they were ready to depart. The villagers gathered around them one last time, thanking them once more for their help and promising they would bury the fallen and burn the body of the beast as Ola wished. They set out for Kolig shortly before noon, a journey which would likely take two days at the slow pace they would be forced to make with their wounded. Adel just hoped all of them would survive the trip.

***

Once the group had departed, the villagers began the task of cleaning up from the battle. Once they had laid the fallen soldiers to rest, they worked as a team to move the body of the massive beast to the center of a nearby field. They began gathering firewood with which to burn it, and before long, the creature's remains were covered entirely beneath a wooden pyre. It was decided that they would light it at nightfall to provide warmth for nearby homes on the chilly early spring night. The Hoyt had used most of their firewood over the long winter, and it would take time to rebuild their stock of resources. There was no wood to waste on a fire in the warmth of the day. Satisfied with their preparations, they turned away to begin the task of disposing of the fallen Hoyt fighters.

Unbeknownst to the villagers, underneath the massive pile of firewood, the beast's body was beginning to change, new legs starting to form from the spot where the old limbs had been severed. As its body began to recover from the trauma it had endured, the beast began to come awake. It did not think, not in the manner of a normal person. Its mind was nothing more than a series of primal instincts, urged on by the commands of its master. It was aware its prey had eluded it and that it must resume its hunt. The magic that had created it had immediately gone to work after the injury. It was like an instinct, its body shutting down out of a desperate sense of self-preservation. If its foes had known it was still alive, they would not have relented in their attacks until its body was utterly destroyed. So, it had lain in wait, allowing its wounds to heal. It would find its prey once more; there was no place it could hide. The magic that created it had already adjusted, accounting for the unexpected manner of attack the prey had used against it. This time, it would not be so easily overcome.

As night fell, several villagers gathered at the site of the pyre with torches. Together, they lit the firewood in several spots and stood by, waiting for the flames to catch. Before long, the fire began to burn rapidly, warmth spreading to the nearby homes. They were utterly unprepared for the scream of unbridled rage that emerged from within the fire and the explosion of burning wood as the fully reformed beast flung itself from the blaze and into their midst.

Chapter Five

It was late afternoon of the following day, and the battered group of fighters continued to push toward the city of Kolig as fast as their weary feet could carry them. As the night crept steadily in on them, Adel found himself with no choice but to face an unpleasant fact: they would not be able to reach the safety of the city by nightfall. The prospect of having to stop and make camp for the second night in a row was an unappealing one. Every hour spent on this trek was an hour that some of these wounded men did not have to spare. He feared many of them would begin to slip away overnight despite their comrades' best efforts to keep them alive.

They were not able to move as quickly as they usually would; the severity of the soldiers' wounds was slowing their march significantly. Those healthy enough to walk had been taking turns helping to carry those who could not. It was not easy, and the strain was taking its toll on all of them. Their very reason for urgency was the thing holding them back; the irony of the situation was not lost on him. Adel had given thought to going ahead by himself and trying to bring healers from the city out to the soldiers. Ola had swiftly talked him out of this idea. With the number of wounded men, they needed every able body they had available to them. If the Hoyt came upon them, it could mean the end of them. Staying together was the only option that made sense.

At this point, Adel was determined to get their group to the bank of the Kival River several miles south of Kolig and then complete their journey in the morning. At least by the river, they would have access to an abundance of fresh water, a resource of which they were running dangerously low. Having the water on one side of their camp would also be a natural line of defense against any attackers who may be lurking nearby. They reached the river as the sun was beginning to slip out of sight behind the western horizon. The injured soldiers collapsed to the ground in relief as the few who were uninjured began bringing water from the river.

Every inch of his body groaning in pain from marching all day, Adel walked down to the riverbank alone for a moment of rest. He knew his aches and pains were nothing compared to those suffered by the soldiers at the hands of the great beast and only allowed himself a few minutes. He had traveled this section of the Kival River many times on the barge with Captain Boyd. The thought of the gruff but gentle captain brought a smile to his face, and he wondered where his old barge was now. He hoped the captain had kept his barge out of Thornata and would not return to this province until the Hoyt had finally been eradicated. He wondered if he would have a chance to see his captain again one day. Most of all, Adel hoped Boyd was doing profitable business safely, wherever he was.

He was about to return to camp when his reminiscence brought an idea to his mind. Perhaps he could get these wounded men to Kolig by dawn after all.

How did I not think of this sooner? His excitement renewed, he rushed to find Ola and Alsea to run his idea by them. He found them building a campfire near the wounded men. The fire was a risk, but one they couldn't afford not to take. The injured needed the warmth if they were to have any hope of surviving the night. He noted most of them were shivering, though from the chill in the air or the pain of their rapidly worsening wounds, he could not be sure.

"Ola! Alsea! I have an idea!"

"Is it that you should help us gather more firewood? Because I think that's a brilliant idea," Alsea grumbled. He did not respond; he knew the past two days had been every bit as strenuous on his companions as they had on him. Instead, he launched straight into his idea.

"We might not need more wood. I think I have an idea that will get these men to Kolig tonight."

"Anything that involves me not gathering more firewood is fine by me. What's your plan?" she asked.

"Kolig is only a few miles upriver. These men are too exhausted to go any farther, but there is another way to get them there. If I leave now, I can get into the city before it is fully dark and find a barge at the docks to hire. There are always stragglers coming into the docks at this time of day. We will sail down the river to this camp, pick up the soldiers, and sail back up to the city; we would be there hours before dawn, and they would not have to march any farther. It could mean the difference between life and death for some of these men." Adel could hardly contain his enthusiasm.

"It is an intriguing idea, Adel. Of course, it would leave the camp less guarded while you are away. If the Hoyt—or even worse, another beast like the one we encountered—were to come upon us, your powers would be sorely missed," Ola said.

"I know, Ola. We've discussed this already, and I understand the risks. It's a gamble, no doubt about it. But look around you. Many of these men have declined horribly today. You can see it as well as I can. Some of them may not live to see the dawn if we aren't willing to take the chance. If we don't do this, I doubt half of them will survive the rest of this journey. If I leave immediately, I can be back within a few hours. I think it's a chance we have to take. A barge is a solution to our problem and the only solution that gives us a chance to make it Kolig with no more casualties."

"You are not wrong, Adel. But you leaving camp still gives me pause. As I said, your powers would be useful in the event of an attack. You would also be at risk in the wilderness on your own. Perhaps I should be the one to go instead. No disrespect intended, but I can cover ground faster than you can anyway," Ola pointed out.

"That's true, Ola. But you know as well as I do that a barge captain will be far more hesitant to hire his ship out to an ogre. It's not fair, and it's not right, but it's the truth. I am more likely to have success, particularly if I spot a captain or crew I am familiar with. I know how men like this think. I can persuade them. I am sure of it," Adel tried to explain, losing more patience with every passing second. Every minute spent arguing was a minute of daylight he was losing.

To his credit, Ola did not appear to take any offense from the remarks. "Would a barge sail at night at this time of year? The river seems clear enough here, but there would still be a risk of hitting chunks of ice in the dark."

"I know some of the men who work out of Kolig, and they know this stretch of the river like the back of their hands. They are also more inclined to take bold chances in the name of gold. If the pay is high enough, they will do it."

"Speaking of pay, how exactly do you plan to pay them for their services?" Alsea asked, speaking up for the first time.

Adel had not considered that particular wrinkle of the plan. He had the savings Captain Boyd had paid him, but even that might not be enough to sway a captain. Not all ship captains were as magnanimous as Boyd. There was no doubt most of them would ask him to pay a large sum for their services. Adel knew that most captains would view a desperate customer as one willing to pay a steep price. He would have no choice but to consult with General McLeod on his plan. He had tried to allow the general to relax as much as possible during their arduous march. Though not as severely wounded as some of his men, the journey had still taken a heavy toll on the aging commander. Adel would've preferred to let the man rest in peace, but it appeared he had no other alternatives, so he hurried over to the general to fill him in on his proposal.

"I will pay whatever it takes to get these men to safety. Here, I want you to take all the gold I have on me. If you need more, you may assure the sailor I will pay them handsomely upon our arrival in Kolig. Here, take this as well," General McLeod ordered, handing Adel a hefty sack of coins and a piece of insignia from his uniform which identified him as the Supreme General of the Thornatan Army. "That should be enough to convince anyone that you are truly asking on my orders. But I don't want you going alone. Take one of your companions with you."

"I had thought to leave them both here in case the camp came under attack by the Hoyt," Adel protested, but the general waved down his arguments. He was too valuable to go alone, and that was the end of it. It seemed as though the sun recognized his urgency and declined to assist him, creeping ever further out of sight as he raced back to Ola and Alsea.

"The general will pay for the boat but insists one of you accompany me. We need to get moving right away. Make up your minds," Adel explained as he rushed to throw a few items in a small pack.

"I will come with you," Alsea declared after a hurried conversation with Ola. "If the Hoyt find this camp, they will attack. Ola is better than I am for defending against a direct assault. Plus, it may take longer to hire a captain with an ogre hovering over your shoulder. No offense, Ola, but being charming falls in my wheelhouse more than yours."

Within minutes, the pair was off, leaving camp and following the Kival River north toward Kolig. The flat terrain was easy enough for fast travel and mostly firm from a hard frost the night before. Adel estimated it was roughly five miles to the city. They could cover the distance within two hours or less if they kept up a good pace. They moved as rapidly as possible, knowing every second they were gone was a second the camp was in increased danger of attack. A barge could make the return trip in an hour at most, and Adel hoped they would find one to hire without delay.

"This was a good idea, Adel. I don't like splitting up, but I'm not sure most of those men would make it through the night and a long walk tomorrow. It's been hard enough up until now, just getting them along this far. It's nothing short of a miracle that none of them died in the cold last night," Alsea remarked, breaking the silence after a few minutes. It was true. Had he not been able to use his power to keep a few fires ablaze in the surprisingly frosty night, their company would've likely been smaller now.

"Being by the river made me think of my days on the barge, and then it hit me that we could use a barge to get those men some help. I agree; it's been a hard journey on them. As difficult as it has been for us, it's been worse on them. Their toughness is remarkable. We are lucky the village was as close to Kolig as it is, or most of them would not have stood a chance of survival."

"Speaking of the village, we haven't had much time to talk about what happened back there. You handled yourself as confidently as I've ever seen. The winter of training has served you well. Those Hoyt scum never stood a chance against us. And that great monster would have killed us all if not for you and the Rawl," she commended.

"Thanks, but I have to ask because I've hardly been able to stop thinking about it. Do you have any idea what that creature was? I've never seen anything like it. Nothing should have been able to withstand the punishment we inflicted on that thing. For a moment, I thought we were all going to die," Adel admitted.

"If it hadn't been for your quick thinking, we may have. I've never seen anything like it either. Did you notice it was wearing Thornatan Army clothing? The same black undergarments they wear under their armor?"

"I did notice that," Adel replied, troubled by the potential implications.

"I don't want to theorize too much because frankly, I don't know. I've never encountered anything like it, and I've been pretty much everywhere in Thornata. But I do not think it was anything natural. If I'm right about that, it may mean the Hoyt are willing to go to disturbing lengths to see you dead. I'm sure you noticed it seemed quite intent on reaching you, as though the rest of us were just in its way," Alsea said.

It was true; the beast had gone right after him several times, virtually ignoring attackers who were actively assaulting it. He had never heard of a predator disregarding enemies who were inflicting mortal wounds on it in the name of killing its prey. But was Idanox truly capable of sending such a creature after him? Even more worrisome, if he was, would he do so again? Questions only begged more questions with no answers to be found. There was no point dwelling on the beast now, he supposed. It was dead and would not trouble them again. They had to hope they would not encounter such a creature again. Their focus needed to remain on what they could control in the present.

The pair continued in silence, the only noise coming from the nocturnal insects beginning to come awake. They had been walking for perhaps twenty minutes when a horrified scream shattered the peaceful night. The scream had come from behind them, a fact that stopped them dead in their tracks. Within seconds, new cries and screams began to fill the air. Horrified, Adel realized they were coming from the camp they had just left. Without pausing to speak, they both turned and began racing back, desperate to reach the camp as fast as their legs could carry them.

They covered the distance within minutes, and Adel raced into the camp with his sword drawn, expecting to find a group of attacking Hoyt fighters assaulting the wounded. Following the sound of crashing blades, he was stunned to find not Hoyt fighters but the same beast that had assaulted them in the village. There was no doubt it was the same creature. The features were identical, and the tunic was torn in the exact spot where Ola had hacked the beast in half. The same twisted snarl was etched across its face, but the eye Alsea had shot out had somehow reappeared in its skull. It was locked in combat with Ola, and two dead Thornatan soldiers were crumpled on the ground a few feet behind it. They had killed this monster, so how was it here now? It was impossible. Snapping himself out of his confusion, he moved to act before it was too late.

Remembering his technique that had distracted the beast during their previous encounter, Adel went to work at once. Reaching out toward the river, he called on his power in the same way he had back at the farm, forming a ball of water and sending it racing toward the beast's face. However, this time the attack did not seem to distract the creature. To Adel's amazement, it was seemingly breathing the water right into its lungs and expelling it out through its snarling mouth. Whatever this creature was, it had adapted to his previous method of assault. Paying the water no mind, it merely continued its brutal assault on Ola, who was steadily being forced to give up ground.

Adel couldn't believe what he was seeing. The mindless beast was forcing Ola into a steady retreat, the orb of water swirling about its face all the while. Ola was stronger than any man Adel had ever met, yet he could not hold his ground against this monster. Each vicious attack forced the ogre to stumble a few steps backward. Every few seconds, Ola's greatsword would find an opening and open a fresh wound on his opponent, but it did not seem to matter one bit to this savage creature. It showed no sign of pain, no indication the many cuts would slow it down in the slightest. Accepting his water attack was not going to affect the beast, Adel released it to conserve his energy.

He spun to look at Alsea beside him and was surprised to find she was not there. Looking around frantically to locate her, he spotted her at last in the shadows behind the beast, creeping up with a long knife in her hand. As Ola broke off from the creature and moved a few paces back, she sprung from the shadows, leaping onto the beast's back and repeatedly stabbing at its head and neck with the knife. The blade struck countless times, plunging deep into the creature's rock-hard flesh with pinpoint precision. Each blow would have been lethal to any normal man, but that was not what Alsea was up against.

The beast cried out, not in pain but frustration, thrashing wildly, attempting to rid itself of her. At last, it managed to throw her from its back, her knife still protruding from the side of its head. Alsea sprung to her feet immediately. Her hand was reaching for her sword the second she touched the ground, but she was not quick enough to avoid the savage kick the beast aimed at her. It struck her with such force that she was lifted from her feet and fell to the ground. She did not move.

Furious, Adel lashed out at the beast, striking it with repeated wind blasts, sending it stumbling backward, away from the vulnerable Alsea. It was merely a delaying action, but Adel had no better ideas.

Determined not to allow this beast to do any more damage, Adel charged while continuing his stream of wind blasts. As he closed the distance, he unleashed one final powerful blast, which knocked the beast from its feet. Adel was on top of it immediately, hacking and hammering with his sword with all his might. He was trying futilely with every ounce of strength he could muster to cut the life from it, swinging at its neck, chest, and head. This loss of composure would have cost him his life if it were not for Ola.

Any delusions his anger-filled mind may have given him that this hotheaded attack would slay the beast were dispelled as soon as it came to its feet despite his relentless and vicious strikes. It lashed back at him with one of its massive axes. His sword was low, in no position to defend the attack, and he likely did not possess the physical strength to hold it at bay even if he could get into position. The blow would have split his head open had Ola not charged back into the fray, knocking Adel aside and absorbing the impact of the axe himself.

Adel looked up from the ground and saw Ola once again locked in a frenzied battle with the beast. This time, it was clear something was horribly wrong. Blood was rapidly pooling underneath the feet of the combatants. Adel had yet to see this creature bleed so profusely, even when its legs had been cut off, leading him to assume that Ola was seriously wounded. His anger gave way to fear and desperation. Ola would not be able to hold the creature off for much longer. He had to get the beast out of their camp, and he had to do it now.

With great effort, he heeded Elim's advice from early in his training at the Temple of the Rawl, clearing his mind and simplifying his thought process. He forced the panic from his brain, taking deep breaths and focusing. The beast was in their camp, and he needed it gone. What was the best way to accomplish this? The answer came to him instinctively, just as it had during his first lessons at the Temple of the Rawl. He reached out once more toward the river, this time summoning far more water than he had on his first attempt.

Once he felt he had gathered enough water, Adel sent it spinning toward the beast, letting it crash into the monster with as much force as possible. The beast stumbled, attempting to regain its feet, but he struck over and over, never allowing his foe to gain a solid foothold, sending it back to the ground every time it found its feet. Each time he knocked it down, he pushed the water slightly closer to the river, dragging the monster along with it. It was a slow process, forcing the monster through their camp, driving it ever closer to the Kival River. Finally, once the beast was clear of any of the wounded, he struck with a massive tidal wave that lifted the creature from its feet. He maintained the attack, sweeping it out of the camp and into the river.

With the beast fully immersed in the water, Adel focused with all his might. He was willing the river's current to gain speed just as it had on the day he had first discovered his power. This was a feat he had not attempted consciously before and was unsure if he was capable of doing it. To his great relief, the river did indeed pick up speed, the current becoming too strong for even this massive beast to fight against for long. It was swept away in moments, but Adel kept his concentration up for as long as possible, though for how many minutes, he could not be sure. He was hoping against hope that the beast would be many miles downriver before the current slowed enough for it to break free of its grip.

At last, Adel could hold his focus no longer, the mental and physical effort taking its toll. He fell to his knees as he broke his hold on the river. He prayed silently to himself that he had not deposited the monster near any unsuspecting bystanders. He was more thoroughly exhausted than he had been the last time he had fended off an enemy attack on the banks of this river, but he knew there was no time to rest, as the moans of pain which soon began to rise into the night air would remind him.

Chapter Six

Adel knew immediately his moment of respite was doomed to be short-lived. The cries and moans arising from the camp around him forced him to set aside his exhaustion and spring back into action. He stumbled to his feet and began assessing the damage done by the beast's attack. His first relief was to find General McLeod on his feet, working his way through the wounded and checking on them. A small touch of panic began to set in as he scanned for Alsea but found no sign of her where she had fallen. He immediately worried he had accidentally washed her into the river along with the beast. A moment later, she limped up beside him, grimacing and wincing with each step. She immediately waved off the arm he offered her for support.

"Don't worry about me; others got it a lot worse. Look at Ola."

Ola was on his feet as well, but Adel was less encouraged by what he saw from the ogre. He was using a ripped blanket to bind a significant wound above his hip, but it was failing to contain the bleeding. The injury was bleeding so profusely that the blood had seeped through the makeshift bandage almost immediately. Adel hurried over to try to assist his friend tending to his injury, a wound which he felt was his responsibility. Had he not attacked the monster haphazardly, Ola would not have needed to place himself between Adel and the axe. If Ola did not recover from the injury, it would be on Adel's hands.

You should be in better control of your emotions, he scolded himself.

"It's bleeding too heavily to bind effectively. Adel, can you bring me a torch, please?" Ola asked as he approached. Adel rushed to comply, not yet comprehending Ola's intent, merely thinking Ola needed help seeing the wound in the darkness.

"Sit down, Ola. You need to rest," Adel urged as he returned with the torch, though the ogre's facial expression conveyed a clear intent to do no such thing.

"There's no time for rest, and it wouldn't do me much good anyway. Rest or no rest, this is going to keep bleeding. I need to use the flame on the wound. I can burn it closed to stop the bleeding. But this torch is not hot enough to do the job. Can you help me?" Ola asked.

This was not a request Adel had ever expected anyone to make of him, and it was not one he was eager to grant. But Ola's wound was severe, a fact for which he had himself to blame. No matter how unpleasant this would be for him, he knew it would be ten times more so for his friend. He passed the torch to Ola, bracing himself for what would come next. He had no choice but to set aside his apprehension and do what needed to be done. If Ola had not done the same in the face of that monster's attack, Adel would be dead now.

"I'm so sorry about this, Ola. If I had been in better control of myself, this might not have happened. It's all my fault," he said, fighting back the tears welling up in the corners of his eyes. He could not remember being this upset since the Hoyt attack on his barge the previous spring.

"It did happen, and there is no point in being upset about it now, Adel. We need to hurry. That beast is not dead, and the longer we stand here talking about it, the more time we are giving it to gain ground on us. The last thing we want is for it to attack us again tonight," Ola admonished, his voice shockingly calm for one suffering from such a horrible wound. Adel nodded, setting aside his guilt and reminding himself of the people who were relying on him. Ola's toughness was remarkable and inspiring, and Adel knew it was now his time to rise to the occasion.

"I'm going to press the flame against my wound. As soon as I do, you need to use your power to make the flame burn as hot as you can for a few seconds. Do not let up until I pull the torch away. If you stop too soon, we will have to do it again, and I assure you this is going to be a very unpleasant experience for me. I would rather not have to do this more than once. Do you understand?" Ola said, pulling the torn blanket away from his side and allowing the wound to bleed freely.

Nodding his understanding and swallowing his nerves, Adel focused on the torch in the ogre's hand. Ola firmly pressed the flame against his open wound, his eyes closing as he did so. Adel immediately reached out with the Rawl, intensifying the fire as much as he possibly could without burning the torch to ash. To his amazement, Ola did not cry out, wince, or show even the slightest hint of pain as the white-hot flame sealed his wound.

How can anyone endure this without so much as a cry? After a few seconds, Ola pulled the torch away from his body, and Adel released his hold on the fire. Ola opened his eyes and examined the blackened scar that had been a gushing cut a few moments earlier. It was not healed, but at least the bleeding had subsided for the time being. Once again, Adel could not help but feel a sense of admiration for the ogre's incredible toughness.

"It will need a healer at some point to prevent infection, but I will be fine until then. Fine enough to get out of here anyway. Thank you for your help, Adel. Alsea, are you badly hurt?" Ola asked.

Adel had forgotten Alsea's injuries in the wake of Ola's needs, but now he turned to find her hunched over in pain. She had taken a brutal kick from the beast to her torso, and Adel worried she had broken bones or was bleeding inside. She briefly allowed him to take her by the hand and used it to steady herself, but then she gently pushed him away. Alsea straightened up, wincing in pain as she did, though Adel knew she was doing her best to conceal her discomfort from him.

"I'll survive. I think that brute may have cracked a few of my ribs, but it's nothing I can't tough out." Adel was about to protest the casual dismissal of her injuries when General McLeod staggered over to them. His face was pale, and Adel was immediately concerned that the aging general was on the verge of collapse.

"We've lost a few more men. The two it encountered before Ola could intervene never had a chance. The stress proved to be too much for two others; it looks like they gave in to their injuries. The rest of the wounded are in terrible shape. There's no time to get to Kolig and hire a barge, and there's no time to wait until morning. We need to leave right now and get them to Kolig. I don't relish the idea of making the trip in the dark, but I don't see that we have much of a choice. That was a clever move to get rid of it, Adel. But I think we would be fools not to assume it's already on its way back," McLeod said through gritted teeth, obviously trying to mask his pain.

It was imperative to get the wounded to Kolig and capable healers as soon as possible. The camp was no longer safe, and there was a good chance the beast was already making its way back here. But there was no way he could go to Kolig. There was no longer any doubt the creature was hunting him. It had located him twice now, and there was little reason to believe it would not do so again. If he led that monster into the middle of a crowded city, it could wreak havoc and death on a scale that was hard to imagine. His mind was instantly made up, and he launched into an explanation of his plan without delay.

"You are right, General McLeod. All of you need to get to the healers in Kolig tonight. If we stay here, it's only a matter of time until the beast returns. If you leave now and follow the river, you should make it to the city by dawn, even with the wounded. I will set off on my own to the west. Once I cross the river, I will march in a straight line as far from the rest of you as I can get. I am certain that thing is tracking me somehow, maybe with some sort of magic I don't understand. I'm confident it will continue to follow me and allow all of you to get to the city safely. Once it catches up to me, I will do everything I can to put an end to it. If I manage to do so, I will rejoin you in Kolig as soon as I can. If I don't, hopefully its hunt will end with me."

There was a moment of silence as Ola, Alsea, and General McLeod processed the plan he had laid out for them. As he had expected, they did not see eye to eye and were none too shy about expressing their opinions.

"Are you out of your mind? If you think for one second that I'm leaving you out here alone with that monster hunting you down, then you need a healer to check you for a blow to the head!" Alsea snorted, immediately wincing in pain from the movement.

"Alsea, we can't lead that thing into a crowded city; you must understand that. I will not have any more innocent people die for being in the wrong place at the wrong time," he argued desperately. He had to make them understand that every second wasted arguing about this was a second they did not have to spare. "I appreciate what you are saying, but it is following me and nobody else. Anybody with me—anybody near me—is in unnecessary danger. If I go on my own, I may at least be able to make sure it does not hurt anyone else. This is the only way to be sure of that. Please, do not fight me on this."

"Adel is right. We cannot lead the beast into Kolig. It is far too dangerous. It would wreak havoc we would be unable to contain, and too many innocents would pay the price for it," Ola conceded, much to Adel's surprise. He had expected Ola would fight tooth and nail against his plan.

"I can't believe what I'm hearing! You swore to protect him, and now you are going to leave him out here to be murdered by that monster? I never thought I would hear you say such a thing, Ola. Go if you wish, but I will not leave Adel behind!" Adel had never seen Alsea this livid, but now it was Ola's turn to get angry. Even the fearless Alsea backed away slightly from the fire that sprung to life in the ogre's eyes.

"Do not presume to know what I am going to say before I say it, Alsea! After all these months together, did you actually believe I would abandon Adel? I meant General McLeod and the remainder of his men should go to Kolig without us. You and I will go with Adel and draw the beast away from them," he explained. The curt manner of his explanation reminded Adel of the early days of their friendship, before the ogre had finally opened up about his past as a slave.

Adel was flattered by his companion's refusals to leave him behind, but this discussion was taking time they did not have to waste. There was no way to tell exactly how far downriver he had managed to wash the beast. It could take days for it to make up the ground, or it could be back at this spot within hours. They could not be sure, and he had no desire to find out the hard way. He had to make them understand that he could not allow them to accompany him.

"Ola, Alsea, words cannot express how grateful I am to both of you for everything you have done for me and everything you are willing to do going forward. But you are both wounded badly, and when the beast catches us again, you would not be able to defend yourselves properly against it. I would stand a better chance on my own," he said.

"You would stand no chance at all," Alsea said bluntly. She wasn't wrong, but it still wounded his pride to hear her say it.

"She is right, Adel. Drawing this creature out into the open and trying to fight it on your own will not work. You have become quite powerful, but you are no match for it. I'm sorry to say it, but it is the truth. You have performed admirably in both of our encounters with it, and you are the sole reason any of us are still alive. But you have been unable to finish it off, and that will not change easily. This is something we have to face together," Ola concurred.

"None of us are a match for it; there is no reason for the two of you to die trying to stop it!" Adel snapped, his patience gone.

His frustration was intensifying by the second. They needed to understand this was his choice to make, and he was not going to allow his friends to persuade him otherwise. Did they think he was excited at the thought of dying alone in the wilderness at this monster's hands? How could they not understand that he was making this sacrifice so they could live? What was wrong with them?

"Hear me out, Adel, please. Your plan is noble but rather flawed," said Ola. "The general and his men need to head for Kolig right away. You, Alsea, and I can head due east to draw the beast in the opposite direction. Once we have given the general enough time to reach Kolig, we can turn north and make for the Temple of the Rawl. It's a long journey, but if we can reach the temple, we will be safe inside. There are ancient protections surrounding it; even this monster will not be able to reach you there. I do not know what magic created it, but it is no match for the powers shielding the temple. I promise you that."

It was not a bad plan, but Adel was still skeptical. A massive stone wall shielded the Temple of the Rawl, and ferocious giants guarded it, but this beast was unlike anything else he had ever encountered. Still, it was a sanctuary better equipped than any other to protect them against the beast; it was undeniable. The validity of the suggestion did not make him forget one pressing concern he had.

"Can the two of you even make it to the temple? It took us nearly five days to travel from the temple to Kolig last fall. Your injuries are quite severe. Do you honestly believe we can make it there before the beast catches us again?" he asked, scanning their faces for any hint of deception in their responses.

"Now you're just insulting us. Besides, there are a few shortcuts I know of that could shorten our journey by a day or two." Alsea snickered, this motion also causing an involuntary grimace. Her injuries were far worse than she was letting on. Ola did not bother voicing his reassurance, merely nodding and sheathing his greatsword.

"Adel, if I may offer my opinion?" General McLeod cut in. In the intensity of the argument, Adel had nearly forgotten the general was there.

"You know I would welcome it, General McLeod."

"You are trying to do something noble here. You are trying to keep the remainder of my men safe, and I am grateful beyond measure for it. But you are overlooking and undervaluing your own importance. Whatever this monster is, it is after you for a reason. To be blunt, I think we will need you if we are going to win this war against the Hoyt. Ola and Alsea are wounded, but they are both capable of making their own decisions in this matter. If they come with you, I feel you will have a better chance of survival. Your selflessness is admirable, make no mistake about it. But please take a word of advice from a man who has seen a lot of death in his life. Do not rush to throw your life away so recklessly."

Adel was silent for a moment. Ola and Alsea both nodded in agreement with McLeod's statement. When the general had cut in, Adel had been hopeful McLeod was going to side with him. He realized in hindsight this had been foolish for him to expect. McLeod wanted him back with the army, helping him stamp out the Hoyt. He would not want Adel to face the beast alone under any circumstances.

It was clear there was nothing he could say to change their minds on this. If they would not be persuaded, he had little choice but to accept their company despite his misgivings. If the beast found them again before they reached the Temple of the Rawl, he had to hope he would be able to protect his friends. The wounded could not afford any more time spent on senseless arguments.

They broke camp without delay, and the injured who were able to walk were tasked with helping those who could not. There was little in the way of discussion; time spent talking was time the beast could be using to close in on them. General McLeod extended a hand to Adel before he departed.

"Thank you for everything, Adel. I hope you can find a way to rid yourself of that monster and rejoin us. Rest assured, I'll be doing everything I can to sniff out that rat Idanox while you are away. When you return, we will go pay him a little visit together," General McLeod said.

"We will, General. I am truly sorry for all the men you have lost. Every one of them is a hero. I'm sorry we can't see you safely the rest of the way to Kolig. Once we rid ourselves of this beast, we will regroup and finally hunt Idanox down and put an end to him and the rest of the Hoyt," Adel said, shaking General McLeod's hand.

"You've got that right, my friend. The day can't come soon enough. I'm tired of seeing this province bleed in the name of satiating that bastard's ego."

With that, the two groups parted ways in the dark of night. General McLeod and what remained of his men began making their way north along the Kival River toward Kolig. Adel and his companions set off to the east, just the three of them once again. They were injured, exhausted, and unsure if they would succeed in escaping the beast. But they knew it was out there somewhere, hunting them as they walked, and they could not afford to give in to their weariness. They had seen no indication that this beast grew tired or that it would halt for even a second in its pursuit. Even an hour of rest now could cost them all their lives tomorrow.

Adel was comforted to have his friends with him, if not entirely happy about it. He had wanted them to go with the general and his men to Kolig; they would've been much safer there. If the beast caught up to them in the wild, just the three of them, they would die. He could admit it to himself, even if none of them were willing to voice it aloud. But as much as he wished they had listened to him, he knew there were no two people in this world he would rather have by his side if he were forced to face the monster for a third time.

Chapter Seven

For the remainder of the night and well into the next morning, Adel and his companions fought through their exhaustion with every step. They trudged eastward as fast as possible, refusing to allow their weariness to overcome them, though it attempted to do so with every breath they drew. The rapidly dropping temperatures made matters worse. Ola and Alsea were able to move with a speed that defied their horrific injuries, though Adel had a bad feeling they would not be able to sustain such a pace for long. He had seen Ola's wound firsthand, and he knew Alsea's injuries were far more severe than she would allow them to see. All the while, they were constantly scanning their surroundings, searching for any sign of the inhuman beast that continued to stalk them. They were all in agreement. It was not a matter of if it would find them again but how soon.

By midmorning, the trio had left any semblance of a trail behind. They were surrounded by wilderness on all sides. This gave Adel a certain sense of relief; at least the beast would be less likely to come across innocent passersby in these thick woods. The people from the small farming village kept creeping into his head. Had any of them perished at the hands of the monster after it repaired itself? He did not know, and he was not sure if he wanted to know. He could only hope none of them had been nearby when the creature had regenerated its legs.

Noon was fast approaching, and they had barely had a moment to pause since fleeing their camp in the night when Adel decided they needed to have a rest. As fearful as he was of their stalker, his friends would collapse if they pushed much longer with no break.

"We should stop here for a bit and rest for a few minutes. I am too exhausted to push on any farther. I can't imagine how you both feel with your injuries," he declared.

To their credit, Ola and Alsea did not show any sign of fatigue, but Adel knew they were too stubborn to admit any weakness. Leaving them to sit for a moment, he made a quick circle around the perimeter of their location, scanning for any signs of the beast or other enemies. Satisfied that they were safe enough for the time being, he made his way back to his companions and took a seat beside them. He passed around a waterskin, watching to ensure they both drank enough. He did not fail to note the pained expressions accompanying their swallowing. The night's march had been hard on them, and things would not improve anytime soon.

"The general and his men should have reached Kolig by now. We have traveled far enough east to draw the creature away from them. We should be able to safely turn north and set out for the Temple of the Rawl," Ola declared.

Adel's thoughts turned to the Temple of the Rawl. He had agreed to flee there for safety but had not thought much about the possible ramifications of the decisions he had made since his departure. They had departed the temple months ago with the expectation that they would assist with breaking the Hoyt occupation of Kolig and then return to continue his training. Instead, they had set off with General McLeod and his men on a hunt for Idanox, a pursuit which had been unsuccessful thus far.

Would Elim and the Children of the Rawl be angry with him for his choice? Would they even allow him to enter the temple with this beast pursuing him? He had not intended to break his promise to the Children, and he still wished to continue his training with them. He was hopeful the Children would have a solution for the monster on their heels, but would they still be open to sharing their knowledge with him? There was no help for it, of course.

He had broken his word, and he would soon have to face the potential consequences of that. He had no better alternative, so he would go to the temple, as Ola had suggested. There was no point in worrying about it now. He needed to keep his focus on the present if they hoped to survive long enough to see the future.

They rested for close to an hour before deciding it was time to push on. Adel noticed Alsea struggling to her feet and moved to help. She batted his hand away briefly before reluctantly accepting his assistance. The stubborn young woman had hardly spoken a word since they had left camp, leading Adel to surmise that her pain was much worse than she was letting on. Once on her feet, however, she finally broke her long silence.

"We should head straight north, directly toward the Bonners. There is a river that runs at their feet, and if we follow it back toward the west, there is a small canyon we can make our way through right into the valley below the temple. It's a rocky path, but it will trim a day or two off our journey. Assuming we don't drown crossing the river, of course. It's a tricky crossing at the best of times, which is why I avoided it last summer when we left the temple."

"The snow on the mountains will be melting rapidly at this time of year. That could make the crossing even more treacherous," Ola cautioned.

"We will take Alsea's shortcut. The pair of you need to reach the temple as soon as possible. I can always use the Rawl to slow the river's current if need be," Adel declared, surprising himself a bit with his forwardness. His companions did not seem to mind his initiative, however, and soon they were heading straight north toward the Bonner Mountains.

They continued all afternoon and well into the evening before Adel once again forced them to stop and rest. As little as he wanted to encounter the beast again, he knew the journey would soon become too much for his injured friends, despite their protests to the contrary. Once again, Adel ordered them to sit while he prepared their camp. He began to gather wood for a fire, against Ola's protests that it would make them too visible to their enemies.

"Ola, if that creature is nearby, it will find us with or without the fire. It isn't following our physical tracks; it is tracking me by some supernatural means. At least with the fire, we can see it coming, and the two of you need some warmth. Besides, I can use the fire as a weapon against anyone or anything that might try to attack us. No offense, but look at the two of you; neither of you are fit to fight, and don't try to tell me otherwise. If the Hoyt or that beast find us, I'll need the fire if we are going to have any hope of surviving," Adel explained, to which the ogre finally relented.

Adel had a fire going within minutes with a bit of help from the Rawl. They did not have much left in the way of food. They had prepared for a journey of about a week when they departed Kalskag, so they had to make do with a few tins of dried plums and pieces of stale bread. Nonetheless, they were happy to rest with the warmth of the fire, and nobody complained about the meager rations.

"We could reach the river in two days if we keep moving at our current pace. From there, we could be at the temple in another day," Alsea said, breaking the silence.

Three more days at our current pace may prove to be too much for them, Adel thought to himself. Yet there was a more concerning thought in his mind. Three days may not be quick enough to elude the beast relentlessly pursuing them. They must assume this creature did not require rest or food in the same manner as they did. If this was the case, every moment they stopped to rest was a moment the beast was gaining ground on them.

"You should both get some sleep. I will keep watch tonight," Adel suggested to immediate protests.

The trio finally agreed that Adel would keep watch for the first half of the night, and Ola and Alsea would each take a shorter shift. They would leave shortly before dawn and head north once more. Once Ola and Alsea were both asleep, Adel sat with his back against a tree and reflected on the drastic changes to his life in the past year.

It had been around this time the year before that he was beginning his final voyage on the barge with Captain Boyd. They had spent the winter docked in the northern port city of Kival, and as they had departed on their first voyage of the year, Adel had never suspected what was waiting for them. It seemed like a lifetime ago, floating down the river on a gorgeous spring day, the Hoyt attack, the blockade, and finally discovering his power. The months since had been nothing short of a whirlwind. If the young man who had set out on that last voyage a year ago could look at him now, he would probably not recognize himself.

Adel wondered if he would have made all the same decisions with the benefit of hindsight. He would probably take a long hard look at whether joining forces with General McLeod was a good idea. He had done some good, but there had been failures as well. This beast would not likely be out hunting for him if not for his partnership with the general.

This line of thinking was doing him no good. The past could not be changed, so why dwell on it? He had to live with the decisions he had made. Wondering what might have been was a course of action that could have no positive impact, and he needed to stop. Instead, he turned his thoughts to the next few days. He needed to focus on things he still had control over.

Could they reach the Temple of the Rawl in time? They were not only racing against the beast that pursued them but also the injuries Ola and Alsea were both fighting through to keep walking. They had both put on brave faces all night and day, but Adel knew it was only a matter of time before the wounds prevented them from traveling altogether. They were as physically tough as anybody he had ever met, but he knew even they had their limits. If either of them perished from their efforts to protect him, he would never forgive himself. These fears and self-doubts continued to invade his mind throughout his watch and made sleep difficult after Ola relieved him halfway through the night.

They departed again shortly before dawn, continuing to march due north toward the Bonners. The forests were steadily thinning out, bringing the massive peaks into full view by midday. Though the more wide-open foothills would give them less cover, Adel was comforted by the fact that they would make it more difficult for the beast to sneak up on them as it had at their camp by the river. He had spent the night with bated breath, waiting for the monstrous creature to appear from the cover of the trees.

They steadily began to climb the foothills, determined to reach the river the following day. Adel found himself looking over his shoulder every few minutes, searching for any sign of the beast below them. Each time, he felt confident he would spot it closing in on them from behind. To his relief, no sign appeared that day.

Adel brought them to a halt again shortly before sunset, seeing the uphill trek was wearing heavily on his injured companions. Again, they had endured the journey without complaint but had barely spoken at all since departing that morning. Their evening meal was even more sparse than the night before, and the following night would be more meager still, assuming they survived long enough to have it. If it took longer than expected to reach the Temple of the Rawl, the shortage of food would become a severe problem. Ola and Alsea were weak enough without hunger adding to their problems. Adel briefly considered going back down into the woods to hunt for food but immediately dismissed the idea. Leaving his friends alone in their current state for any length of time was not an option.

This night, there was minimal discussion, Ola and Alsea finding spots to sleep and drifting off shortly after their arrival. They did not even have enough strength to argue with him about keeping watch. Adel was racked with guilt; he should have been more insistent that they go to Kolig with General McLeod. This journey was slowly killing them, one step at a time. Adel feared their injuries would be too severe by the time they reached the Temple of the Rawl for them to be saved. There was no helping it now, but Adel vowed to himself that he would be more of a leader if a similar situation occurred again.

Morning came quickly for Adel even though he had kept watch all night, refusing to wake his wounded friends. They were not happy about it, but they were also too weak to do much complaining. They were off again as the sun was rising, determined to make the river by midday. Ola and Alsea trudged on with inhuman courage and resolve. As the noon hour arrived, they stumbled down to the banks of the river. Once again, Adel insisted they stop for a brief break to only hushed arguments. He looked at them with new reverence. Not only had they made it this far, but they had done so quicker than any of them could have hoped. Perhaps they could reach the temple without encountering the beast again after all. For the first time since before their first encounter with the beast, he felt optimistic.

He had an idea for making the remainder of their journey easier on the pair, but he was determined to find them some food first. He scavenged the riverbank, never leaving sight of his friends. After close to an hour of seeing nothing but empty berry bushes, he was about to admit defeat when he spotted a barge floating on the river. He glanced around. His friends were several hundred feet away, and he had no backup, but they needed the food, so he made a break for the shoreline, yelling and waving his arms.

The barge slowed down to examine him but did not come to a stop. It was a large vessel, larger than the one Adel had served on under Captain Boyd. Such a boat would no doubt have plenty of food stores to spare a little for them. A man Adel presumed to be the captain stood near the port railing and eyed him curiously.

"Do you have any food you can spare? I will pay you for it. Please, we need something, anything at all," Adel called out desperately.

"How much do you have?" the barge captain called back.

Reaching into his bag, Adel withdrew a gold coin, held it up for the man to see, and tossed it out to the boat.

The man caught it, examined it for a moment, and then disappeared out of sight. Adel jogged to keep pace with the ship, fearing the man was going to take his coin and leave. He could use the Rawl to bring the boat to a forceful stop, but he had no desire to take anything from these men by force. But a moment later, the man returned with a small cloth sack, which he flung toward the shore.

Calling out thanks to the man as the barge moved away, Adel raced to untie the bag. It held a small amount of rice and even a few spices. It was not much but would make them a thin soup they could eat before heading downriver. It may be just enough to keep his friends' strength up for the remainder of their journey to the temple. He hurried back upriver to where they rested and found Alsea on her feet, apparently about to set off in search of him.

"Where have you been? We thought that beast caught up to us and got you," she said.

"I'm sorry to worry you. Sit down and rest, please. I was finding something to eat. You two need something to keep your strength up." Adel waved her off, gathering a few sticks together for a fire.

"You're cooking now? We are wasting time. We have to get downriver and make the crossing before nightfall," she argued back.

"No, Alsea, we need to eat. The two of you are on the verge of collapse, and don't bother trying to deny it. We've hardly had anything to eat since parting ways with

McLeod. I feel like I could fall over at any moment. I can't imagine how you feel. We are not walking downriver today either. No, don't argue with me right now. Can you just help me cook this, please? I'm serious. Don't bother arguing with me because it will be a waste of your strength. I'll explain my plan. I promise."

They were clearly quite confused, but they were also correct that time was of the essence. He could not stop and explain his plan at the moment. Leaving Alsea to finish the soup, he moved over to the riverbank. This idea had occurred to him on their walk that morning, and he hoped desperately that it would work. Drawing upon his power, he focused on the water and exactly what he wanted.

The power of the Rawl worked quickly, freezing the water near the shoreline into a substantial chunk of ice within moments, but he continued to work. He needed the ice to be thick enough to support all of them yet buoyant enough to ensure they would not sink. It was no easy task, and for the most part, he relied on the Rawl to form the raft instinctually. By the time he was done, his eyelids were beginning to droop, and he was ready for some rice, which Alsea had just finished.

"We will eat now, and then we will get on the ice. It will act as a raft and carry us down the river to the canyon," Adel explained. "We can lay down our bedrolls so we aren't sitting directly on the ice. It won't be comfortable by any means, but it will be faster than we could walk, and it's safer than trying to cross on our own. Most importantly, it will keep us moving all afternoon while we have a chance to rest. From what Alsea has said, it's several miles to the canyon. At our pace, we will never make it by nightfall on foot. Hopefully, when we reach the canyon, we will all be rested enough to keep walking until we reach the Temple of the Rawl."

"You never cease to impress me, Adel," Ola said, the first words he had spoken all day. Was it Adel's imagination or did the ogre's blue skin look lighter than usual? Could ogres go pale? Deciding it did him no good to dwell on this now, Adel smiled his thanks for the compliment.

They ate hurriedly, then Adel snuffed their fire and began moving their belongings onto the ice raft. After that morning, he had serious doubts about their ability to complete the journey on foot. To his great relief, he found the chunk of ice held all their belongings with no issue.

Then came the actual test as Ola and then Alsea stepped tentatively onto the makeshift raft, but once again, his fears were alleviated as the ice held firm. Uttering a silent thanks to the power of the Rawl, he climbed on to join them. Reaching out toward the current of the river with his power, he began moving them away from the shore and then thrusting them downriver.

While not exactly reminiscent of the barge he had spent so many days on, Adel found the ride downriver on the block of ice surprisingly comfortable. More importantly, it allowed them to rest for the remainder of the day as they floated downriver to the canyon. Alsea said once they reached the canyon, they could arrive at the Temple of the Rawl within hours. For the first time in days, Adel allowed his mind a moment of relaxation. However, the peaceful ride was to be short-lived as Alsea cried out.

"Adel, look over there!"

He spun in the direction she was pointing to find the last thing he wanted to see. There was the great beast on the river's southern shore, stalking toward them with both massive battle-axes gleaming in the late afternoon sun. It did not slow as it reached the water, merely walking through the river until the water became too deep and then paddling toward them with a speed which should not have been possible while carrying two heavy axes. How could anything be so powerful? What would it take to kill this thing? The monster should have sunk like a stone, yet on it came.

Adel acted out of instinct, knowing it would be the end of them if the beast reached the raft. Ola and Alsea had no strength left, and even at full strength they had been no match for this monster. He struck out with his power, not at the creature itself but rather at the water around it. He focused his energy the same way he had as he'd created the raft. The water around the beast began to freeze, locking it in place, but it lashed out with the axes, crushing the ice in its path as it continued its mad rush toward them.

Adel refocused his energy, knowing if he did not execute this attack properly, he would likely not have the strength to try again. He was not injured, but he had hardly slept for five days, and he knew it was only a matter of time before it caught up with him. He struck once more, this time with more power. He brought a whirlwind of water up around the beast's body and then froze it in an instant. He turned his focus to the water around it, freezing a vast stretch of the river near instantaneously. This time, the beast was unable to smash its way through, completely frozen in the ice block Adel had created. Using the last of his energy, he sent a blast of power through the water beneath them, speeding the current to carry them away from the beast as fast as possible. The monster stayed frozen in place in the water, a macabre ice sculpture rising from the river.

Adel collapsed face-first to the ice, Ola and Alsea trying to steady him. The night of no sleep, followed by the exertion of using his power on such a large scale, had brought him to his absolute limit. Alsea was easing him gently down, keeping him from hitting his head on the ice raft.

"That was amazing, Adel. With the nights as cold as they are, the beast will be trapped for a full day at least. That's more than enough time for us to reach the temple," she said.

Adel was so exhausted he was barely able to acknowledge she was right. The pursuit should be over for the time being, but he was far from reassured. Once they reached the Temple of the Rawl, they would have to find a solution to this monster that continued to hunt him. No matter how long the ice delayed it, it would come again; he was sure of it. Even this ominous thought was not enough to keep him from giving in to his weariness, and he drifted off to sleep right there on the ice raft despite his best efforts not to.

***

"Adel, wake up. We've reached the canyon. You have to guide us to shore." Alsea's voice shook him from his slumber.

He sat up sharply, blinking and attempting to see through the dark evening sky. He had been asleep for hours and hoped he would have enough energy for what was needed now. He focused once more on the current, this time pushing them toward the northern bank of the river with the last of his energy reserves. He was able to get them there, albeit slowly, and they gathered their belongings and clambered to shore.

Adel was looking around in the dark for a place to set up their camp for the night when loud footsteps broke the evening silence, crashing toward them. The beast had found them again.

He ripped his sword from its sheath, spinning in every direction in search of their foe. However, his fears were quickly put to bed as something far more massive than the beast emerged from the shadows of the canyon. He looked up to see the familiar face of the giant Klaweck, one of the gigantic protectors of the Temple of the Rawl, looking down at them. Adel fell to his knees, overcome at last by exhaustion and relief.

Chapter Eight

Far to the north of the remote mountain canyon where Adel and his companions were collapsing from exhaustion, Idanox felt a different type of weariness setting in on him. He had traveled east to the Thornatan capital city of Oreanna, planning on setting his final plan into motion at last. Yet now that he'd arrived, he found rallying his Hoyt fighters would prove to be a far more difficult task than he had anticipated. Looking back at his years of hard work, for the first time in a long time, he wondered if it had all been for naught.

He was staying in an abandoned cottage north of the city walls near the shore of the Kival River. It was a dilapidated hut surrounded by similar structures. The

Thornatan soldiers rarely patrolled this area, keener on protecting the more beautiful and developed center of the city. The problems faced by the type of people who lived in such poverty were of little concern to the duke. It was yet another instance where his willful lack of empathy for those beneath him would come back to bite him. It allowed the notorious Hoyt leader to hide here, right on the outskirts of the capital, undetected. It had allowed him to sway many people who lived in such conditions to fight for him.

The wealthy Idanox had never lived in such poverty, but it was a necessary sacrifice for the time being. Repulsive though he found it, the army would never suspect a man of his means to be hiding in a place like this. He had been here for three days and had yet to see a single patrol in the street outside. His lieutenants were still wary of visiting the shack in the light of day, so here he sat this late evening, awaiting their arrival. The later it grew, the more he suspected they were stalling. No doubt, they did not wish to bring him news he did not want to hear, as they had every other night. In the past, he had been known to take out a foul temper on bringers of bad news.

Their meeting last night had left him in a foul mood, which had yet to abate. His lieutenants had reported that the number of Hoyt fighters reporting to their assigned locations was less than half of what they had been expecting. They had lost many men to the meddlesome Rawl wielder in the Battle of Kolig, yet they still should've had a sufficient force to assault the capital. However, many men were not reporting as they had been instructed, men who had no excuse for such tardiness. Many had likely been hunted down by General McLeod and his attack force in recent weeks. Many more were likely cowards who had chosen to give up the fight and return to the safety of their squalor-filled lives. When he came to power, Idanox would see to it that each and every one of them was hunted down and brought to justice for their cowardice. A commitment to the Hoyt was a lifelong pledge, and he would see to it they remembered it.

He could understand their hesitation to continue fighting even if he could not forgive it. The Hoyt had banded together as a group of men who were tired of their governors overlooking them, determined to take control into their own hands. In the Hoyt, they had seen the opportunity to seize control of their own futures, to forge a better existence for themselves and their families. Whether their grievances were legitimate or not was irrelevant. Idanox had given them a figure to rally around, and they had rushed to his side with near-religious zeal. Now, with the results he had delivered far from impressive, many had become disillusioned with his leadership. His messages of the grandeur waiting for them had fallen flat. He would already be sitting in the duke's palace if it were not for the meddling of the Rawl wielder and his men's inability to put an end to it.

His chief lieutenant, a man named Glover who had been with the Hoyt since the beginning, arrived shortly before midnight. Two others came soon after, junior lieutenants whose names Idanox could not recall. The battles that had gone against them had cost the Hoyt dearly. Many of his most trusted commanders had been killed or captured by the army. The emergence of the Rawl wielder was to blame, emboldening the army to fight back with a fervor they had not shown before. Before the boy had come into the picture, the army had been content to allow the Hoyt to prey upon the smaller communities and trading caravans across the province. Now they were fighting back, and he was left with these bumbling incompetents to try to win a war. They would not have been among his first choices, but fortunately, his own mindpower would be sufficient enough for the job at hand.

"I assume you all ensured you were not followed?" Idanox asked as they all took seats around a dusty table in the kitchen of the shack. All three nodded in response, though he lacked confidence in their ability to ensure any such thing. With any luck, the army would think these fools would not be worth their time to follow. They were certainly not the type of men he would allow into positions of power if he had any better options available to him.

"A few more men have reported to their assignments, sir. I estimate we could muster a force of close to twelve hundred by the end of the month," Glover declared tentatively. His optimistic tone did not fool anyone. Glover was dim, but Idanox knew the man understood his news to be bitterly disappointing.

Idanox had hoped for a force of close to three thousand men for his planned assault on the capital. Oreanna was the best-defended city in the province, the high walls surrounding the city making it a formidable target. In the four hundred years since the city had been built, the outer wall had never been breached by an attacking force. That was not to mention the fact that it housed the largest garrison of the Thornatan Army in the province. Idanox believed they could overcome these challenges, but it would be a suicide assault without enough men. He had not brought the Hoyt this far to be defeated so easily. Idanox was a man who cared about his legacy. The fool who led other fools into certain death was not how he cared to be remembered.

"Winter is still just beginning to break, sir. We could wait a few more weeks. Perhaps more men will report," one of the junior lieutenants suggested.

"We can only wait for so long. We must have control of the capital before the end of spring. Any later and we will not have enough time to bring the entire province to heel before winter. If the people haven't been convinced by next winter that we should be in charge, they will spend the entire winter planning insurgencies against us. If we allow that to happen, next spring will bring the arrival of our bloody downfall. A short-lived reign for the Hoyt," Idanox snapped.

This was true enough, of course, but it was far from Idanox's primary motivation for hurrying the attack. While the peasants may indeed revolt, this was not his chief concern. Failing to seize control of Thornata soon could have grave consequences for him personally, but this was not anything he cared to share with these fools. He did not need their questions. He needed a solution, and he needed it now. He had made promises that were already long overdue, and continued delays would not be tolerated forever.

"Have you heard anything about the Rawl boy, sir?" Glover asked, cleverly changing the subject. Perhaps he was more intelligent than Idanox suspected, though this would be no crowning achievement.

"The beast has not yet brought me his head, but we have not heard any reports of him interfering with our recent affairs either. After seeing what that beast is capable of, I do not doubt the boy will be dead soon if he is not already," Idanox replied. He had no patience for Glover's stalling inquiries; however, an idea came to him even as he brushed the question aside. Glover was a fool, no doubt, but he had stumbled on a possible solution to their problem, albeit quite accidentally.

The dark mage Srenpe had traveled to Oreanna with him, suggesting he should be nearby when his beast returned from its mission. Idanox had not seen him since they had arrived in the city, but the mage could potentially be the answer to his problems. Idanox was now remembering the ferocious ease with which the mage's beast had dispatched his men in Kolsvard. Could the mage produce more of these formidable beasts? Could he perhaps provide a dozen of them? If so, the lack of Hoyt forces may prove to be less of an obstacle in the days ahead than he had feared. The thought of several such monsters tearing their way through dozens of Thornatan soldiers in the streets of Oreanna was an enticing one.

"Glover, I want you to find the mage Srenpe and bring him here to see me tomorrow night at this time. Tell him he will be well compensated for his time," Idanox said, his visions of horrific bloodshed becoming more spectacular by the second. If Srenpe could deliver a second time, the Thornatan Army would have no idea what hit them.

"What shall I tell him is the reason for the visit?" Glover asked.

"He needs no reason other than the gold he will receive," Idanox said, brushing off the question. The mage would not care what the reasons were as long as he was handsomely paid for his time. Glover's question had solely been to satisfy his own curiosity, about which Idanox could not possibly care less. The man's job was to do as he was told without asking questions, and he would do well to remember it.

"Very well, sir. Should we also begin preparations for the men who have already assembled to begin their journeys here?"

"Yes, begin with the men in the southern reaches of the province; it will take them longer to arrive. Split the men into several encampments in areas the army's patrols don't normally sweep. Keep them far enough from the city to avoid detection but close enough to arrive within two days if summoned. I also need you to acquire some boats. Build them, steal them, I don't care how you do it. We need enough to carry a sizeable portion of our forces."

"Do you mean to attack Oreanna from the river?" one of the junior lieutenants asked, not bothering to conceal his skepticism.

Simpleminded fool, Idanox thought, irritated by the interruption.

"No, but we need to make them believe that is our plan. If most of the army's forces move to defend the docks and water gates, an attack on the walls on the opposite side of the city will be much easier to execute. Splitting our foe's strength gives us our best opportunity to defeat them," Idanox explained, wishing once more for competent assistance. There was no help for it; this was the best he had available to him. He had no choice but to make the best of it.

Idanox rose from the table, indicating to the men their meeting was over. They left in a hurry, only pausing to insist what a pleasure it was to serve him. Idanox made his best effort to pretend their comments meant something to him, though in truth he was eager to be rid of them this night. Their naivety was exhausting, and dealing with it was a chore he did not care to perform. Though in months past he had enjoyed the feeling of being treated as a distinguished leader, he lacked the energy to respond appropriately of late.

Once he was finally rid of their presence, Idanox retrieved a bottle of liquor from a nearby cabinet. He rarely indulged in such things but found himself needing it this night. He was surrounded by fools, a situation which was unlikely to change anytime soon. The constant strain of single-handedly overseeing this war was aging him prematurely, and it grew more noticeable with each passing day. Nights like this one made him yearn for his old life. The life of a wealthy timber mogul had been comfortable, if less than fulfilling. He had always known he was destined for greater things, meant to be in a position of real power. He had built the Hoyt by playing to the deep-seated desires of men too poor and naive to know better. Now he had to deal with the challenges of leading such a group through complicated and finely orchestrated plans. They were far from qualified for such tasks, but of course, that was why they followed him in the first place.

Nearly all his fortune had been spent on this war. Idanox had once been perhaps the wealthiest man in Thornata, and now he was living in a shack, hiding from the army. His business rivals would've been delighted to see it, thrilled to see their arrogant rival living in such squalor. The costs of running the Hoyt had stripped away his gold reserves, and the military had seized his massive home here in Oreanna. There were limits to how far his charisma and silver tongue would carry this struggle. At some point, his fighters would expect payment for their services. He had brought them along this far with the promise of better lives in the future. If this attack on the capital failed, he feared the few men who remained would see him as a fraud and walk out on him as well.

If the attack succeeded, on the other hand, things would become much more comfortable for him. Once the city was in their control, they could break open the duke's gold vaults, and the money within would keep his men happy for a long time. The gold would mean nothing to his Thrawll allies, if he could even call them that. They were no doubt impatient with the constant delays by now. They cared nothing for riches, only for the agreement he had made with them. He could only hope the delay caused by the Rawl wielder's interference in Kolig would not prove to be fatal to this campaign. If it were, it would be disastrous to Idanox as well. His Thrawll allies had made the cost of failure perfectly clear to him when their deal was struck.

He wondered again if the beast had killed the boy yet. He had little doubt it would succeed after seeing it in action against his own men. He hoped Srenpe would be able to produce more for him, monsters that could turn the tide of the battle to come. The battle plan was already forming in his mind, the best way to utilize these beasts and their devastating power and ferocity. Idanox retired to bed with images of a bloody and gruesome victory swimming in his liquor-addled mind.

Idanox slept well into the following afternoon, waking to find the midday sun seeping into the shack through the cracks in the curtains. He stumbled from the bed and retrieved dried meat and stale bread from the kitchen. His men had not brought him fresh provisions in close to a week. He would need to remind them of their responsibilities when they arrived later. His head was aching; he had overindulged in the liquor the night before. He barely had time to admonish himself before a sudden pounding at the front door brought him crashing back to reality. Was this a raid by the army? His men were under strict instructions to not visit this shack in the light of day.

Retrieving his sword from underneath the bed, he made his way cautiously toward the door. Idanox had never been much of a fighter, but he would not go quietly if the army had come for him. He would not be the duke's prisoner, to be trotted out in front of the commoners and have his failure mocked and ridiculed. They would never have the satisfaction of seeing him swing at the end of a hangman's rope. He cautiously drew back the curtains enough to see a sliver of the street outside. He could not see the person at the door, but there was no sign of a patrol. He leaped back in shock at the sound of a voice on the other side of the door.

"I'm not here to arrest you, Idanox. You sent for me, and I am here. Can you open the door? I don't have all day."

Of course the mage would not heed his instructions to wait until nightfall. Srenpe had made it clear at every opportunity that he was no servant of the Hoyt and had gone out of his way to prove it at every turn. Irritated by Srenpe's constant refusal to follow his requests, Idanox opened the door wide enough for the red-robed mage to slip inside before closing and latching it behind him. He wheeled on the mage as soon as the door was securely locked, not bothering to mask his irritation.

"Did Glover not explain that you were meant to come at night?" Idanox asked, giving the mage the benefit of the doubt in spite of himself.

"He did, but I assumed if you required my services again, you might prefer to discuss such matters privately. I wouldn't want any of your men to worry that they are about to be the subjects of a graphic demonstration. After all, I can't imagine they appreciated the beauty of my last display," Srenpe japed, infuriating Idanox further with his arrogance.

"I'm not paying you to make assumptions about what I want," Idanox snapped, his throbbing headache leaving him in no mood for the mage's mind games.

"You do plan on paying me again, do you? Because at the moment, I am standing in this squalid shack purely out of the generosity of my heart. You did not summon me here simply because you enjoy my company? That is good because I do not find yours to be particularly pleasant either, Idanox. I'm sure it's not something the sycophants who follow you would ever admit, but you can be rather insufferable. I feel we are at the point in our working relationship where I can be open with you about such matters."

"Perhaps I should ask for my money back. I still have not seen any evidence that your beast has killed the boy. Maybe I should invest the money in somebody who can actually do the job they were hired to perform!" Idanox shot back, already weary of the mage's endless streams of japes and insults.

"Idanox, you wound me. My creature shall not fail, even if its quarry is more formidable than a handful of Hoyt brutes. If it makes you feel better, I can assure you it is alive and well and tracking the boy as we speak. But I suspect you did not ask me to come here so you could moan and complain about everything under the sun. If you did, it is not at all becoming of a man of your stature. Though judging by the aroma of your lovely home, I suspect you may have overindulged last night. Again, not very becoming of a man such as yourself, but these things happen. What is it you want from me?"

As much as he disliked the sneering mage, Idanox could not help but admire his bluntness, albeit deep down. They were not all that dissimilar, he and Srenpe. For one, neither of them cared much about the opinions of others. Perhaps it was the reason they felt such disdain for each other. Strong men did not appreciate the threat a fellow strong man could pose. Still, the mage could be useful to him, and perhaps a more delicate touch could help him here. Swallowing his pride and wishing the whole time he could kill the man and be done with it, he set to work on wooing the arrogant Srenpe to his cause.

"Your beast was quite magnificent, I must admit. Seeing it in action was truly a sight to behold. I was wondering if it would be possible to create another," Idanox said, trying his best to conceal his contempt.

"Of course I could. But why would I?" Srenpe's arrogant reply was already intensifying Idanox's hatred for him. Assuring himself the end result would be worth his irritation in the short term, he plowed forward, refusing to give Srenpe the satisfaction of seeing him react.

"Because you would be paid handsomely, just like you were for the first," Idanox said. There was no point in trying to butter up a man like Srenpe; he was smart enough to see right through any effort to do so. The only thing a man like Srenpe would respect was the straightforward truth.

"I have gold, quite a bit of it, largely thanks to you. While it is always nice to have more, perhaps we could reach a different sort of agreement this time." Srenpe's tone was different, almost hungry.

This was not a response Idanox had expected. Speculating on what besides money might interest a man like Srenpe brought a chill to his spine. He had never heard the mage sound this eager, and he was anxious about what ambitions could elicit such a response. Once again, he wondered if he had made a horrible mistake by forging this partnership. But he did not have any other solution to his problem; he needed the mage's help. It could not hurt to hear the man out. Almost afraid of the answer he would receive, he asked his question.

"What type of agreement do you have in mind, Srenpe?"

"Let's not dance around the matter anymore, Idanox. You need to take control of this city, and you don't have the resources to do it. It turns out frustrated pig farmers and stable boys grow tired of fighting for free, even for a cause as noble and righteous as yours. Do not despair, for even an insurmountably brilliant man such as yourself could never have suspected this to be the case. You don't need one beast; you need at least a dozen to ensure you succeed in your assault on Oreanna. That was what you were thinking, was it not? If you get me the materials again, I will provide these for you at no charge up front," Srenpe declared.

No charge up front? Idanox was immediately suspicious. In all his encounters with the mage, Srenpe had never expressed interest in anything other than enriching himself. He could not imagine Srenpe developing a charitable nature out of the blue. If he did not want money in exchange for his services, what was he after?

"I assume you would not do this purely out of a spirit of generosity." Idanox was almost afraid to ask, knowing instinctively that the answer would disgust him. If Srenpe was offering these beasts for free, he must've had something truly sinister in mind.

"The government of this province and the Order of Mages have long worked together to eradicate magic they consider to be dangerous, or so they claim. It's a ridiculous lie, of course. They hoard such powers so others may not have access to them. Those in power fear what would happen if those they deem beneath them were to gain control over such things. It's one of the great injustices that occurs in this province. They say there are vaults in the basement beneath the duke's residence containing magical artifacts and spellbooks they feel need to be locked away. Burying knowledge is a horrific crime, in my opinion. My payment will be that I will be the first to access these vaults once you have taken the city. With the help of my creatures, this outcome will not be in doubt. I may remove anything from the vaults that I see fit and use it as I please."

It was an intriguing offer. Idanox did not care one bit about spells or magical artifacts but could not help but feel a certain apprehension about what Srenpe intended to do with them. But he knew the mage was not likely to settle for anything less. Srenpe knew what he wanted, and he knew he held all the leverage. He did not like making concessions to anyone, particularly when he did not fully understand the possible ramifications of doing so. But this would hopefully be a small sacrifice compared to the reward it would yield him.

"Very well, Srenpe. Provide me with enough of your beasts that we successfully take control of the city, and the pick of the vaults is yours."

"It is such a pleasure for me to do business with you and your wonderful organization, Idanox. Your constant efforts to serve as a champion of the common man are the utmost height of nobility and selflessness. I assume you do not want me to do the transformations here. This hovel you are living in would get quite crowded, would it not? Such a noble sacrifice for a man of your stature to make, living in such squalor in the name of the greater good. Have your men find me a larger space, a warehouse like last time perhaps, someplace secluded. And they will need to supply the raw goods, of course. I daresay a dozen should do the trick. Have them send for me once they have the preparations ready, and I will provide you with the warriors you need to make this city yours."

Idanox nodded his understanding, and the mage slipped out the front door without another word. Alone once more, Idanox took a seat, resisting the urge to retrieve another bottle of liquor. He did not like being in business with this dark mage, but what choice did he have? Without the help of Srenpe's beasts, he would fail in his endeavor to seize control of the province, and failure was not an option. For Idanox, it had never been an option.

Chapter Nine

The harsh early spring wind had finally begun to ease as Adel made his way up the long stone staircase leading to the top of the wall. The massive stone wall towered at least sixty feet above the ground below, completely encircling and protecting the Temple of Rawl within. Adel had spent most of his day sleeping in the same chamber he had occupied during his last visit, exhausted from the arduous trek from Kalskag to the farming village and then to the temple. Now awake, he found himself restless, desperate to take some sort of action. With nothing else available to him, he climbed the wall, though he feared what he might find once he reached the top. The beast had not appeared again since their encounter on the river, but its pursuit throughout their trek left him in no doubt that it would find him once again.

This was the third time Adel felt the urge to climb to the top of the wall in the past day. Every time he had woken from his slumber, he had been unable to fall back asleep until he had assured himself the beast was not down below. Each time he reached the top and looked out tentatively, confident he would find the mindless monster standing at the gates below. Each time thus far, he had breathed a sigh of relief. The moments alone at the top of the wall gave him time to reflect on the improbable escape they had made to reach the Temple of the Rawl.

They might not have completed the journey at all if Klaweck had not come upon them when he had. Ola and Alsea had been pushed to their absolute limit over the past few days. Adel suspected they'd likely been within hours of succumbing to their injuries. The giant had lifted them both, albeit with vocal protests, and carried them here to the temple with Adel rushing to keep up. The Children of the Rawl had welcomed them and immediately began tending to their injuries. Not many words had been exchanged other than Elim promising Adel they would speak once he had rested. His sleep had been uneasy and restless despite his exhaustion.

Adel had woken this last time to find the temple quiet, his companions and the Children apparently still resting peacefully. He had discovered food waiting for him in the temple's dining room, which he had devoured hungrily before coming outside to climb the wall. Adel reached the top at last and found himself greeted with a truly spectacular view of the surrounding valleys and mountains. Once again, it seemed like yesterday he was admiring these same mountains on the first trip of the spring for Captain Boyd's barge. The moon was faint, but there was still enough light for him to scan the area below the wall, reassuring himself there was still no sign of the beast. It was a small comfort. He knew it was out there somewhere, just waiting for him to expose himself again. Sooner or later, another confrontation with the monster would need to happen. Its hunt would not end until one or both of them were utterly destroyed.

Elim had assured him they would be safe inside the temple walls, and Klaweck had pledged that he and his fellow giants would patrol the surrounding mountains. They would deal with the beast if they found it lurking nearby. Yet Adel could not shake the uneasy feeling that they had not seen the last of it. But there was no sign of it this evening, so he allowed himself to breathe slightly more comfortably. Perhaps Ola had been right; maybe it could not reach him here within the temple. He turned back toward the stairs to find Elim approaching. The old man had come up the stairs without making a sound, causing Adel to jump slightly in surprise. After their harrowing flight from the beast, he found he did not much care for people sneaking up on him.

"My apologies, Adel. I did not mean to startle you. Keeping an eye out for your hunter, I presume?" the old man asked, and Adel nodded. "It must be quite the formidable beast indeed, given Ola's and Alsea's injuries. I would not have thought any creature living capable of inflicting such wounds on two such skilled fighters. Your fear is well-placed. But I assure you it cannot harm you here, Adel."

"If you had seen that monster in action, you would be concerned too. I've never seen anything like it," Adel replied.

"After seeing Ola's injuries, I do not doubt it. As I said, I did not think there was a creature alive that could do that to him," Elim admitted, standing next to Adel and gazing out over the surrounding mountains and valleys. "Still, you need not concern yourself with it while you are here. This temple is protected by more than stone walls and giants. It would take something far more powerful than a dark magic beast to reach you here."

There was no anger, no trace of an accusatory tone in the older man's voice, but Adel could not help but feel responsible. He should have returned to the Temple of the Rawl after the battle at Kolig, as Elim had requested. If he had, his companions would not have been injured. So many things could have been different if he had kept his promise. Perhaps Elim was hiding his anger to be polite. Adel could not shake the suspicion that the Children were furious with his decisions over the past months.

"They will both recover fully?" he asked.

"They will. They will both need a significant amount of rest over the coming weeks, but fortunately, Wulfgar was a healer before joining us here. He has retained his skills these many years, though he mainly treats the sprained ankles of delicate old men nowadays. Still, he is certain they will return to full strength with sufficient time and rest."

"I'm sorry, Elim. I feel like I let you all down. We should have returned after the battle at Kolig like I said we would. I felt like we could end this war in no time if I agreed to help the army deal with the Hoyt. I overestimated myself and my abilities, and now Ola and Alsea are badly hurt because of it. I was a fool. Do you want me to leave? I can understand if you do." Adel had not meant to let it all spill out, but he could not contain his feelings of guilt any longer.

"Adel, do you remember what I told you when last we spoke? I believed then that you would prove yourself worthy of becoming the master of our order. It's a belief which has only strengthened since that day. Your willingness to throw yourself into the middle of a war was misguided yet at the same time admirable. You felt as though you could make a difference and save lives, and you were willing to place yourself in considerable danger in the process. From what Ola and Alsea have told me, you have done just that. Do you honestly expect me to condemn you for this?" Elim asked.

The older man's reply was a welcome one to Adel, even if he felt it did not fully exonerate his poor judgment. However, he also understood that stewing in his guilt would not be a productive use of his time. He was back at the temple, back among the Children of the Rawl, which was an opportunity for him to continue to hone his skills. The past few days had shown he still had much to learn about the mysterious power. He would be foolish to squander such an opportunity, one which could hold an answer to the riddle posed by the beast on their trail.

"If Ola and Alsea need a lot of time to rest, I suppose this would be a good opportunity to continue my training. If you are still willing, of course," Adel suggested, unsure of Elim's current attitude toward him.

"Of course we shall continue, my dear boy. I was coming to ask if you would be rested enough by tomorrow afternoon. You have done quite well at expanding your skill set on your own, but there is still much you can learn. I daresay you are prepared for more advanced techniques and to learn some of the more sensitive secrets our order protects," Elim replied.

Adel's curiosity was immediately piqued. What type of secrets and advanced techniques was Elim referring to? The pair began making their way back down the stone steps, Elim inquiring about the different manners in which Adel had utilized his powers since their last meeting. He seemed particularly impressed by Adel's idea of creating an ice raft to hasten their journey downriver, commending him for his creativity. Recounting the lightning strike on the warehouse brought up painful memories for Adel, but Elim assured him they would work on perfecting the attack together. Not once did Elim indicate any anger or disappointment, for which Adel was immeasurably grateful.

Adel retired to his chamber upon their return to the temple, thinking about everything Elim had said. It seemed the Children held no grudge against him for his poor judgment, so perhaps it was time to forgive himself. Every decision he had made had been with the best of intentions, though this fact still did not justify his mistakes in his mind. He supposed this guilt would be his burden to bear, one he might carry with him forever. Was such guilt an inevitable consequence of becoming a leader? These thoughts were continually swirling through his mind, and it took a long time for him to find sleep that night.

The next afternoon, Adel made his way to the chambers where his companions were resting to find an ancient member of the Children named Wulfgar in the corridor. Wulfgar advised both were recovering well but sleeping and he may wish to wait a day or two before visiting. Wulfgar reassured Adel he would inform him of any changes to their condition but stressed it was best to leave them undisturbed for the time being. Disappointed he would not have the opportunity to speak with his friends, he made his way to the main chamber of the temple, where Elim was waiting for him.

"Welcome, Adel. I know you are still weary from your long journey, so I thought rather than practicing today, we could discuss the Children of the Rawl, this temple, and our place in the world," Elim said. "We covered the basics when you were last here, but there is still much you will need to know if you are to become Master of the Rawl."

Adel was relieved to hear Elim did not want him to train with his power; his night had been far from restful. There was a lot he still did not know about this world he had found himself thrust into, and this was an excellent opportunity to learn more. Eager to begin, he asked a question that had been on his mind since his return to the temple.

"You assured me last night that the beast could not harm me here. Ola said something similar when he suggested we return here to seek safety. He said there were protections around the temple that the beast would not be able to breach. Can you explain what he meant by this? The walls are tall and thick, but after seeing this monster in action, I would not doubt its ability to breach them. Klaweck and his giants cannot be watching every second of the day and night."

"The Temple of the Rawl was built centuries ago by the first Rawl wielders who came to the Empire. They selected this location because of the mountains and the natural defense they provided, but they understood as well that geographical defenses would not be sufficient. When one possesses a unique power, some will never rest until they have attempted to steal it or snuff it out. Men fear what they do not understand. You are young, but you are still old enough to understand this. This temple's defenses would need to be more comprehensive than those of any other structure in the world. So, as they constructed this temple and the walls surrounding it, they infused the stones with their own power, strengthening them to a point where it would take an attack so powerful that it is nearly beyond comprehension to breach them. That power still runs through the stones to this day. If this creature tracks you by following the scent of the Rawl, as I suspect it does, these ancient protections guard against that ability as well. Within these walls, your power, while immense, is dwarfed by these centuries-old barriers."

"How is that possible? If this temple was built centuries ago, I assume all the builders have been dead for a long time. Is this correct?" Adel asked, and the older man nodded. "But then how is their Rawl power still running through the walls of the temple? Does a Rawl wielder's power not die with them?"

Elim didn't respond immediately; he seemed to be contemplating something. After a few moments, he silently beckoned for Adel to follow him. Elim led him out of the main chamber and into a series of winding corridors, turning in every direction. The journey revealed a system of passages far more complicated than any Adel could have imagined. After countless twists and turns, they reached a large chamber with a stone staircase that descended beneath the temple. Adel had never been to this part of the temple before. The air felt different, as though an incredible power was running through it. It reminded him vaguely of the feeling of the air around him during his most powerful expenditures of the Rawl, though it dwarfed anything he had ever produced. The sensation made the hair on his arms stand straight.

The walls of the staircase were lined with dormant torches. With a wave of his hand, Elim brought them to life, presumably transferring a flame from a torch elsewhere in the temple. The simple display reminded Adel how much he still had to learn; he had never even attempted such a thing. In the light, Adel could see this chamber bore no more adornment than any other in the temple. Without a word, Elim proceeded down the stone staircase, a perplexed Adel following. They reached the bottom of the stairs to find a large stone door. It was almost an exact replica of the door that granted entry to the temple from the outside world, though on a much smaller scale. Elim came to a halt in front of the door and finally began to speak again.

"The room beyond this door is known as the vault. This door can only be opened by correctly using the Rawl in a precise manner. If even the slightest mistake is made in the process, the door will refuse to open. You will learn how to open this door once your training is complete and you have officially been named the Master of the Rawl.

Such securities are necessary, and you will understand the reasons for this shortly. For the time being, please take a step back while I open it."

Adel complied, taking a step back as Elim turned toward the great stone door. Reaching out, he placed one of his wrinkled hands on the surface of the door. Adel watched in amazement as a series of Rawl powers seemed to play out at the tips of his fingers, rushing water, burning fire, flashing lightning, and frigid ice all appearing and vanishing in the span of a few seconds. He still had a lot to learn indeed. Within seconds, Elim had completed his ritual, and the stone door slid open.

Elim stepped into the vault first before motioning for Adel to follow. Adel stepped into the room, his eyes darting in every direction, trying to take in as much as possible. The vault was a large round room, the walls the same marble as those in the rest of the temple. The chamber rose high above them, the light descending from several small windows carved twenty feet above their heads. The walls were unadorned except for a set of about two dozen books set in a nook on the far side of the chamber.

It was the center of the vault that immediately drew Adel's attention. There was an artifact seated on a pedestal in the exact center of the great round room. This object was unlike anything Adel had ever seen. From a distance, it appeared to be a perfectly shaped glass orb, but as he drew closer, he could see whatever this thing was, it was not made of glass. The more he examined the object, the more it became clear that he could not identify the material from which it was made.

The orb's surface seemed to be in constant movement, as though he could reach out to touch it and his hand would pass right through its surface. The sphere was roughly the size of his head and looked impossibly fragile, though his instincts told him this appearance was misleading. There was more to this orb than merely a visible appearance; there was a power that seemed to emanate from it, a power that felt familiar to him. It took him another moment to realize this was the source of the energy he had felt at the top of the stairs.

"It's quite beautiful, isn't it?" Elim asked, snapping Adel from the trance the orb had placed on him. "You are not the first to lose yourself staring into its surface, and you won't be the last."

"What is it?" Adel asked, his eyes never leaving the orb's swirling surface.

"The first Children of the Rawl called it the Vindur. It is a name derived from a language that has long since passed from the world. In ancient times, this is what the first men who came to Thornata called the wind, or that is a rough translation of the ancient word, at least."

Yes, it made sense to Adel now. The apparent motion across the orb's surface was indeed reminiscent of blowing wind, the surface shifting back and forth in unpredictable waves. The moving surface gave the orb the appearance of being alive. No object had ever made him feel this way simply by standing in its presence. Elim seemed to sense his confusion.

"The Vindur is an artifact of ancient times; it was here before the Empire was formed. We cannot be sure if a person created it or if it existed before life itself, a creation of nature. What we do know is that it contains a seemingly infinite amount of energy that takes shape in the form of wind, hence its name. The builders of this temple recognized this, and they realized the potential of such an object. They decided to channel their own power through this orb while building the defenses of this temple. You see, Adel, they recognized that they would die, and with them, their powers would pass from this world as well. However, this orb is everlasting. So, by doing this, they ensured the defenses they put in place would last as long as the Vindur rests within the walls of this temple," Elim explained.

"Would it be possible to draw from the power of the Vindur itself?" Adel asked, still unable to pull his eyes away from the swirling orb.

"For an experienced Rawl wielder, it would certainly be possible, which is another reason for keeping it safely within this vault. In theory, it could potentially give its possessor unlimited capacity to manipulate wind energy. Just think of being able to use your power with impunity and never grow weary. I'm sure you can imagine all sorts of wonderful uses you could make of such power. Unfortunately, not all people are as good-natured as you are, Adel. Such a tool in the wrong hands could cause death and destruction on a scale the likes of which this world has never seen."

"You are referring to the Thrawll. We keep it here to keep it out of their hands, don't we?" Adel asked. The tales Elim had told him of the mysterious race of Rawl wielders were returning to his mind. The thought of such creatures getting their hands on an instrument of such power was terrifying.

"Obviously, that would be a worst-case scenario. Any Rawl wielder with bad intentions could potentially turn the Vindur into a weapon of incredible destruction."

Adel reached out with his power, wanting to brush against the power of the Vindur for a moment. What he felt was unlike anything he had ever imagined. Adel remembered the many times the use of his power had left him exhausted, yet within this orb, he could feel energy that would never be spent. The possibilities were endless.

As he allowed himself to feel the power of the orb rushing through his body, Adel toyed for the briefest moment with the thought of using it as a weapon against the beast that pursued him. Such power could reduce even that impossibly powerful monster to dust within seconds. He lingered on the thought for a long moment before dismissing the idea as reckless. It would require removing the Vindur from the temple, something the Children would certainly never allow. He wondered again how such a thing could exist as he withdrew. Perhaps the Children were right. Maybe it was best that the Vindur stayed safely locked away in this vault. Such power was best left contained in a safe place.

"I'm glad it's locked away in this vault, where we can keep it safe. This must be the most powerful object in the world," Adel said.

"It is a good thing indeed; however, you are mistaken on one count. The Vindur is not the sole object of its kind in the world. Think of how you use your power. You manipulate not only the wind, but water, fire, ice, and even lightning as well," Elim said.

"You mean to tell me there is another orb with unlimited capacity to manipulate fire? And another for water? And others?" Adel asked, his mind racing once more.

"That is exactly what I am telling you."

"Are they in other vaults? Do we have them all locked away?"

"No, we do not possess the other orbs. They are scattered across the Empire. We know the locations of some, others we do not, but only the Vindur resides within this temple. It is the lone orb under the control of the Children of the Rawl."

The idea of weapons of virtually limitless power lying about where anybody could potentially seize them was not a comforting thought. Imagining such an object in the wrong hands sent a chill down Adel's spine. Still, it was somewhat reassuring to know they had one safely locked away, and it could potentially be used to combat another if necessary. He vowed to himself that once he did become

Master of the Rawl, he would set about hunting down the rest of the orbs. They could not be left adrift in a world with so many evil people who would seek to abuse their power.

There was so much information for him to process that he did not know where to begin. Elim seemed to sense this and took his arm, guiding him out of the vault. The great stone doors slid shut as they exited the vault and began making their way back upstairs and through the labyrinth of passageways. They came back out into the main hall and found a table with food and drink waiting, sustenance Adel found he badly needed. The morning had been as mentally exhausting as any he could remember. How much more did he have to learn about this mysterious power he possessed?

"I daresay you have learned enough for one day. Tomorrow morning we will resume your more practical training, but for now, take some food and rest," Elim said, motioning for Adel to join him for lunch.

Adel nodded and took a seat at the table, his mind racing with thoughts of the Vindur. Yesterday he never would have imagined such objects could exist. Each time he thought he was beginning to gain a thorough understanding of his power, something new was thrown at him. Once again, he felt his real training had only just begun.

Chapter Ten

The arrow was racing through the air, closing in on its target at blistering speed, when the gust of wind caught it, bringing it to a complete halt mid-flight. A split second later, the wind changed direction, sending the arrow winging with the same blistering speed into the bullseye of the round hay target. Alsea dropped the bow to her side, and she turned toward the doorway Adel was standing in, her expression a blend of exasperation and amusement.

"Can't a girl have an honest target practice without some cocky Rawl wielder spoiling her fun?" she asked playfully, setting her bow aside and walking over to embrace Adel.

"Even cocky Rawl wielders need practice, Alsea. If I can stop your arrows, I should be able to stop whatever any Hoyt thug has to throw at me. Besides, a girl has had several hours of honest target practice today. All while she is supposed to be resting in her bed and recovering from her injuries, I might add," Adel said, wagging his finger at her like an old woman scolding her granddaughter for neglecting her chores.

They had been at the Temple of the Rawl for several weeks, and Alsea was recovering well from the injuries inflicted by the great beast. Both she and Ola were well enough to move around freely and even engage in some light training, though the Children of the Rawl had urged them not to test their limits too soon. Adel had taken it upon himself to monitor this aspect of their recovery closely. He had found himself constantly interrupting them from various activities he deemed too strenuous. He suspected his constant interruptions were beginning to wear on them, though their well-being mattered more to him than their exasperated attitudes.

His own training had continued as well, and he had begun to master Rawl techniques he would not have even imagined were possible during his first visit to the temple. He had spent the better part of the past week perfecting his use of lightning strikes, this time on a far more controlled scale than he had been forced to utilize in the warehouse attack. Under Elim's direction, he had even begun to master the ability to create smaller bolts of lightning he could use to strike more accurately and with less collateral damage than a full strike. Elim had said that in time he might even master the ability to produce the devastating attacks at the tips of his fingers. Such mastery would give him the ability to attack with unmatched precision.

"Are you already done with your training for the day? I had hoped Elim would keep you busy late today and I could get more target practice in without your interference. I'll make sure to tell him he isn't working you hard enough," Alsea teased, smiling despite the exasperation in her voice.

"I am never too busy to play mother hen to you and Ola. I caught him swinging that massive sword of his around like a pack of hungry wolves was attacking him. It's as though the two of you are trying to make my life difficult. Why exactly do you need more practice? I have been watching for a while, you know. I saw you plant six shots in a row dead center before I decided to interrupt you. For that matter, I don't think I've ever seen you miss."

"Don't be a fool, Adel. We are not trying to make your life difficult. That is just a lucky side effect of our hard work. A wise man once said struggle is merely nature's way of making us stronger, and we do love to see you struggle." Alsea snickered, flashing him one of her dazzling smiles. "You will walk away from this stay at the temple a better man, you mark my words."

"Oh, is that what it is? Well then, perhaps I should be thanking the pair of you for all your hard work making me stronger. You know, I didn't just come to interrupt your archery practice; I'm not that mean. Well, actually, I am, but that's beside the point. I was coming to ask if you cared to have supper tonight, the three of us. Our time here has been productive, but I think we need to discuss our plans beyond our stay. I assume you have no objections. You seem quite eager to get out and about once more."

"You will hear no argument from me. The Children are always gracious hosts, but you know I'm not particularly eager to stay put for too long. I was not born to live in confinement. I love these gardens, but would it kill them to pretty up the inside of this place a little? Maybe a vase of flowers or two? Something for you to think about when you become Master of the Rawl."

"I figured as much. I'll take your advice on decorations to heart. But you know I have to ask this, so please don't give me a sarcastic answer. How are you feeling? Do you honestly believe you have recovered well enough to go back out there? You know what will be coming after us," Adel said, his eyes scanning her face for any hint of deception.

"Honestly, Adel, I feel as good as new. I feel ready to go out there and deal with that monster and then Idanox and the Hoyt. I'm getting restless being cooped up here. I'm ready to go shoot that beast in the face."

"It will probably just smile and keep coming forward. Well, here, I brought you a gift to help liven up your chambers. At least you won't be able to complain about having to sleep in such a drab room," Adel said, offering her a small handful of yellow wildflowers. It was still too early in the spring for them to be in full bloom, but a quick jolt of Rawl energy had sped them on their way. She blushed slightly and smiled as she took them from him.

"Thank you, Adel. Not just for the flowers, but for everything you've done. I wouldn't have made it back here after that beast's attack if it weren't for you."

"You wouldn't have been involved in the beast's attack if it weren't for me," Adel reminded her, and she giggled. "So, I will see you at supper tonight?"

Alsea agreed, and they separated and headed to their respective chambers to wash and change their clothing. Adel had difficulty keeping the image of Alsea's smile out of his mind, but he had decided there were some matters he could not allow himself to pursue. Whatever his feelings for Alsea were, he had to set them aside. There were more important things to worry about than his desires. The injuries his friends had suffered had reinforced his belief that he had to view matters differently. He had to act less like a friend and more like a leader if they were going to survive what lay ahead of them.

He arrived in the dining room to find Alsea and Ola already waiting. The Children had set them a generous feast of bread, fish, and roasted vegetables, and they dug in without much conversation. They ate in relative silence, Adel noting the ravenous manner in which his friends consumed their food. It only affirmed his suspicion that they had been pushing their injured bodies too far the past few days. When the meal was completed, Adel decided it was time to get things started.

"First of all, I want to say how relieved I am that you have both recovered from your injuries, though not quite as completely as you try to lead me to believe," he said, giving each of them a stern look. "After all of this time together, I consider you both to be dear friends, and I am forever grateful for the friendship you have given me."

"I'm glad I recovered too. My life just wouldn't be the same if I had died," Alsea joked, once again flashing her mischievous smile. Adel allowed himself a brief chuckle, though the joke hit a bit too close to home, as he still felt their injuries fell on his shoulders.

"I thought it would be a good idea to meet and discuss our plans for what comes next once you are both fully recovered. I plan on returning to Kolig and rejoining General McLeod and his forces. I promised him I would help him deal with Idanox and the Hoyt, and I am not going to go back on my word. With that being said, I want it understood that I do not expect either of you to come with me. There would be no judgment whatsoever if you chose to stay," Adel said.

"I will be by your side whenever you choose to leave the temple and will stay by your side no matter what," Ola declared immediately, as Adel had suspected he would.

"I will too, but you already knew that without asking," Alsea added.

"I suspected you would both say as much, but I had to make it clear. You have both been badly injured while following me, though I know you do not think I am to blame. I could not have you with me going forward without stressing that I would understand completely if you chose another path."

That was the simple part of our discussion, Adel thought to himself. He had known neither one of them would leave his side, but now they had more complex matters to discuss. His trepidation about allowing his good friends to continue with him would have to be put aside. He knew no protest would sway them from their insistence to stay with him. Now they were decided, they needed to figure out what to do about their most pressing problem.

"There is still the matter of the beast. Klaweck and his giants have found no trace of it in the valley below, but I think we would be fools not to assume it is still out there hunting for me. Elim believes the protections placed around the temple are likely throwing it off my scent. Once we set off, those protections will be gone, and it will come after me again. If we are going to rejoin General McLeod, first we need to figure out a way to deal with it. We cannot rejoin the army with that monster on our tail. I considered asking Klaweck to accompany us until it shows itself again but decided against it. The protection of this temple is his priority; this monster is a puzzle we need to solve on our own," Adel said.

"Whatever this creature is, it seems capable of healing itself from nearly any injury. I cut the beast in half, yet it came back to attack us again. I must assume those villagers did not burn its carcass soon enough. I have a bad feeling some of them may have paid a horrible price for that mistake," Ola said, voicing a dark thought that had occurred to Adel more than once, even if he had not been willing to voice it out loud.

"If we were to find a way to burn it to ash, I have a hard time believing it could recover from that. Whatever magic formed this creature, it can only heal from so much. If we manage to annihilate its body, that should be the end of it, right? Of course, the problem is that it is not going to stand still and let us burn it. In fact, I think we may want to anticipate a rather angry response to our attempts," Alsea chimed in.

"I don't think we can count on Ola being able to cut it in half again. The next time we face this monster, it will most likely just be the three of us. There are no soldiers to distract it this time, and it also seems able to adapt to my Rawl attacks. Its attention will be solely on us; this will complicate matters," Adel pointed out.

"Can this creature think? It seems to be nothing more than a mindless marauding monster that will do anything to achieve its goal. It wants to kill you—that much is easy enough to see—and it is willing to slaughter anyone who gets in its way. But is there a mind inside of its head?

Is it able to think, to use logic and reason? Can it anticipate what we are going to do?" Alsea asked.

This was not a question Adel had spent a great deal of time considering. However, he thought it wise of Alsea to bring it up. If this creature were capable of strategic thinking of any kind in addition to its incredible brute strength, the challenge ahead of them would be all the more difficult. However, if it was indeed the mindless monster they suspected, perhaps that was a weakness they could use to their advantage. Assuming this to be the case was a gamble, but it was one they may have to take.

The idea came to Adel quickly, and he wasted no time in sharing it with his companions. They listened intently and made suggestions for minor ways in which the plan could be improved. By the end of their discussion, they were in agreement on the best way to attempt to put an end to the beast. With their plan in place, that left just one matter up for decision.

"Now we need to decide when we are going to leave. I know the two of you feel much better, but I still think we should wait at least another week. I know you are both restless, but please hear me out. You may be well enough to train and walk around the temple, but an encounter with this beast is another matter entirely. If we aren't all at full strength, I don't think we will survive this confrontation. This is going to be our last chance. If we fail, I don't think any of us are going to survive long enough to try again."

"Whenever you decide is best, I will be ready," Ola replied predictably. He would never admit to needing time to recover. It was not lost on Adel, however, that Ola had not immediately objected to the idea of more rest.

"I am as stubborn as Ola, but I think it for the best if I admit I think you're right, Adel. Don't get used to it, though," Alsea said, shooting Adel a wink. "I think we could both use another week of rest. And we should both use the time to rest and stop making Adel chase us back to our beds like children. He has training of his own to focus on."

Adel mouthed her a quiet word of thanks for this last suggestion.

With all three of them in agreement, they went their separate ways again, Alsea giving Adel a parting embrace once more. Adel was not tired after the meeting; so many thoughts were racing through his mind that he suspected he would find sleep impossible even if he tried. Instead, he went for a walk, wandering the corridors of the Temple of the Rawl, exploring every room he came across before finally ending up in the main hall. He found Elim sitting at the table where he had knowingly used the Rawl for the first time, reading silently.

"It's getting quite late, Adel. You should probably get some rest," Elim suggested kindly.

"I don't think I could if I tried tonight," Adel replied.

"Yes, I have noticed you struggling with this of late. It is a problem most great leaders face," Elim said, closing his book and setting it down on the table. "Adel, since you are awake, I have something I need to ask you."

"What is it?" Adel asked, wondering what information he could have that a wise man such as Elim did not.

"I noticed Alsea was carrying flowers earlier after she spoke with you this afternoon. But it is still too early in the spring for such flowers to reach maturity. Where did you find them?"

"Oh, I remembered them from last year. I went to them in the courtyard, but they were not fully grown yet. I used the Rawl to help finish the process," Adel explained, confused about why he would care about such a mundane detail. Surely Elim was familiar with every plant growing within the walls of the temple after so many years?

"I see. Perhaps I should have explained this to you sooner, Adel. I am not angry—you had no way of knowing better—but you need to understand this. Even though it is possible, the power of the Rawl should never be used to alter the life cycle of another living thing."

Alter the life cycle? Was that what he had done with the flowers? Adel had given it no thought; he had assumed it was nothing more than a simple way of performing a kind gesture for Alsea. What harm could come from such a simple act?

"I can see you are confused, Adel. Allow me to explain. What you are doing when you cause flowers to reach maturity faster than they normally would is altering the flow of time itself. Such an act is dangerous, and you never know what impacts it could have. There are stories from centuries ago of the Thrawll using such tactics as a weapon against their victims to devastating effect. I know you would never do such a thing, but I must stress upon you the importance of avoiding such uses of the Rawl. Even small acts of time manipulation can have unforeseen impacts. Time is one of the fabrics that weaves together to form this world and the one about which we know the least."

Adel took a deep breath. He had not thought of what he was doing as manipulating time itself. It had never even occurred to him that the Rawl was capable of doing such a thing. In hindsight, he realized he should have recognized what he was doing and the potential dangers involved. Imagining the ways the Thrawll may have used this ability in the past sent shivers down his spine.

"Thank you for explaining this, Elim. I am sorry. It will not happen again."

"No apology is needed, my friend. I blame myself for not explaining this sooner. I should have known a fast learner like yourself would test such uses of the Rawl sooner rather than later. You are too intelligent not to consider such possibilities. But enough about this matter. Have you made up your mind about what you are going to do next?" Elim asked.

"I am going back to rejoin General McLeod and hopefully help him end this war with the Hoyt. There are too many innocent lives at risk across the province for me to do otherwise. Ola and Alsea both insist on coming with me, and we will leave in a week. I believe we have a plan for how to deal with the beast hunting me."

"It sounds as though your plans are set. This should be a comforting feeling. Why do you think you are restless tonight?"

Adel considered this for a minute. It was something he had been struggling with the entire time he had been wandering the temple's corridors. After a minute, he felt he could articulate what he was feeling and began to respond.

"I'm not as confident as I was after the battle at Kolig. When General McLeod first asked me to join his men, I did so because I felt I could help them in their fight against the Hoyt. I felt my powers could save lives, could help end this conflict sooner. After stopping that flood from wiping out the army, I was so sure of myself, so sure of my powers. If I could do that, I felt I could do anything. But after the ambush in the warehouse, and now the attacks by this monster, I'm not so sure anymore. I feel my inability to keep people safe has let everybody down. I've failed to live up to everyone's expectations of me, and even more so, the expectations I have of myself. Now I am terrified my plan for this beast will not work, and Ola and Alsea could be hurt again—or worse."

Elim was silent for several seconds after Adel's reply, his face pensive and kind. Once he seemed satisfied Adel had no more to say, he began wording his response. Every word was carefully chosen, as was usually the case when he spoke.

"You are hard on yourself, Adel. As I said earlier, this is typical of a great leader. It was something I could sense in you when we first met, and I am happy to see my suspicions confirmed. All great leaders doubt themselves, and all great leaders blame themselves when their plans go awry. I would say any leader who is always convinced he or she is right is a leader who will inevitably fail, often with grave consequences. Not to say the opposite is a guarantor of success because, frankly, it is not. But given a choice, I would rather follow someone with your outlook," Elim said.

"You still want me to be your leader, don't you? I'll be honest; it isn't something I thought much about while I was away from the temple. I was so preoccupied with finding Idanox and stopping the Hoyt that it just didn't enter my mind very often. Do you still think I am the right man for the job?"

"More than ever, my young man. Since the day I met you, you have conducted yourself with nothing but honor, dignity, and selflessness. You do not seek power or leadership, which makes you the ideal candidate to wield both. I do not know if your fears and doubts are something you will ever be able to conquer entirely. I do not even know if you should want to rid yourself of them completely. Perhaps these doubts and fears are what will save your friends' lives or your own one day," Elim said.

Adel thought about what the older man had said. Was it true that good leaders all experienced these emotions? He thought about Captain Boyd, the man from whom he had learned more about leadership than any other. He could not recall any instance of Boyd expressing doubt or fear, except perhaps when the Hoyt attacked the barge and the lives of his men were in danger. Maybe another aspect of being a good leader was not ridding yourself of fear and doubt, but rather concealing them so those who followed you could not see them. Maybe merely creating an image of confidence and ability could prove as valuable as the real thing in the minds of those following.

"Thank you, Elim. You have been most helpful, as always," he said before heading toward his chamber. He had not overcome his doubts, but perhaps this new perspective would allow him to succeed in spite of them.

Chapter Eleven

That same night found Idanox waiting impatiently in a heavily thicketed area a mile outside of Thornata's capital city of Oreanna. The night had finally come. All preparations were in place, and by the time the sun began to rise on the eastern horizon, Thornata would have a new ruler. It was a surreal feeling for Idanox, realizing everything he had worked for was within his grasp at last. He reflected briefly on a similar night almost a year earlier, standing on a hill overlooking the city of Kolig and thinking similar thoughts.

This time will be different, he told himself. This time there would be no mistakes and no Rawl wielder to interfere with his meticulously laid plans. The city's gates stood wide-open, the result of the sheer arrogance of the soon-to-be-former duke. No word of this attack had leaked to the army. The defenders of Oreanna were utterly unaware of the death and destruction that was about to descend upon them.

Srenpe stood in silence a few feet to Idanox's right. Idanox had insisted Srenpe be present for this, against the mage's vocal protests. He was still impatiently waiting for the mage's first creation to bring him the Rawl wielder's head. If the group of beasts the mage had provided for the night's battle failed their mission, Idanox would have no more patience, and Srenpe would be the one to pay the price for it. For his part, the mage insisted the first beast was still alive and well, continuing its hunt for the boy who had been such a thorn in the Idanox's side. He also pointed out that there had been no news of interference from the boy in weeks, which Idanox begrudgingly had to admit was true. While he would've preferred the certainty of knowing the boy was dead and gone, he would settle for his absence for the time being.

Srenpe had produced twelve new killing machines on schedule as requested and assured Idanox they would not fail in their task.

They had better not, Idanox thought darkly, for he only had half of the forces he had once hoped to bring against Oreanna. He had invested years of his life into making this night come to fruition, and he was not comfortable with the number of men he had at his disposal. Between the Rawl wielder's massacre against their forces at Kolig and the high number of desertions, the Hoyt were stretched thinner than they had been since the early years. Seizing control of the capital of Thornata was a much more daunting task than the trading caravans and small villages they had assaulted in those days. None of it would matter, though, if they succeeded tonight. If they failed, he might not survive long enough to punish Srenpe for his failure.

"Are you able to tell where your beasts are?" Idanox asked.

"They are still just north of the city; your men must be rowing slowly. You should try to find men who are not quite so lazy. Or is it a matter of poor physical fitness?" Srenpe replied, needling Idanox as always. "One would think former farmers and stable boys would be in better shape."

The mage had appeared downright annoyed when Idanox had demanded he be present for the assault and had offered several excuses as to why his presence should not be necessary. Every passing day found Idanox hating Srenpe more and more. He would love nothing more than to see the infuriating mage lying in the dirt, bleeding out.

Soon enough, Srenpe, you arrogant fool, he thought.

"My men are doing their jobs. You'd better hope your beasts do the same. I have invested a lot of resources in you, mage, and thus far I have received nothing resembling results," Idanox warned. The arrogant mage merely smirked in response.

The Hoyt did not have a sufficient force to take the city by force from outside the walls. They also did not have a large number of men inside the city walls who had infiltrated the army as they'd had in Kolig. Idanox's original plan was to fabricate an attack by the river and then send a large contingent of men to seize the duke's palace while the army was preoccupied repelling the feint. It had been a risky plan, one with plenty of opportunity for failure. Once Srenpe had agreed to help, he had adjusted the plan accordingly. Having the beasts at his disposal allowed him to improve the battle plan significantly.

There would still be an attack by the river, but this would no longer be a simple feint. Instead, it would be the key to a Hoyt victory. At this moment, his men were rowing the twelve beasts into the city in three small rowboats, which would not be deemed threats to any soldiers watching the river. Once they were inside the city, the creatures would unleash chaos. They would kill every soldier in sight, along with anybody else who got in their way. As the army scrambled to respond, his men would gather at the palace and take the duke captive. The Hoyt men Idanox had chosen for this job had been slipping into the city for the past two weeks. This left only a token force of a hundred men outside the city walls, dedicated to protecting their leader. If this attack failed, they would likely be all that remained of the Hoyt by dawn.

That is why we will not fail, Idanox thought. Finally, his pieces were in place, and the attack could begin.

"The boats have reached the docks," Srenpe announced, breaking the silence. How he was able to pinpoint the exact location of his monsters was a mystery to Idanox, but it was an ability that had proven useful on this night. The time had come to unleash hell on the unsuspecting city of Oreanna. It was an unfortunate but necessary sacrifice. It was a small price for the people to pay in exchange for having Idanox as their new leader.

"Very well. Signal the attack," Idanox instructed.

The mage raised his staff straight into the air, and for the briefest moment, there was a faint purple light emanating from its tip. Just as quickly, the light was gone, and he lowered the staff to its normal position. Idanox raised a curious eyebrow, but Srenpe merely nodded to indicate that the attack had begun. A split second later, the distant sound of screams from the city confirmed as much. Idanox's mouth twisted into a wide grin, his lone regret that he could not witness the attack up close.

***

Even Idanox's twisted mind would have taken little pleasure from the scene unfolding inside the city. At the same moment that Srenpe's staff had ignited with his dark magic, the beasts had sprung into motion. Their suddenness shocked the Hoyt men who had ferried them into the city. A pair of city guards patrolling the dock area had been the first unfortunate victims, though the beasts had intentionally killed them slowly, allowing them time to scream out in fear. This was all part of Idanox's plan, of course. The city at large had to become aware of the beasts for the strategy to be effective. Therefore, the first victims had to suffer. Every fighting man in the city needed to be drawn toward the monsters. This was the only way for the success of the plan to be assured.

The screams drew the attention of every patrol in the area, dozens of city guards descending on the docks to find themselves confronted by a dozen monstrous creatures the likes of which they had never seen. Thornatan soldiers began to respond as well, some of the most seasoned fighters in the entire province, none of whom had ever fought anything like the beasts attacking their city now. The creatures, armed with massive battle-axes and broadswords, hacked and hammered their way through all attackers, walking through any injuries they received in return as though they did not even matter. The Hoyt fighters accompanying them could only stand back and watch, their expressions torn between horror and awe.

Within minutes, the beasts broke free of the forces struggling to contain them to the docks and began rampaging through the city streets. Horns were blowing, people were screaming, and the whole time Idanox stood in a forest just outside the city, his twisted face curled into a gleeful smile at the sound of it all. After about ten minutes of continued chaos inside the city, he turned to Srenpe.

"I daresay they should have the soldiers well enough occupied by now. Send the second signal," he instructed the mage.

Srenpe raised his staff skyward once more. This time there came one, two, and then three quick flashes of green flame that shot into the blackness of the night sky. This was the signal his men inside the city had been told to watch out for while they lay in wait. This was their message that it was time to launch their assault on the duke's palace.

It will not be long now, Idanox thought. This assault could not possibly have gone any smoother thus far. After the countless fiascos since Kolig, a flawlessly executed plan brought joy to his heart.

Another hour passed before one of his men finally emerged from the city. The Hoyt fighter informed him the palace had been taken and the duke was in their custody. Idanox turned to Srenpe, who raised his staff one last time, igniting a series of colorful yet silent flashes. They waited in silence for several minutes until two of the freshly created beasts appeared before them, answering their master's call. Idanox had requested they escort him into the city. This was for his own protection. It would also send a message to the people of Oreanna about the abilities of their new ruler. He noted with delight the copious amount of blood and gore adorning each monster's body.

It had been a wise foresight, indeed. Idanox was barely a few yards inside the main gates of the city when a Thornatan soldier emerged from behind a stack of crates and rushed toward him, brandishing a sword. Idanox barely spared the man a second glance as his one of monstrous bodyguards swiftly put a brutal end to the pathetic assassination attempt. Anyone who shared the man's reckless bravery would meet the same fate. He found himself hoping he would have the chance to see such a thing unfold.

He turned to give Srenpe a nod of approval and noticed the mage had not followed them into the city.

The coward likely does not want his face associated with the Hoyt, Idanox thought to himself. Srenpe was a man who always hedged his bets. It mattered not as long as his pets did their duty without question. He continued through the city streets, his massive bodyguards flanking him closely, a broad smile stretching across his face as he took in the carnage around every corner.

Citizens of Oreanna had begun to file out into the street, drawn from their homes by the screams of battle, followed by the eerie silence that filled the city now. Most of these people knew who he was. This city had been his home once, and he had been quite well known in those days. His wealth and riches had once made him a man to be admired. Many of them had dreamed of their children growing up to reach his level of success, too stupid to understand why such things could never happen. Most of them did not bother to disguise their hatred or disgust now, and some hurled insults at him. He did not respond; the opinions of peasants meant nothing to him. They could call him what they wanted for now. By the time this night was over, they would have no choice but to call him their ruler.

The closer he drew to the center of the city, the more visible signs of the battle he saw.

The beasts have done their work well, he thought as he passed what appeared to be the torn and bloody remains of a Thornatan army squad. Angry citizens attempted to attack him twice, and his monstrous bodyguards made unpleasant examples of them. There were no more attempts at violence against him after that. He had found peasants were like misbehaving dogs. They would only take so many smacks before hiding and whimpering in a corner.

As he approached the duke's palace, he saw several dozen Hoyt fighters gathered in front of the main doors, surrounding a small group of prisoners. There, front and center, was the duke of Thornata, a man he had met on numerous occasions while he had lived in this city. A man who had never shown him the respect he was due. A man who was about to pay the price for those many slights. A wiser man would have seen Idanox's potential and the potential of a partnership with such a brilliant man.

As he approached, he noticed the rest of Srenpe's beasts gathered to the left, nearly out of sight. To his delight, their skin and torn clothing were covered with the remnants of their victims. It was a sight which would serve to intimidate his enemies further. He was pleased to see they had all survived the battle and were here now; he intended to put on a show that might dismay some people.

If that happened, having the beasts nearby could prove to be a good thing. Satisfied that all aspects of his plan had worked to perfection, he turned his attention to the duke, a broad smile on his face.

"So sorry to disturb your sleep, my lord. But you have been asleep for a long time, haven't you? If only you had woken up sooner and realized how many of your subjects have suffered needlessly under your incompetent regime. If you had, you would not be in the position you find yourself now," Idanox said. He took care to raise his voice so it would carry to the crowds of civilians who were cautiously beginning to gather nearby.

"Idanox, you always were a miserable bastard. You are still nothing more than an arrogant fool with more money than sense. I always knew you were a fool, but you have surprised even me tonight. You cannot possibly think you will get away with a move like this," the duke said, insolent as ever.

Taunt all you want. We will see who the fool is soon enough.

"Nothing more than an arrogant fool with more money than sense? Odd, but if that is indeed all I am, it seems to qualify me to be the ruler of this province. Maybe you should reflect on what that statement says about you, my old friend," Idanox said, noting with pleasure that more civilians were beginning to gather around to witness the exchange. The more witnesses present, the better his purpose would be served.

"You are a murdering tyrant, a filthy, worthless, flea-bitten thief!" the duke cried out for all to hear. He spat at Idanox, striking him in the chest.

That is unfortunate, Idanox thought. He would have enjoyed the opportunity to continue the show for the crowd's benefit, but he could not let such an insult pass in public, not even for a second. His new subjects needed to know that such actions bore immediate consequences. The duke would need to face his punishment here and now. He turned to the crowd with his arms held wide.

"My brothers and sisters of Thornata, I speak to you as one of you. I speak to any person who has ever felt the rulers who live in this palace do not care about you. I speak to any person who has ever felt the oppression of this man's incompetent rule firsthand. I speak to you as a wealthy man, one of the few who has long profited from the duke's selfish policies, policies which were written to keep all of you intentionally in poverty. Thornata deserves a ruler who will help us all move forward into a new age of prosperity. I pledge that I will be this for you, that all I have, I will give for the good of my countrymen. But before we can move into the future, the past must be killed. The oppressor of the past must go so we can move forward into a bright new future together." Idanox strained his voice so as many people as possible could hear him, then he turned to one of the beasts by his side.

"Kill him. Make it nice and messy," he instructed, turning from the crowd momentarily so that they could not read his lips. He shot the duke one last smile, a smile which grew wider at the expression of sheer terror that was returned.

The beast advanced on the duke without hesitation, raising its massive battle-axe. It did not strike with full force; as always, it had taken note of Idanox's instructions. The duke died a slow, painful, and public death in front of hundreds of his former subjects. The crowd gasped and cried in shock, horror, and disgust. When it was finally over, Idanox could still hear crying and retching emanating from the gathered civilians. It was unfortunate they had to witness such brutal things, but Idanox had learned long ago that visual examples were far more effective than verbal threats.

"My friends, I am sorry you all had to see such things. Sometimes evil is needed to combat evil, and this was one such instance. Hopefully, with the traitor to our people gone, we can move forward and finally prosper as the province of Thornata deserves. We will serve as standard-bearers for all the downtrodden people across the Empire. We will show them that change can benefit all people, not only those fortunate to be born into wealth! Thornata will be a shimmering beacon of hope!"

If people were at all excited by this prospect, they did not express it, raining him with more shouts and jeers.

Fools, he thought. *They should be showering me with cheers and praise for the service I just did them.* The truth of the matter was that if any of these peasants could not prosper on their own, there was little he could do to help and little he cared to do to help them. Branding himself as a champion of the common man had helped him build the Hoyt into a formidable fighting force. The same tactic was facing more resistance from these people. Their opposition mattered not. They could choose to accept his rule or die in the name of their misguided principles. There was no other option for them.

"Idanox! You are under arrest for crimes against Thornata. Order your men to lay down their weapons and surrender at once!" someone shouted.

Idanox squinted through the early morning haze; the sun had still not risen high enough to burn it off. He was mildly surprised to find the source of the voice to be a Thornatan Army captain at the head of several dozen Thornatan soldiers. They must have scattered and regrouped, though instead of fleeing the city, as any sane man would have done, they had boldly decided to attempt to put a stop to the inevitable. He noted the expressions of relief on the faces of the gathered civilians. They must've thought Idanox and the Hoyt would be defeated in short order. Apparently, yet another visual demonstration was needed. Their faces were full of hope. It was an emotion he would need to steal from them at once.

"I have no intention of surrendering, my good man. It is you and your brothers who need to lay down your weapons. I have great respect for the men of the Thornatan Army, and I hope you will lay down your weapons and come and speak with me like gentlemen. I believe we can accomplish much together, the Hoyt and the Thornatan Army, working as one. There is no need for further bloodshed," Idanox called out, under no delusions that the men would do any such thing.

There was no response, at least not a verbal one. The men continued to advance on him, approaching the duke's palace, which now belonged to him. Had he brought only the Hoyt fighters with him, they may have been in danger. The soldiers came close to equaling their numbers and were better trained than his own men. But he had a trump card, one which would both rid him of this problem and set a supreme example of why the citizens of Oreanna should not attempt to resist his rule.

"Kill them all," Idanox instructed his group of beasts, pointing to the advancing soldiers.

As one, all twelve beasts started toward the attackers, their battle-axes and greatswords in hand. The soldiers continued without hesitation, apparently thinking a mere dozen opponents could not possibly stop them.

Oh, my friends, if only you could understand how mistaken you are. They met the beasts a hundred feet from where Idanox stood watching, and it looked as though they might as well have walked into a brick wall.

To their credit, the soldiers fought bravely, but they had never faced creatures such as these. These were creatures that could absorb the most grievous of wounds yet fight on with a strength and ferocity no ordinary man could ever dream of matching. Idanox could not help but feel the slightest touch of respect for the men. Not a single one attempted to flee the carnage. Every last one of them fought and died for their city and their people.

Brave men are destined to become dead brave men, Idanox thought darkly to himself, noting with satisfaction the expressions of profound horror on the faces of the witnesses. They would heed his commands now; he was sure of it. They would not like it, and he did not care if they did. Their happiness mattered not a bit to him. All that mattered was their silent obedience.

The battle lasted no more than a few minutes, and his beasts returned to his side, blood still dripping from their weapons. The people of Oreanna offered no more shouts or jeers of protest, only frightened, solemn silence, which pleased Idanox greatly. Perhaps now they would be more receptive to what he had to say. They would not want him to provide them with another demonstration, after all.

"My friends, this has been a difficult night for all of us, but as you can see, the sun will still rise and shine bright as it ever has. I come to you not as a conqueror but as a savior. Please accept this opportunity I have laid before you and accept this chance to see your lives change for the better. Please return to your homes and think long and hard on what you have witnessed here today. Tell this tale to every man, woman, and child you know. Tell them what happens to those who stand in the way of progress. The people of Thornata will prosper, and any who attempt to stand in the way of that will pay a heavy price."

To his pleasure, the crowd of citizens silently obeyed his command to disperse, thoroughly disheartened by the shocking displays of violence they had witnessed. He couldn't hear so much as a whisper in their midst as they shuffled away from the palace that now belonged to him. He was confident he had broken their spirits sufficiently and that they would not cause any problems in the immediate future. The tale he had given them to spread was bloody and frightening enough that even those who had not witnessed it firsthand would be terrified enough to fall in line for a time.

Turning to his men, Idanox immediately began giving instructions. The city was to be scoured for any surviving soldiers. He could not allow them to rally a force with which to attack him. Any high-ranking officers were to be taken alive if possible; they would prove valuable to his plans in the days ahead. Just as in Kolig, any protests were to be met with ruthless brutality. Messengers were to be sent to all major cities of the province. They were to be informed that the Hoyt were now in control of Thornata. The leaders of those cities could kneel to Idanox or suffer the same fate as their former duke. Idanox hoped this would bring some of his more reluctant servants back to his side.

He made his way through the duke's palace, a luxurious symbol of power. He had been plotting this day for so long, and it was hard to believe it was finally happening. It was almost as gaudy as the mansion home he had once kept in this city before trading in his life of luxury for insurgency. Idanox had always enjoyed riches and luxuries. As he moved through the chambers of the palace, he even noticed with outrage pieces of artwork that had once resided in his home. The duke must have felt deserving of them after the army raided his mansion, the corrupt pig. They were back with their rightful owner now, and he was in the place he had always deserved to be.

He reached the duke's bedchamber to find Srenpe waiting for him. The mage was lounging in a chair near the window looking quite bored. Idanox was vaguely irritated by the mage's forwardness but set his anger aside. This was a day of celebration, and even the insolent Srenpe could not steal that from him. Besides, the mage's beasts had done their job to perfection, and he could at least appreciate that much.

"That was some demonstration you put on out there, Duke Idanox," Srenpe said.

"People need visual examples to truly understand the consequences of their actions. Your beasts did their job well. Will they stay in my service now?" Idanox asked, eager to keep the monsters and the level of control they afforded him.

"That depends. Are you going to maintain your end of our bargain?" Srenpe asked.

"I am a man of my word, Srenpe. You may take whatever you see fit from the vaults; my men will not interfere. All I ask is that you come and hear me out if I request your services again," Idanox said.

"I admit you do pay quite well. I will hear out any requests you have of me in the future, and you may retain the services of my creations. They will follow any order you give without question, as you have seen. Good luck in your future endeavors, Duke Idanox," Srenpe said, rising from his chair and sinking into an exaggerated bow before heading out the door without a glance back.

Alone in the bedchamber, Idanox allowed himself one final moment to truly relish his most significant accomplishment to date. Years of planning and hard work had led to this moment; he could finally call himself the ruler of Thornata. He had convinced countless men to give their lives in support of this cause, men whose lives had been meaningless enough to him. Still, he could not help but be somewhat humbled by their exceptional sacrifice.

He would enjoy his rest this night, but he knew this victory was the first skirmish in a more prolonged battle that was still to play out. He still needed to bring the rest of the province to heel, a task that would be easier with the capital under his control but far from simple. More work would begin when he awoke, but for now there was time to lie in this bed he had won for himself and enjoy for one morning the fruits of his labor.

Chapter Twelve

Adel made his way through the winding corridors of the Temple of the Rawl, trying his best to remember the way to the vault Elim had shown him weeks earlier. He had woken to find a note in the kitchen from the old man asking him to meet in the vault for a quick word before his departure. As he wound his way through the seemingly endless maze of identical passageways, he could not help but wonder if this was a test of his navigational abilities.

The corridors of the Temple of the Rawl were so intricate he could not help but wonder if he would ever learn his way entirely. Even after all these weeks, there was still much to learn about this new world in which he found himself. Each time he began to feel comfortable, something new was thrown at him. As he passed doorway after doorway, he wondered if he would ever know the purpose of each chamber within the temple. Adel could not help but feel as though his training had barely scratched the surface.

When he finally came to the staircase leading down into the vault, he breathed a sigh of relief. He had begun to fear he was lost in the endless maze of passageways, which would've made him look quite the fool on the morning of his departure. Once again, Adel felt the familiar tingling of immense power in the air around him. He wondered if his power had helped guide him here, following the Vindur as a navigator on a ship at sea might follow the stars to find their way.

He descended the stairs to find the door of the vault already open and Elim waiting within. The Vindur sat on its pedestal in the middle of the chamber, its gleaming surface immediately drawing Adel's eye. Its shimmering surface glowed brighter than the most exquisite diamond.

Forcing his eyes away from the glistening orb, he approached Elim, who extended a hand. Adel shook it, and Elim gave him a warm smile.

"So today is the day you depart once more. While it pains me to see you leave so soon, I understand the need. Your skills have been honed, and your powers have reached a level the young man who departed this temple last year would never have imagined. You should be proud of all you have accomplished in such a short time, Adel. I do not doubt for a second that you will succeed in your endeavors ahead," Elim said.

It was true. He would never have suspected when he left the Temple of the Rawl last year that he would be capable of the things he could do now. If the deckhand from the barge could see him now, he would probably not recognize himself. Adel sometimes felt as though he had grown more in the past year than he had in his first sixteen combined. He felt old, as though the past year of trials and challenges was only now taking its full effect on him. This was nonsense, and Adel scolded himself for thinking in such a way. He was still a young man, and his actual trials had yet to begin. The war with the Hoyt would not be a battle won easily no matter how far he had come in his training.

"It's all thanks to your training, Elim. I would not be half the Rawl wielder I am now without your help. I doubt I would even be alive for that matter. I owe the Children of the Rawl a debt I can never repay."

"Do not sell yourself short, Adel. Training is worthless without a willing and capable student. You have earned everything we have done for you. No debt is owed for any of it. I am so proud of the strides you have made. You are no longer the naive boy who first came to this temple last year. You are truly a man now, one worthy of wielding the power you possess. That is why I have asked you to meet me down here before you depart."

The old man beckoned for him to follow, so Adel fell into step behind him as he led the way across the vault. As they walked past the Vindur, Adel could feel the immense power emanating from the ancient artifact. Once again, his mind struggled to comprehend how an object of such power could exist. He wondered once more what it would feel like to hold the orb in his hand, to feel the full might of its power coursing through him, a curiosity that he forced from his mind.

Elim led him into a small alcove that Adel had not noticed his first time in the vault. Inside the alcove waited a set of armor on a stand.

The armor was the same dark green color as the robes worn by the Children of the Rawl. It appeared to be made of hardened leather, lighter and more flexible than plate metal yet still sturdy. Elim gestured for Adel to try it on, so he did, fitting the guards into place over his clothing. It fit perfectly and did not hinder his movement at all. Tapping his chest with his hand, Adel felt as though this was the best possible protection he could ask for without sacrificing his mobility. The leather was hardened to the point that Adel suspected it would stop all but the most vicious of strikes.

Still, let's not test this theory in a real fight if we can avoid it.

"This armor has been worn by the Master of the Rawl over the centuries. We would be honored if you wore it now. We feel you have earned that right, and besides, it may help keep you alive in the days ahead. I do not doubt you will find yourself in many more dangerous situations before returning to us again. Perils are inevitable with a cause such as yours. Hopefully this armor will help see you safely through them," Elim explained.

Adel was touched to hear the Children of the Rawl saw him as fit to wear the armor of their leader. He re-solved himself once more that he would not make them regret their decision to train him. Adel thanked Elim, clasp-ing the wise man's hand once more in farewell. Elim had been a mentor to him since he had come here for the first time, but at this parting, Adel felt a genuine friendship be-tween them. It was a feeling he could recall being skeptical would ever occur the last time he had been to the temple, yet the friendship had blossomed nonetheless. He left the vault, making his way back through the winding corridors, this time with more confidence as he chose his route.

I'm dressed like a leader, and I might as well walk like one, he thought proudly to himself. To his delight, he did not get lost, and he soon emerged into the courtyard where Ola and Alsea were waiting for him.

"Looking sharp, Adel," Alsea said, gesturing to-ward his new armor. "Green is a good color for you. Hope-fully you don't get too many red stains on it."

"The armor suits you well, my friend. Hopefully it does not have to do its job too often in the days ahead," Ola said.

"Thank you both. I will try to be worthy of the honor of wearing it. Shall we be off?"

They set off without further delay, making their way down the stone steps into the valley below. When they reached the floor of the valley at last, they found Klaweck waiting for them. Even after several meetings, Adel felt the same sense of awe staring up at the impossibly massive giant.

Out of all the strange things about this new life, I don't think I will ever get used to being around giants, Adel thought as he smiled up at the gentle face towering above them.

"Farewell, my friends. I wish you good fortune in your journey ahead. We have seen no sign of the beast that is pursuing you, Adel. Still, show caution once you are clear of the valley. I do not doubt it will find your trail once more now that you have left the Temple of the Rawl. Rest assured, the temple and the Children will be well protected in your absence. Be safe, my friends," Klaweck said

They set off eastward across the valley toward the narrow gap that would lead them back down into the foothills. They had decided not to take the shortcut through the canyon to the south. Their plan for the beast required a certain amount of wide-open space, which the narrow canyon would not afford them. Their idea was to march east at a hard pace, keeping their eyes open for a suitable location as they did. They could only hope and pray their pursuer would not find them too soon. Elim had surmised the protections around the temple had confused its senses, throwing it off the trail. If he was correct, they should have enough time to find the location they needed. If he was not . . . That was not a thought Adel cared to entertain.

It was nearing noon when Alsea called them to a halt.

"I think this spot will do as well as any other," she said, her eyes sweeping the surrounding area as she pointed out the various landmarks, which would serve them well.

Looking around, Adel found himself in agreement. There were a few trees and the perfect amount of open space. The creature would not be able to easily sneak up on them here. Adel looked to Ola, who was also nodding in agreement, and they immediately went to work, not wasting any time on further discussion. They did not know how long it would take the beast to find them; it could take days, or it could be a matter of minutes. If it was the latter, their careful planning over the past week would be for naught.

Ola pulled a small shovel from his bag and immediately began to dig. Meanwhile, Adel and Alsea retrieved long branches from nearby trees, using their knives to carve them into the desired shape as quickly as possible. They worked rapidly, desperate to complete their task, knowing the beast could come upon them at any moment. There was no talking while they worked; there was no need for it. They had gone over the plan repeatedly during the past week, and each of them knew their role so well they could've done it in their sleep. The only breaks in the work came in the brief moments they took to steal glances at their surroundings, reassuring themselves they had not yet been discovered.

The bulk of their work was done within the hour, an hour which fortunately passed with no sign of the monstrous creature. Adel breathed a sigh of relief. They had been able to prepare for the beast's arrival properly. When it did arrive, at least they would have a fighting chance. All that remained was to build a campfire, which Alsea did in a hurry, bringing a roaring flame to life within minutes. Adel would typically have used his power to assist but contented himself with letting Alsea do the work. They had already agreed it best if he saved every bit of strength possible for the confrontation ahead.

The three took seats around the fire, the tension palpable as they waited for the inevitable stone to fall. A fire was a risk they were usually unwilling to take, a sign pointing to their whereabouts. But on this day, they wanted their hunter to find them. It was time to put an end to this pursuit, time for a final confrontation. This time, at least it would happen on their terms. They would prevail, or they would die, but at least it would be over. Adel suspected they were all thinking the same thing, though none of the three were eager to put their feelings into words.

"I will be shocked if it does not come upon us in the next few hours," Adel commented. He wasn't telling them anything they didn't suspect themselves, but he was almost as desperate to break the painful silence as he was to put this matter to rest.

"I agree. It was quick enough to find us every other time. Now that we are outside of the protections surrounding the Temple of the Rawl, I am sure it has found our trail and is well on its way," Alsea agreed. Her eyes were darting nervously in every direction, as they had been ever since the trio had left the temple. Adel noticed her fingers nervously strumming the handle of her knife.

With nothing much else to say, the tense silence resumed. The afternoon was fading away, much to Adel's disappointment. Whenever the beast did arrive, he would much rather face it in the light of day. This confrontation would be dangerous enough without the added challenge of limited visibility. The greatest weakness of their plan was the fact that it required absolute precision. One misstep by any of them could mean the end of all of them. Darkness would only increase the chances of such a mistake.

Every hour, one of the three would take a turn sweeping the perimeter, searching for any sign of the beast, though Ola suggested they stop this when night fell. It would be too dangerous for one of them to be alone in the dark with the monster potentially close to their camp. Adel and Alsea were quick to agree. None of them cared to be caught alone by that monster in the pitch-black night.

As night fell and the blackness set in around them, Adel found himself hoping he was wrong, that the beast would not come upon them until the next day. Their plan was a good one, and he believed it would work. But he understood it would be all the more challenging to execute correctly in the darkness. His heart raced in his chest, refusing to slow its rhythm no matter how hard he willed for it to do so. He noticed Alsea's foot was tapping rapidly, and Ola's hands were continually adjusting their grip on the pommel of his sword. At least he was not the only one suffering from nerves, which was mildly reassuring. The moon briefly gave them some light before thick clouds obscured it. Before long, the only light available to them came from the glow of their campfire.

Adel had just begun to believe the beast would not reach them until the following day when it appeared without warning. It moved with an elusiveness that should have been impossible for a creature so large. In every other encounter, it had made no effort to conceal itself. Perhaps their time in hiding had allowed it to evolve its hunting techniques. He recalled the way in which it had seemingly evolved in between their first and second encounters, shrugging off his Rawl attacks the second time around. It was within twenty feet of them before he spotted it. Had it not been for the dancing glow of the firelight bouncing off the massive battle-axes it wielded, he may not have seen it at all until it was too late. Crying out to his friends, he sprung to his feet, ripping his sword from its sheath and hoping they were not too late.

Ola met the beast first, grabbing ahold of it and flinging it back away from their campfire with all his might. He was trying to put as much distance between them as possible to give Adel and Alsea enough time to get into position. Adel raced for his assigned area as cautiously as possible, reminding himself that a single misstep could ruin everything. He did not look back to see how effective Ola's attempt to slow the beast was. He could not afford even a second of distraction. He had to trust in Ola's ability to do his job.

The beast recovered from Ola's throw in less than a second, spinning back around and locking its eyes on Adel. It started toward him, but Ola was in its path again, striking out this time with his greatsword in an attempt to slow the beast. He managed to strike the creature twice with wounds that would have instantly crippled any normal man. But the creature was no ordinary man, and it continued unfazed, swinging its battle-axes toward Ola as a man might try to swat at a fly. In position up on a tree branch, Alsea cried out for Ola to abandon his assault, and the ogre deftly leaped out of the monster's path. As they had suspected, it did not pursue Ola after he moved aside. Its objective was Adel, and it instantly turned its attention on him once more, now advancing unchallenged.

The crack of Alsea's bow split the night three times, each arrow finding its mark and sinking into the belly of the massive beast. They did not slow the creature for even a second, though the three companions had not expected they would. It was closing in quickly, and Adel lashed out with the power of the Rawl, using powerful wind gusts to attempt to knock the creature off-balance. Maintaining these brief attacks, he began to move once more, sidestepping toward the exact spot where he needed to be. This was the most delicate part of the plan. If he took a wrong step, he would be dead, and the plan would fail instantly. Alsea sunk one last arrow into the beast's gut as Adel deftly sprung toward his position, his feet hitting their marks with pinpoint precision. With each step, the monster responded, angling to take the shortest possible path to its prey.

He reached his designated spot, the beast square in front of him. There was just one thing left to do now. He let his sword fall limp at his side, halted his Rawl attacks, and stood perfectly still, waiting for the beast to attack. It did not take long. The creature rushed toward him with the same reckless abandon as always, utterly oblivious to the four arrows still protruding from its body. Adel locked eyes with the beast as it charged. There was no emotion in those eyes, merely an innate, instinctual need to kill. Had this creature ever been human? If so, there was nothing left of the man it had once been.

Adel could not help but wonder one last time if this would work as the beast closed in on him. If it did not, he would be dead before his friends could come to his aid. His question was answered a split second later. He felt a rush of relief as the beast stepped right onto the patch of twigs and leaves they had used to conceal the gaping hole they had dug in the earth. The leaves and sticks gave way beneath the gigantic monster's weight, and it crashed down into the pit below, vanishing from sight with a primal scream of rage.

Adel hurried to the edge of the hole, peering over the side cautiously, aware that an attack may still be incoming. To his great satisfaction and relief, he found the beast had fallen directly onto the long branches they had carved into jutting spikes, thoroughly impaling itself. If this caused the monster any pain, it did not show it. It was attempting to rise but could not. They had positioned the spikes in varying angles. The tactic had worked. The beast was having a difficult time climbing to its feet. It was unable to pull itself free from all the barbs simultaneously. A frightening sound split the night as the beast let out another scream of rage, causing Adel to take an involuntary step away from the pit. Even in its trapped state, the creature was terrifying, its inhuman eyes glaring up at him with murderous intent. The spikes were working, but they would not hold the monster indefinitely.

"It worked! Hurry!" Adel cried to Ola.

Ola raced toward the pit with a torch he had retrieved from their campfire. He stopped a few feet short of the pit and tossed the torch into the hole. The grease they had rubbed on the spikes and the tips of Alsea's arrows did its work. It accelerated the rate at which the pit began to burn, feeding the flames as the primal roars continued to rise from the hole. Once there was a sizeable flame, Adel went to work as well, using his power to hasten the growth of the fire even more. He brought the flame to as hot of a burn as he felt was safe and held it there for several long minutes, waiting for the beast's enraged screams to stop.

When Adel finally felt he had held the flame for long enough, he reached out with the power of the Rawl, stealing the air from the fire and extinguishing it instantly.

Gathering around the edge of the pit, the three friends squinted cautiously through the smoke, their eyes blinking against the heat. There was no hint of movement, but the three were not reassured. They stood in a circle around the smoking pit, weapons at the ready. It was over an hour until the smoke finally cleared enough to reveal that everything within the hole had been entirely burned to ash.

The beast was finally gone, and Adel was confident there was no challenge they could face in the days ahead that would rival the one the vicious monster had provided. It was as though a heavy weight had been lifted from his shoulders. Together, the three of them had accomplished what had felt impossible days earlier. If they could survive that monster, they could survive anything else Idanox threw at them. It was finally time to rejoin the Thornatan Army and put an end to the Hoyt once and for all.

Chapter Thirteen

Idanox found the challenges of ruling a province to be quite similar to those of governing a ragtag band of outlaws. In particular, he found the minor yet grueling annoyances provided by both to be nearly identical. For years he had thrived as a wealthy man with industries to run. He had found it was relatively easy to get anything he wanted, provided he could afford to pay for it, which Idanox always could. In those days, there were always men eager to provide him with anything he needed in exchange for a few coins. In industry, men were predictable creatures. Ruling over people was another challenge entirely, one he was still not sure he particularly enjoyed. For some reason, these people felt a ruler should have compassion in his heart for those under his rule. They seemed to believe he should genuinely care for their well-being. These were traits Idanox had never been blessed with, nor did he much care to pretend otherwise.

He had been in this meeting with his commanders since midmorning, and they showed no signs of shutting up anytime soon. They had gathered to apprise him of everything going on in Oreanna. These meetings were becoming daily affairs, each longer and more tedious than the one before. Idanox found himself increasingly annoyed that they were apparently incapable of managing themselves without supervision for more than a day. So here he sat every morning, listening to them drone on and on about the mundane aspects of managing a conquered populace. He had considered having a few of them killed for their incompetence, but they needed every able body they had to keep their operations in the city running smoothly.

More Hoyt were finally reporting to the city, most of them full of wild excuses explaining away their tardiness. But still, he did not have the numbers to throw away those willing to help his cause. For the time being, he had no choice but to accept their excuses and move on, but there would be a day of reckoning soon enough. They could not expect to appear suddenly, after victory had finally been secured, without facing the consequences.

"The shop owners in the marketplace are not happy about the new taxes we have levied on them, and I fear some may begin to revolt," one fool was saying, thoroughly oblivious to the daggers Idanox was glaring at him. How long had this oaf been under his command? His face wasn't particularly familiar. Still, could he honestly not hazard a guess at what Idanox would advise him to do in such a situation?

"The first merchant who revolts can be strung up by his wrists in the middle of the market for a few days with no food or water. Flog him every few hours to make the point even stronger. That should send the message to the rest of them that revolution may not be the best idea," Idanox said, wondering all the while why he had to explain this to them. "The same can be done to any merchant who does not pay the full amount owed. Proper punishment will ensure the crimes are not repeated. Taxes are not optional; we have a province to run."

Competent help was so difficult to find. Of course, the Rawl wielder had robbed him of some of his better lieutenants the year prior. This thought sent Idanox's mind to an even darker place. There was still no sign of the beast Srenpe had sent after the boy. The mage's creations had won him this city, but where was the first beast? He had thought the boy would be dead weeks ago, yet he had received no evidence to prove it.

"We still aren't having much luck with the army commanders we captured. They continue to swear they will not fight for us no matter what threats we throw at them. Shall we kill a few of them to send a message?" another commander asked.

Typical, Idanox thought. These morons believed any problem could be solved with brute force and intimidation. No wonder they had never found prosperity until he came along to gift it to them so graciously. Once they found one solution, they believed it could be applied to any problem. The army commanders were a limited and precious commodity, one which could not be wasted on delivering messages. A more delicate touch would be needed, one he doubted any of these fools possessed. Such a sensitive and essential matter would undoubtedly require his personal attention.

"None of them are to be harmed without specific instructions from me. We are going to need every army commander we can sway to our cause in order to keep the grunts in line. Hunt down as many of their family members as possible and lock them up as well. They are not to be harmed. Inform me when we have gathered a good number, and I will come down and deal with the commanders myself," Idanox said. "Perhaps I will be able to make them see reason. I can be quite persuasive when needed."

The meeting finally ended as the late afternoon was drawing near, leaving Idanox irritated with his men's incompetence. Without a doubt, they would return the following morning with another series of asinine questions for him to answer and problems for him to solve for them. Being the lone intelligent man in a room full of imbeciles was tiring and hungry work. He retired to the duke's dining room and barked at the servants that he was hungry.

He had forced the entire household staff to stay on, serving his needs as they had once served the former duke's. After several years of living in camps in the wild, being waited on in a mansion once more was a welcome change. He had been concerned a disgruntled cook might think to poison him, so he had gathered the entire staff on his first morning in the house. He had lined them up and introduced them to one of Srenpe's beasts. He explained in no uncertain terms that if he died or was harmed in any way, the creature would proceed to massacre every living person it found in the mansion. Their expressions of terror assured him none of them would be stupid enough to try any such thing.

They had his meal prepared in short order; he had made it quite clear he was not a patient man. He had needed to threaten one serving girl with a beating on the first day of his residence, but the speed of their service had been adequate since then. They were not as accommodating as the servants he had once employed in his own mansion, but they would learn eventually, even if it took a few floggings. It would not surprise him if his household servants proved to be more competent than the men he was forced to entrust with the command of his forces.

Despite the continued annoyances, the past week of ruling had gone smoother than he had anticipated. There had been little in the way of civilian resistance after his graphic demonstrations the night he had seized the palace. People may have hated him for his brutality, but there was no questioning its effectiveness at keeping the peasants in line. Loathe though he was to admit it, he likely had Srenpe's beasts to thank for the total lack of uprising. The creatures had the bulk of the city's populace quivering in terror after their horrific displays of violence on the night of the battle.

Only the captured soldiers in the dungeon still resisted him, and they would soon be reminded of the consequences. Their courage in the face of inevitable defeat was no longer admirable to Idanox; it merely made him question their intelligence. He would need commanders capable of logical thinking, and he was not likely to find many within the ranks of the Hoyt. It was the price one paid when working with the simpleminded. He needed to force the army commanders to see reason; it was critical to his continued success. They would no doubt fight and resist him the entire time, but they would learn obedience soon enough, and the only question was how heavy the price would need to be for that to happen.

He had just finished his late lunch when a knock at the door interrupted his rest. It was one of the Hoyt who had been assisting him with governing the city—a fool, but one who was useful for completing the more mundane tasks associated with ruling. Every leader needed men like this, just barely smart enough to complete their assigned tasks while not smart enough to ask for more in return for their service. Still, if he had come to interrupt Idanox with more trivial nonsense, the Hoyt leader's patience was wearing thin. Punishment may be in line, no matter how useful the man had proven himself in recent days.

"Sir, the mage Srenpe is here and has requested an audience," the man said, much to Idanox's surprise. The mage had not returned to the palace since the night of the attack on the capital. According to his men, Srenpe had spent nearly all his time in the artifact vaults. He stayed there for hours each day, poring over the tomes and artifacts found within.

"I will receive him in my study," Idanox said, and the man hurried away. He wondered what had brought Srenpe to speak with him. Had the first beast finally succeeded in killing the boy? Excitement flooded through him as he realized he might finally be on the verge of receiving welcome news.

Idanox kept Srenpe waiting for a while, wanting to make sure the mage understood the Hoyt did not operate on his schedule. It was quite satisfying to be on this side of the partnership for a change. The mage had been useful to his cause, but Idanox still did not like the man in the slightest. Srenpe's blatant disrespect toward him at every opportunity was an offense he would never be able to forgive.

When he finally entered the study, he found the mage lounging in a chair, his feet resting comfortably on the desk. The arrogant fool shot him the usual smirk as he entered the room.

"All hail Duke Idanox, the rightful ruler of Thornata, champion of the common man, and slayer of tyrants!" Srenpe said, raising his staff in salute but other-wise not moving an inch from his relaxed position.

Insolent as always, Idanox thought. *Count yourself lucky to still be breathing, Srenpe.*

"Do you need something, Srenpe? I am quite a busy man these days, as I am sure you can imagine. The duke of a province has many important matters that require his attention," Idanox said.

"I do not need anything from you, my friend. I have found all I could ever need and more inside the vaults you have so graciously opened to me. Thank you again for your hospitality, by the way. No, I have come to give you a bit of news. I feel it is news that is worthy of interrupting even the important matters requiring His Excellency's attention," Srenpe said mockingly, his foot still resting infuriatingly on Idanox's desk.

"Very well. What news do you have for me?" Idanox asked, his patience with the mage running thinner with each passing second. He was the duke of Thornata now, and his uses for the mage were few and far between. Srenpe would be wise to tread more carefully.

"It concerns the creature we sent out in search of the Rawl wielder. I am afraid it has been destroyed. Rather unfortunate, as I'm sure you would agree. It was such a beautiful specimen. Future generations of Thornatans will owe so much to dear Quentin for his great sacrifice," Srenpe said, continuing to lounge as though this news was not concerning to him in the least.

Idanox was more furious than he had been in a long time. This mage had promised his beast would not fail, that it would return to him with the boy's head in hand. Yet here he was, telling him the beast had in fact failed, that his indestructible creation had not been fit for the challenge of killing a mere boy. His mind was already working out the most painful ways possible in which to have this useless mage killed. He would make Srenpe regret every witty jape he had made at his expense, and he would ensure the mage's suffering lasted for days.

"I assume I will be receiving my money back?" Idanox asked, his tone low and threatening.

"If you feel like coming over here and taking it from me," Srenpe replied, dropping his foot from the desk at last, his hands gripping his staff menacingly.

The reply caught Idanox somewhat off guard. The mage had always been bold, but he had never spoken in such a threatening and direct manner. For a moment, Idanox wondered if he could draw his sword and strike the mage down before he could react. A cooler head prevailed, and he decided such a course of action would not be smart. He had made a fortune and built the Hoyt by making slow, intelligent, calculated moves. Now was not a time to change that—not with a man as dangerous as Srenpe. The mage would pay for his failure, but it would have to wait for the right time. The mage smirked slightly at the sight of Idanox's hand moving away from his sword.

"Wise move, Idanox. I will remind you once more that I do not serve you, and I do not serve the Hoyt. This pathetic excuse of a regime you are trying to build is of no concern to me. Remember what I told you at our first meeting. I am not one of the simpleminded fools who have fallen in line with your message. I provided you with a service in exchange for payment, and there are no refunds. Make no mistake, Idanox; trying to kill me will be the last mistake you ever make in your blunder-filled life. Send your men after me, and I will send them back to you in pieces. Then I will come for you, Idanox. I have tolerated your arrogance throughout our partnership, but I will not allow you to sit there and threaten me. If you think living in this palace I won for you makes you more intimidating, you are sorely mistaken. Consider this your only warning. If I ever see your hand inch toward your sword again, you will beg me to kill you before I am done having my fun with you. Believe me when I say nothing would bring me more pleasure than hearing you squeal in agony. Now, if you are done with your bravado, we may continue our discussion like civilized men."

"Well, what do you intend to do about this, Srenpe? You promised me your beast would kill the boy, yet now you tell me it has failed," Idanox said, his best diplomatic voice going to work. He had angered the mage, and little though he liked to admit it, even to himself, that could prove to be a fatal mistake. The best thing to do now was to smooth things over, doing his best to show no fear in the process, though he could feel his heart racing.

"Is there something wrong with your ears?" Srenpe snapped, bold as ever. "I did not say the beast failed; I said it had been destroyed. It is fully possible it managed to kill the boy but was forced to pay with its own life. It would die without hesitation if it meant the success of its mission; it has no instinct telling it to do otherwise. There is no way to know for sure. But I assure you it would have killed the boy at all costs even if it meant dying itself. You saw its obedience for yourself in that warehouse. I removed dear Quentin's capacity to do otherwise."

"So, you are telling me the Rawl wielder may be dead or he may still be out there scheming against me? And you have no way to know for sure?" Idanox was far from reassured.

"Idanox, you are in control of this city and this province. Are you seriously concerned about what one little boy may be able to do to you? Rawl wielder or not, how much of a threat can he truly be at this point? You sit in the seat of the duke, and I assume you are taking steps to bring the army under your control. Even you are not foolish enough to believe your Hoyt brutes are all the forces you will require in the long term. Need I remind you that you have twelve more of my creations at your beck and call? As long as they are nearby, the boy is no threat to you, assuming he is still alive, which I very much doubt to be the case."

He did still have a dozen beasts at his command, and the threat posed by the Rawl wielder was significantly decreased. With the capital under his control, General McLeod and any commanders in other parts of the province would be hesitant to attack. They would understand the enormous cost of civilian lives that would result from a prolonged battle in the streets of Oreanna. He was displeased with the mage but could not argue with his logic. Dead or alive, the boy was likely no longer a threat.

"Very well, Srenpe. Perhaps you are right. Still, there are two of your creations out in the hall. I have selected them as my protection detail. Can you alter them so they will attack the boy on sight if he does ever try to come near me? One can never be too cautious," Idanox said.

"An interesting idea—one I wouldn't have thought you to be capable of producing. I can adjust the beasts so they will sense Rawl power being used nearby. If that happens, they will attack the wielder immediately and will not stop until he is dead. Would this suit your needs sufficiently?"

"Yes, that will be enough. If the boy is out there, he will likely try to flee the province after encountering the first beast. If he is stupid enough to come here and try to stop me, he will be the cause of his own demise the moment he uses his power. I like that. There is a certain poetry to it," Idanox replied.

Srenpe snorted in derision before rising from his chair and walking into the hallway. Once in front of the beasts, he raised his staff toward each of them, muttering a few indecipherable words. There were a few dull flashes of purple light, though it was far from the dazzling display the mage had put on when creating the first beast. Idanox wished he could know for sure what the mage was doing. Magic was shrouded, a mystery he did not comprehend. There were few things Idanox hated more than something he could not understand. After a few moments, Srenpe turned back to him.

"It is done. They will attack any Rawl wielder the moment they use their power in your presence. This will only work if you keep them by your side, so I would not use these two to keep the peace in the city. The others should be more than equal to that assignment," Srenpe said.

Satisfied with this resolution, Idanox thanked the mage for delivering him the news and dismissed him. He then made his way to the duke's wine cellar and retrieved an excellent vintage to retire with for the evening. There would be more work in the morning, more bumbling fools to irritate him and fires to put out. At least he was as confident as he could be that the boy would no longer be a problem for them. There was not a man in this province who was capable of being a problem for him anymore.

Chapter Fourteen

Adel deflected the incoming blow with his sword, but there was no time to feel satisfied with himself. The next attack was coming in so fast he would not be able to move his sword into the correct defensive position. He used his feet instead, deftly stepping away, hoping to throw his opponent off-balance.

Don't be naive, he thought. *Alsea is never off-balance.* Sure enough, she was already in position to strike again, faster than his brain could react. It was like fighting three opponents at once; Alsea was a whirlwind of untamed aggression and pinpoint precision.

Adel parried the swing she made for his ankles, then the one aimed for his head. Alsea was lightning fast, but he had become skilled enough to successfully deflect her attacks—or most of them anyway. One cracked him in the ribs, and he hadn't even seen it coming. One moment he thought he was in an excellent defensive position, and the next moment a sharp pain was radiating up the right side of his body. Raising his hands immediately in defeat, he dropped his sparring sword and dipped into a mock bow in acknowledgment of her superiority. The bow was also a discreet way to double over in pain without her noticing. After all the time he had spent with her, he was still amazed that a relatively small woman like Alsea could deliver blows with such devastating force.

His pride urged him to continue the sparring session, but the rapidly growing welt over his ribs pleaded otherwise. Alsea did not have the brute strength and impossible reach of his usual training partner, but she moved with a swiftness that was hard to believe. Alsea also had a knack for stringing her attacks together faster than his mind could process them. By the time he had successfully parried one strike, she already had her next three moves planned out. It was a frustrating yet immensely useful learning experience to spar with her. It was a reminder that no matter how far his skills had come, there would always be more to learn.

"Well fought, Alsea. I don't know if I'll ever be able to keep up with you," Adel said, trying his best to hide the fact that he was gasping for air. The sharp stinging pain had begun to ease into a dull throbbing ache where he had absorbed the final blow. He silently thanked Elim for the armor the Children had gifted him, knowing the pain would likely have been far more intense had it not dulled Alsea's attack. In fact, he probably would have been nursing a broken rib were it not for the stout leather protection. On the other hand, maybe the armor gave Alsea the confidence she needed to hit him harder.

"It's all in the footwork, Adel. Your parries are as good as anybody I've ever faced, but sometimes the best way to block a strike is to not be near the strike. A swing and a miss can often leave our opponent off-balance and vulnerable. This also leaves you in a superior position to counterattack. If you don't have to use your sword to deflect your opponent's attack, your sword can be wherever you want it to be. Defending in such a way takes a long time to master, though. I don't recommend you start trying to dodge every attack the next time we're in a real fight. You also seem much more tentative in your attacks against me than you are when I watch you practice with Ola. I'm flattered you don't want to hurt a delicate little girl like me, but sometimes the best defense is a good offense. I can't stab you if I'm too busy bleeding out in the dirt," Alsea replied, shooting him a teasing wink.

It was true, even if he would never admit it out loud. He loved the challenge training with Alsea provided him, but he could never bring himself to attack her with full conviction. He knew it was rather stupid on his part. It was highly unlikely he would ever be capable of hurting a fighter of her caliber no matter how hard he tried. Still, it was an issue he did not have when sparring with Ola. The ogre was as good a friend as he had ever had, but it was different with Alsea. He knew that despite his best efforts to prevent it, he would always think of her differently than any other friend. The thought of swinging his sparring sword at her with all his might was something he could not bring himself to embrace. It was a reluctance he had paid for every time they had trained together.

Three days had passed since they had finally defeated the monstrous beast. They had reached the far southeastern foothills of the Bonner Mountains. They would reach Kolig in two days at most and would once more be thrown into the midst of the war against the Hoyt. Adel and Ola had finally resumed their sword training now that the ogre was back at full strength, but Ola had left camp that night to try to find game for their supper. Alsea had volunteered to spar with him instead, an opportunity Adel would never pass up.

"We should probably get a fire going. If Ola manages to get us something for supper, I want to get right to cooking it," Alsea said. "I don't know about you, but I'm starving."

Adel reluctantly set about building a campfire. The sweltering early-summer heat made the prospect an unpleasant one, but if Ola returned with meat, it was better to be prepared. It was a quick task for him; his power allowed him to build an intense fire from the smallest of sparks in moments. Alsea joined him shortly after he had the logs burning, having retrieved several containers of water from a nearby spring. She sat next to him, giving him the opportunity to examine her more closely, and he was amazed by what he saw. If she had broken a sweat during their sparring session, he could find no trace of it.

"How are you adjusting to wearing the armor?" she asked, passing him a waterskin. He averted his eyes with a blush, hoping she had not noticed him looking at her and gotten the wrong idea.

"To tell you the truth, it hasn't been much of an adjustment at all. It's so well made I don't feel it hampers my speed at all, and it's so light that I don't tire from wearing it. Even on a hot day like today was, it isn't too tiresome to wear, not to mention I would probably have a few broken ribs right now if I weren't wearing it," Adel replied with a smile. The one she shot back made him grateful to be sitting. Had he been on his feet, his knees may have given out at the sight. As it was, he had a hard enough time keeping the swig of water he had just taken from running down his chin.

His feelings for her were an issue that was not going away no matter how hard he tried to ignore or suppress them. He had not known many women over the years. His companions on the barge had exclusively been men, and his only real exposure to women had been during their mostly brief stays in the cities. He had been young, and though he would occasionally admire a beautiful woman in a tavern or on a dock, he had never felt an impulse to act. It was different with Alsea; he had never had these feelings before, feelings he knew he could not act on without jeopardizing everything. This young woman saw him as her leader, and he could not take a chance of exploiting those feelings, even unintentionally. His feelings would have to remain a secret. If he let them be known, it would place their friendship in jeopardy, and he was not willing to risk it.

"We haven't seen any Hoyt since we left the Temple of the Rawl," Alsea said, shaking him out of his thoughts. "It makes me wonder if they trusted that beast alone with the task of hunting you down. If so, it was a serious mistake on their part. Though after seeing it in action several times, I cannot fault their confidence too much. On the bright side, after beating that thing, I think we can best anything they have to throw at us. It's as though things are finally starting to fall in our favor."

"I wonder what they are up to lately. I am sure they are not sitting idly. Idanox has ambitions he is not going to set aside while he waits on his beast to kill me. We've been out of contact with the army for weeks; anything could have happened in that time. It will be good to get back in touch with General McLeod and be in the loop again. I suppose it's always possible they've found and killed Idanox, but I doubt it. He's proven to be quite slippery thus far." Adel was grateful she had given him something else to dwell on.

"Idanox is nothing but a coward, sending other men to do his fighting for him. Still, he is a dangerous man. I've found a weak man with a silver tongue can do much more harm than a strong man with a steel sword," Alsea said, her fists clenching. "Don't forget, I was in Kolig when the city fell to the Hoyt, and I saw firsthand the brutality they are capable of displaying. People were tortured or executed for the most minor of offenses against the Hoyt. Some of them, I think, were cases of the Hoyt killing for the entertainment of doing so. Idanox's brutes are brainwashed to do his bidding no matter how cruel his orders. Maybe they were always that way, and he simply gave them an outlet with which to express it. Either way, we have to do everything we can to make sure the snake never gains control of an entire city like that again."

"That will never happen; I am sure of that much," Adel reassured her.

"I hope not. The day before I slipped out of the city, I came upon two of them in an alley. They had cornered a girl who could not have been more than thirteen years old. They had obviously drunk their fill at a tavern just before. I imagine they failed to pay for their drinks on the way; they seemed like the type. I heard them muttering what they were going to do to her. I couldn't hear all of it, just enough to get the gist of their intentions. After I left them in a bloody heap in the alley, I decided it was time to get out of Kolig and back to the Temple of the Rawl. I had been lying low, trying to help people in any way I could, but that was too much for me to stand. I needed to get back to the temple and get help. I was making my way out of Kolig when I overheard their plans for the army and the dam. I didn't know anything about you yet, of course. I was hoping Ola would be able to help me put a stop to it. If you hadn't discovered your power when you did, there might not be a city of Kolig standing right now. So many innocent people would have died in that flood. Those are the type of men we are up against, Adel. That is why we must not fail. If we do, people like the poor girl in the alley or the little boy you saved in that village will be the ones who suffer the most."

Adel sat in silence, digesting her story. She had never shared many details about the things she had seen in Kolig during the Hoyt occupation. He had known she must have seen a number of unpleasant things, but hearing them put into words gave the events life that they had not held for him before. His hatred of the Hoyt had always burned intensely but was now hotter than ever. He would not allow such horrors to happen again—not while he was still breathing.

"I'm sorry you had to see those things, Alsea. I can't imagine how difficult those memories are for you to carry. But it's a good thing you were there for that girl."

"I often wonder what happened to her after that. I wonder if she survived the rest of the occupation, if she was able to avoid more attacks like that one. I hope she's okay," Alsea said, staring off into the distance.

"Well, you gave her a chance at survival, and I don't think we have to worry about the Hoyt ever being in such a powerful position again."

He was confident after what had happened at Kolig that the Thornatan Army would be on high alert for any such attempts to seize a major city. The Hoyt operated mainly on the element of surprise, and if they tried to do it again, they would catch nobody off guard. There was little doubt that the Hoyt were now at their weakest. They would never be in a better position than they had been when they seized Kolig last year. Adel was confident that when they rejoined General McLeod, he would have good news to share with them about the state of the battle with the Hoyt. Hopefully they had discovered Idanox's whereabouts and could put an end to this war swiftly.

"Have you given any thought to what comes after the Hoyt are defeated?" Alsea asked.

In truth, it was not something he had given much consideration. He had thought of little besides defeating the Hoyt since they had attacked his barge the previous spring. His rage at their attack, which had grown with every atrocity he had witnessed since, had wholly consumed him. For the better part of the past year, every decision he had made had been with the intent of putting an end to the gang of outlaws. What would come next?

Elim seemed confident he was worthy of becoming the Master of the Rawl, but he did not know much about what the job entailed. After learning of the existence of the Vindur, he had given thought to hunting down the other infinitely powerful orbs. That was a lofty goal, though, and he did not know where to start with that. What exactly were the responsibilities of the Master of the Rawl? In all his conversations with Elim, they had never gotten into many specifics. Such things had seemed so far in the future that there was no need to discuss them. Now, with the end of the conflict with the Hoyt possibly imminent, he felt like a fool for not giving his options further consideration.

"To be honest, no, I haven't given it much thought. Elim seems to think I should become the Master of the Rawl, but I don't know much about what it means," he said, embarrassed though he was to admit it.

"Don't feel bad. I don't know much about it either. There has not been a Master of the Rawl the entire time I have served the Children, though I know they have wanted to find someone worthy of the title. Elim leads them for now, though I sense he grows weary of doing so. I think you would be responsible for finding and guiding other people like you, people who possess the power of the Rawl, and leading them into battle if that should ever become required. The Children are powerful, but as you may have noticed, they are well past their prime," Alsea said. "The Children don't talk about it much, but I have a feeling they are afraid. I think they sense something coming, some sort of threat. Not the Hoyt, but something bigger, more dangerous. Elim once told me the Hoyt are a symptom of a more serious disease that is beginning to take hold of the Empire. I don't really know what he meant by it."

That was an interesting, if somewhat daunting, prospect. Adel still felt like he had so much to learn. How would he be able to guide others along a path he was still traversing himself? He knew he should not doubt himself, his friends had told him so continually, but it was unavoidable in some instances. At least he did not have to worry about this until the Hoyt were defeated. Once that was done, there would be plenty of time to figure out what came next.

"I'm not sure how good of a teacher I would be, but I will do my best if it is expected of me," Adel said. "The thought of a battle that requires multiple Rawl wielders is a prospect that scares me. Elim told me a little about the Thrawll, enough to make me hope I never have to face one in a fight. I have a feeling they are the more serious disease he told you about."

"I think you will be an outstanding teacher, Adel. You have learned so much in such a short time. I'm sure there is still more for you to learn on this journey. You have experienced so much; you will have so many lessons to pass on to others. Besides, you already have the most important aspect of being a great mentor," Alsea said.

"What aspect is that?" Adel asked.

"You are a great friend. Sometimes friendship is the most important thing a mentor can offer. Think about it. How much did it help you in your sword training to have

Ola as a friend? If he had been nothing but a random stranger who did not care about you, learning from him would have been quite a challenge, don't you think? Imagine having some virtual stranger beat you senseless night after night. Would it feel like learning? But the two of you formed a friendship, and look how rapidly your skills have improved," Alsea said. "I know you don't see it, but you have reached a level of skill many men never reach even with years of training and practice."

It was a fair point. His sword training had drastically improved as he had become friendlier with Ola, and likewise, the practice had also given them something to bond over. It had helped with building a friendship when Adel had previously felt like no more than a burden to the taciturn ogre. It was similar with Elim. As their friendship had grown, so had Adel's comfort with their training. Perhaps it would be the same with other Rawl wielders he would meet.

"I just hope once you are Master of the Rawl that you will still have some use for me," Alsea joked. "I know I can be a nuisance to have around, but I occasionally help out. I promise I won't hit you so hard next time if you keep me around."

"There will always be a place for you anywhere I go," Adel assured her.

This remark seemed to surprise Alsea, her head cocking slightly to one side. Adel knew immediately his comment had gone too far, that he had been too eager to reassure her and had overstepped. Comments like that would betray his true feelings if he were not careful. To his surprise, she shot him yet another of her dazzling smiles.

"I'm glad to hear it, Adel. There's no place I would rather be," she said.

What did she mean by that? Surely she meant only as a friend. Still, Adel could not help but read more into the comment. Was it possible she felt the same way as he did? Even if she did, would it not still be wrong for him to pursue it? He noticed his palms beginning to sweat and his knees trembling slightly. He could not help himself; he had to know for sure. Clearing his throat, he tried to think of the best way to pose his question.

"Good news! I got us some rabbits!" Ola's yell broke the silence, causing Adel to leap about two feet into the air in shock and immediately cast aside his question for Alsea. Looking over at her, he was relieved she seemed not to have noticed his startled reaction.

The ogre was returning with their supper, and his questions would have to wait for another night. As he rose to prepare a pot, he could not help but notice a look of disappointment on Alsea's face. Was she as disappointed as he was that they had been interrupted? Knowing he was in for a long night of confusion, Adel took the rabbits from Ola and set to work on preparing their supper.

"How did the sparring go?" Ola asked as he took a seat beside the fire with them.

"Apart from Alsea trying to cut me in half, not too bad," Adel replied jokingly.

"Well, I figured if one Adel is so wonderful, wouldn't two Adels be even better?" she shot back with a laugh.

Adel laughed along with the joke, but his mind was somewhere else. If he had not been interrupted, what would her response have been to the question he was going to ask? Maybe it was for the best; he had refused to ask the question earlier for a reason. He should've been grateful Ola had interrupted his moment of weakness. He couldn't allow himself to give in to such temptation again. His relationship with Alsea could never be more than it already was; he would've been a fool to think otherwise. He ate his supper and crawled into his bedroll that night, still trying to convince himself.

Chapter Fifteen

I danox donned his black leather armor and cloak, determined to look as dignified and intimidating as possible this night. The audience he would address would not be one easily swayed, but he hoped having the proper appearance would help his cause ever so slightly. If not, he would have no choice but to resort to violence again. Ultimately, it made no difference to him. However, he thought he might instill more loyalty if he could persuade them with words rather than blood. To achieve this, it was better if he appeared more as the leader they needed than the outlaw they despised. His men had still not been able to sway any Thornatan Army commanders to join their cause, so tonight he would take a crack at them himself. Unlike his men, he would not fail no matter the cost. For Idanox, failure was never an option.

Not that I will be the one bearing the cost of tonight's work, he thought to himself.

Midnight was approaching when he received word from his men that everything had been prepared as requested. He had wanted this to take place late at night; it was the time he felt at his most powerful. Idanox had always felt more comfortable in the shadows of the night. The human mind played tricks on its owner in the dark, illusions which could work to his benefit. The light of the sun could instill hope, and that was something he could not allow these men to feel. He beckoned for his two monstrous bodyguards to take their positions beside him and walked calmly from the duke's palace and out into the city.

The prison was quite a walk from the palace, but Idanox made the journey unconcerned with only his creatures at his side. No person in this city would dare attempt to harm him as long as they accompanied him. If by chance they did, they would die a most unpleasant death, and the story of their demise would discourage others with similar notions. He was their ruler now, and there was nothing they could do to change it. Every time he passed a set of fearful eyes in the street, eyes which darted away when they saw him watching, his satisfaction grew by leaps and bounds. This was the destiny he had always been bound to, and it had come to life at last.

The prison of Oreanna was a foreboding stone structure used to house criminals and traitors to the province or the Empire. His predecessor had been a pathetic excuse for a man, and under his rule the prison had been scarcely populated. Under the control of the Hoyt, that would be changing, and Idanox had begun by imprisoning every senior army officer who had survived the sack of the city. His men had spent the better part of the last week rooting them out of their hiding places and stamping out the beginnings of uprisings. The commanders would join his cause, or there would be severe consequences, as they were about to discover. They were used to the soft touch of the former duke. They would find Idanox to be far from forgiving of their refusal to follow orders.

He reached the main entrance of the prison to find two of his men waiting for him. They greeted him and led him inside, locking the door behind him. He noticed the apprehensive glances they shot his bodyguards and smirked in satisfaction. While he did not question the loyalty of his own men, it was still reassuring to have protection against an assassination attempt from within the Hoyt as well. Now that he was in a position of true power, it was always possible one of his lieutenants would experience delusions of grandeur and be tempted to act on them. Perhaps the added intimidation the beasts provided helped to further motivate his men to succeed in any task he set them.

"I was told all the preparations had been made. Is this true?" Idanox asked the men as he approached.

"It is, sir. We have gathered the commanders into the smallest cellblock, as you requested. You will be able to address them all from the center of the cellblock with no issues. The others are waiting in another area. Shall I bring them now?" one man answered.

"No, I will talk to the soldiers first. Perhaps they will finally see reason. If not, I will tell you when to bring them in. There is no need to levy these particular threats until they have rejected me in person. Now, take me to them," Idanox instructed.

The two men led the way through the prison's dark corridors, most of which were lined with empty cells.

That will be rectified soon, he thought. There would be no shortage of people who would need to be taught respect under the new regime. They would fill these cells soon enough. Idanox understood something his predecessor had never been able to grasp: this prison could be a valuable tool for controlling the populace. The Hoyt would turn this prison into a place so terrifying that the people would much prefer falling in line to being imprisoned within its walls. Frightened people tended to be obedient people.

After several minutes, they arrived in a small cellblock in the center of the prison. Eight cells lined the walls of the small rectangular room, each holding a Thornatan soldier. Most were still clad in their army attire, their facial hair unkempt from their time in imprisonment. None of them appeared to be particularly pleased to see him. Idanox found if he stood in the center of the room, he could address them all at once. He rotated to make eye contact with each of them as he spoke, wanting them to feel as though he were addressing them personally.

"Good evening to you, my friends. My men tell me there has been a terrible misunderstanding, and I have come to set matters right. They tell me you do not wish to fight for our cause. Tell me, are you not all sworn to serve the duke of Thornata? As of now, that is me. Please, tell me, why are you now forsaking your vows? I would never have expected such acts from men of your reputations. I have always held the men of the Thornatan Army in high regard," Idanox said, figuring he may as well attempt to start this diplomatically. He had little hope it would work, but at least none would be able to accuse him of unnecessary brutality. Whatever unpleasantness occurred this night, at least he gave them a chance to avoid it.

"We do not serve a duke, Idanox, and if we did, we would not recognize a usurper like you. We serve the people of this province. We defend those who cannot defend themselves. We serve those who seek to make a better life for themselves and their families. We fight on their behalf against scum like you who would seek to destroy them. We don't serve some self-absorbed rich man who thinks wealth gives him a right to rule," one of the men spat at him. Idanox locked his icy stare on the man. This one would be the first to feel his wrath if these fools did not come to their senses. Still, he had to keep trying. Now that he was in a position of such power, optics were important no matter how little patience he possessed for them.

"If you do truly serve the common people of Thornata, answer me this, my friend. Why do you refuse to follow us? You must realize it is the blood of the common people that will be shed if this war continues. It is the common people's lands that will burn, their lives that will be lost, their children who will suffer. You claim to serve the common people, yet you are allowing your stubborn pride to take precedence over their safety. I respect men who refuse to accept defeat, but allowing your brothers and sisters to suffer due to your pride is a terrible crime. Is their well-being not more important than your own stubborn refusal to accept defeat? I do not see your stubbornness as courage. I see it as treason, not against me, but against the people you swore oaths to defend," Idanox said, trying to reason with the men as best he could. He had already accepted that a more visual demonstration would be needed, and now he was just going through the motions.

"Oh, they will be safe under your rule, will they, Idanox? I was at Kolig when your thugs opened the floodgates of the dam to try to drown us in the river. The floodwater would have washed away half of the city and thousands of people along with it. Countless farmlands downriver would have been destroyed, and how many people would have gone hungry because of it? How many children would have starved to death over the long winter because of your savage and merciless tactics? Fortunately for us, your men were no match for a boy!" It was the same soldier, and he was apparently quite proud of his own audacity. His smirk left Idanox furious, and he struggled to conceal it. This fool would not be feeling good about himself for much longer.

"My friends, you are all so silent. Does this man speak for all of you? Are you all truly willing to see your people bleed and suffer to keep your pride intact?" Idanox asked, his arms outstretched, imploring somebody else to speak. None of them spoke a word, the proud fools. They would learn soon enough. His predecessor may have been a weak fool, but the new duke of Thornata was not a man to be trifled with—not without consequences. It was time to teach them a lesson they would never forget.

"Very well, sir. When you see what is about to happen next, remember that I gave you this opportunity to see the error of your ways." He sighed, turning to his men. "Bring this one's in first, please."

The two men vanished down a nearby corridor and returned a few minutes later, minutes which were spent in silence except for the occasional curse hurled at him from the same soldier's cell. This one was quite vocal, but he would learn obedience soon enough. How much it would end up costing him, he would soon have the opportunity to decide. The Hoyt men returned, leading a group of five people.

Idanox noted the three children right away, the eldest of whom could not possibly have been older than ten. They were accompanied by a woman who Idanox surmised to be the soldier's wife and a man who looked as though he could be his brother. Idanox turned back toward the soldier's cell, shooting the man a smirk similar to the one he had received a few minutes earlier. The soldier no longer looked quite so confident, his face turning ghostly white at the sight of his family.

"I told you all to get out of the city," he stammered in their direction.

"Isn't it frustrating when people do not do as they are asked? I'm sure you told them it would be for their own good, didn't you? Yet they disobeyed even though you wanted nothing but the best for them," Idanox said, rather enjoying the sudden change in the man's attitude and demeanor. "You are experiencing a taste of the frustration you and your comrades are causing me. Just like you did with your family, here I am, trying to help you make a decision that is in your own best interest. But you refuse to hear me out."

"They have nothing to do with this, Idanox. I am the soldier; I am the one who defied you. Please, punish me however you see fit. Please, please do not punish them for my crimes," the soldier cried out, tears streaming from his eyes. All of the bravado and arrogance had evaporated instantly. It was a pitiful sight, one Idanox soaked in for a few seconds before striding over to face the man directly. He met the soldier's tear-filled eyes and smiled.

"I am punishing you. What do you think this is, my good man? You were given a choice. You could have pledged yourself to my cause, and if you had, your family would be safe at home instead of shivering in this cold and miserable prison. You have nobody to blame for their situation but yourself. Remember that while you witness what is about to happen," Idanox said.

"Please, please, please, I'm begging you." The man was practically bawling now, a pitiful look for a soldier. Idanox smiled again and pointed toward the man's brother.

"Cut his throat. No, wait, that would be over too quick. Kill him, but make it last a while," he told the beasts standing guard.

One of his beasts stepped forward, not hesitating for even a second. It reached out with one hand, clasping the back of the terrified man's head and holding him in place. The other hand drew a long knife from its belt and began to hack mercilessly away at its defenseless victim. The beast took its master's order to heart, and it felt like an eternity before it finally allowed the man to fall to the floor, bleeding out, his agonized screams dying at last. Even a man as cold as Idanox had to force himself not to flinch away at the sight of the savage violence. It would not do for his future servants to see any sign of weakness in him. The three children grabbed their mother's legs, screaming in terror, their eyes locked on the blood-soaked monster that had just dispatched their uncle.

"Silence!" Idanox screamed, and they ceased their screaming at once. Now their terror-stricken eyes glared up at him with hatred and fear. One emotion meant nothing to him; the other brought him great satisfaction. Now these men would understand what real power was. Perhaps the rest of them would fall in line with less of a fight. If not, his men had collected family members for each of them.

The arrogant soldier had fallen to his knees inside his cell, openly weeping. The display had been a brutal one, and he feared it might have rendered the man useless to him. Such things were not easily forgotten, and maybe this man was damaged goods. Perhaps he would be better off killing this one as a message to the others. But Idanox knew he would need as many senior officers as possible if he was going to control the army. Idanox walked over to the door of the man's cell and began to speak again.

"Do you understand now what the consequences of your resistance are, soldier? Or does one of your children need to pay the price for your crimes before you understand?" he asked.

"Yes, yes, I understand. Please don't hurt anyone else, please. I will do whatever you ask of me, Duke Idanox. I promise I will never falter in my service to you. I will fight and slay any enemy you command," the man blubbered, all semblance of composure lost.

"No! We cannot cave in to him, men! We cannot give him what he wants! The Thornatan Army can never stoop to the level of serving the Hoyt!" Another soldier in a different cell had finally found the courage to speak up; that was a mistake.

"Release this woman and her children at once. They are not to be harmed as long as our friend here keeps his word. We will need to have somebody keep tabs on them just in case he has any more defiant outbursts. For the time being, we will give him the benefit of the doubt. After all, we are not in the business of terrorizing women and children. But it seems one of his comrades does not quite understand what we are hoping to accomplish here, so can you please bring in some more guests?" Idanox said.

It would prove to be a long and difficult night, even for a man who had grown as numb to senseless bloodshed as Idanox. Several of the men gave in to his demands without resistance to save the lives of their family members, but most of them were defiant at first. He was forced to kill two children of one, a particularly stubborn fool who took a great deal of effort to break. Their lives were irrelevant to him, or so he kept telling himself, but Idanox knew the sight and sound of those two would stay with him for a long time. He had long believed his capacity to feel remorse had been purged from his mind, but that belief was tested before the night was done. In the end, all the soldiers gave in and agreed to serve him to the best of their ability. It was the result he had known was inevitable, though he could never have predicted the effect it would have on his mind.

Dawn was beginning to break by the time they were done, and Idanox ordered his men to release all remaining hostages and even allowed them a few moments with their captive soldiers as a show of good faith. Once the family members were gone, Idanox had all twelve men released from their cells and food and water brought for them. They needed to see that he could be as just and merciful as he could cold and ruthless. He then commanded them to sit around a long table while he sat at the head.

"I'm glad you were all able to see reason tonight, gentlemen. I didn't want to have to execute any of you. Your service to Thornata has been and will continue to be invaluable. I do not doubt the Hoyt will be made stronger by your service," Idanox said. The men glared at him, some through still-teary eyes, but their hatred meant nothing to him. He did not need their love; he had more than enough of that for himself. He needed them to do their jobs and understand the consequences of failure. He was satisfied he had broken them sufficiently enough that no resistance would be immediately forthcoming.

"The group of you will be split up and assigned to various tasks. I will need some of you to gather what troops remain in hiding within the capital and bring them over to our cause. They are necessary to keep the peace in this city. I assume you will have no trouble locating them. After all, you will know your own hiding places better than anyone, won't you? Some of you will need to travel to the other major cities and stress the importance of obedience to the men stationed there. Men of your stature will command a level of respect my own men cannot dream of matching. And finally, I will need some of you to begin the work of reforming a standing army, one which can be dispatched to deal with any threats which may present themselves," Idanox instructed.

There were a few murmurings of consent, but none of them seemed to want to meet his gaze. They simply stared down at the table like children who had been caught in the middle of some wrongdoing. While seeing them so downtrodden was a pleasant thing for him, it was not quite sufficient.

"We do not seem to be clear on how this works, gentlemen. When I speak to you, I expect a response. I will forgive the transgression this time. It's been a long night, after all. From now on, you will remember to reply to me. Now, each of you will rise one by one to receive your assignment. When you receive it, I expect you shall conduct yourselves more properly; you are addressing your duke, after all," Idanox said, his voice low and menacing.

He made his way around the large table, and each man rose to receive his new assignment. Each man met his gaze and responded to him out loud, some more meekly than others, but all to his satisfaction. They were fast learners, this group. It was a trait that would serve them well if they hoped to survive the weeks ahead. He hoped they would prove useful, for it had been an exhausting night, and he did not care to repeat it with a different group. These men already had the respect of their fellow soldiers. Rounding up more officers would take time he did not have to waste.

"My men will see that you are all outfitted appropriately for your assigned task. I feel I must stress upon each of you one last time how crucial it is that you keep the promises you have made here tonight. As you have already seen, my men know where your family members can be found. If you attempt to stir a rebellion, they will die. If you attempt to flee from your duty, they will die. If you attempt to do anything which has not been specifically instructed to you, they will die. I will take no pleasure in such acts, but I will not hesitate. I hope I have sufficiently stressed upon you how serious I am. Go forth from this prison, my friends. Go forth and serve Thornata with honor and distinction," Idanox said, flourishing his arms for effect.

The sun had fully risen by the time Idanox returned to the duke's mansion, giving the word to his men that he did not wish to be disturbed for anything that was not an emergency. He also made it clear that any man who interrupted his rest for anything which was not a crisis would be punished most severely. The beasts would be stationed outside his door, and they would give any man pause about disturbing him. When he retired to the duke's bedchamber, he took a long look at himself in the mirror that adorned the wall.

His hair was grayer than it had been the last time he had seen his reflection, and more thin lines crisscrossed his face. But it was his eyes that genuinely shocked him. They had seen things these past few years that he could never have imagined in his old life. He had thought his life as a man of means had prepared him for this future. He had jumped at the first opportunity that had been presented to him to claim what he had always felt was rightfully his.

Idanox lay down in the bed he had won with bloodshed and death, wondering—as he had many times over the past few weeks—if he had made the right decision.

Chapter Sixteen

It brought Adel a great sense of relief when they crested the final ridge and came within sight of the city of Kolig. The trio had pressed hard over the past few days, wanting to rejoin General McLeod and his men as soon as possible. They were hopeful the general had rebuilt his strike force of elite soldiers and would have information on Idanox's whereabouts. They had been away for so long that they had no idea what had been happening in the conflict against the Hoyt. They were eager to find out what progress the army had made against the band of murderers and thieves in their absence. When they had parted, the Hoyt had been all but forced out of the southern reaches of Thornata. Adel was hopeful those successes had continued in their absence. With a bit of luck, the army would have the Hoyt on the run. The trio was optimistic they would be able to finish the war with the Hoyt within weeks.

Adel noted as they entered the city gates that the city lacked the usual hustle and bustle he had become accustomed to during his countless trips through Kolig on the barge. There were still people milling through the street, but the overall mood seemed relatively subdued. The typical sounds of children at play and merchants aggressively hawking their wares were nearly nonexistent. The soldiers at the gates stole second glances at them as they passed, though this was far from an unusual occurrence when traveling with Ola. As they made their way through the streets toward the army barracks, they found the same somber feel had seeped over the entire city. Adel was with apprehension as they drew near to the barracks. What had happened to steal the life from this ordinarily vibrant city? His optimism had already been replaced by anxiety. He could only assume whatever had happened was not a good thing.

They were met outside the barracks by one of General McLeod's men, who stopped them before they could walk inside and asked them to follow him. He led them away from the barracks and down several alleyways and into a dilapidated old building that appeared to be an abandoned shop. Asking them to wait, he said he would bring the general to them. They waited for what felt like an hour, exchanging confused glances and whispers before the door opened once more and General McLeod entered. He shook their hands warmly, but his grim smile betrayed that something was troubling him. Adel could feel his optimism continuing to slip away before McLeod had so much as opened his mouth.

"I'm glad to see all of you in one piece. I was beginning to fear maybe that beast had finished you off until we heard of the bounties. I figured Idanox would not bother to put money out on the heads of dead men. I've had my men keeping an eye out for your arrival ever since. I had hoped to catch you before you could enter the city. I apologize for the state of your accommodations," General McLeod said, gesturing to the dusty shop.

"Bounties? There are bounties on us? Forgive our confusion, General McLeod. We have not had much in the way of contact with the outside world, though I am happy to report the beast is no more." Adel was confused, and a glance at Ola and Alsea confirmed that they shared his confusion.

"You don't know anything about what has happened? We've been getting the news in small bits until two days ago when a few army commanders arrived from Oreanna. I hardly dared to believe the rumors could be true until I heard it from their mouths. The Hoyt have seized control of Oreanna and killed the duke. Idanox is currently ruling as duke in the capital and doing so with an iron fist from the sound of the reports we are receiving."

Adel could not believe what he was hearing. It felt like he had been slapped across the face. A few weeks ago it had felt as though they had come close to stamping out the Hoyt completely. Now they had managed to seize the capital of the province? How could this have happened? They had fought so hard to stop this from happening, yet they had failed. He could not imagine a worse defeat than seeing Oreanna, the capital that had never fallen in battle, in the hands of the Hoyt. The image of Idanox in control of the capital of Thornata was one he could not stomach. A feeling of intense guilt washed over him. If he had found a way to destroy the beast sooner, perhaps he could have helped prevent this from happening. It felt as though all the fighting they had done, all the lives that had been lost, had been in vain.

"How were they able to seize Oreanna, General McLeod? We killed and captured many of their men in the early spring. I thought we had crippled their ability to mount a large-scale assault against any city, let alone one as well defended as the capital. They must have somehow caught the defenders off guard; they could not have had enough men left to seize the city in a direct assault," Ola said.

"You're right; there was no hint an attack was coming. If there was, I would have mustered as many men as possible and marched to Oreanna right away. Instead, I was here, completely unaware of what was going on up north. Our intelligence is still spotty at best, but it sounds as though most of the Hoyt were already inside the city walls before they launched their attack. And I'm afraid the news gets worse. There are reports of monsters that sound awfully similar to the one we encountered after our battle in that village. I presume that's how they were able to turn things in their favor. You are right; I doubt they had enough men to pull this off without help from more of those unnatural beasts. Unfortunately, the reports indicate they may have as many as a dozen of them at their disposal."

The sinking feeling of dread that Adel was feeling kept getting worse. More of those beasts? They had been hard-pressed to rid themselves of one of the indestructible monsters, and now there were more? Enough of them to enable the Hoyt to overpower the extensive military force guarding Oreanna? Not to mention the fact that Hoyt fighters were now in control of the capital of Thornata. This meant they also had a disturbing number of civilian hostages under their thumb, for Oreanna was one of Thornata's most heavily populated cities. Only the northern port city of Kival was home to more people. How could they hope to beat the Hoyt now?

"I don't want to pile on, as I know this is already bad enough, but I'm afraid the news from the capital gets worse. Idanox has persuaded a number of Thornatan army commanders to join his cause and rally their subordinates to take up arms against any who resist him. I can't imagine the threats he must have levied against them to pull this off, but he did, and now it is another problem for us to deal with if we hope to win. I don't know how many have pledged themselves to the Hoyt, but I have a bad feeling the number will continue to grow," General McLeod continued, sending Adel deeper into despair. "No man in my army would willingly serve Idanox, but desperate times call for desperate measures. You can never predict what a man will do if he feels his loved ones are in peril. We have to be prepared for the possibility that we will have to fight not just the Hoyt but Thornatan soldiers as well."

"This doesn't seem possible. It's like a bad dream. I thought we were doing so well against the Hoyt," Adel muttered, sinking to the floor with his face in his hands. How could the tide have turned against them so abruptly? The confidence he had built during their weeks at the Temple of the Rawl had evaporated in the span of a few minutes. What a fool he had been, thinking he could return to the struggle and put an end to this war quickly.

"The past is gone, and dwelling on it cannot help us now. We have to act in the present to the best of our ability and hopefully save the future for the people of Thornata," Alsea exclaimed, speaking up for the first time, placing a reassuring hand on his shoulder.

Adel felt a rush of gratitude; once again, she had managed to say exactly what he needed to hear at the precise moment he needed to hear it. Wallowing in despair was no solution to their problems. There were thousands of people now under the thumb of Idanox. That number would grow as the Hoyt solidified their grip on the other major cities. They could not change what had happened, but perhaps they could change what would happen next. They needed to act right away; every day lost was a day Idanox could use to strengthen his position.

"Well said, Alsea. I have been assembling a new strike force in your absence, and we are almost ready to move against the Hoyt. The problem now is that Idanox is coercing soldiers over to the Hoyt; we do not know where spies may be lurking, even in our barracks here in Kolig. He has put bounties out on Adel and Ola. The sums are high enough to entice many men to try to claim them. No offense, Ola, but you are not exactly hard to spot. It is likely the Hoyt already know you are in Kolig. I do not like to think any of my men might try to claim the bounties, but these men aren't exactly well paid for their service to Thornata. It only takes one tempted man to wreak havoc. That is why I thought it would be safer to meet here rather than in the barracks." General McLeod was a continued source of bad news.

"We can slip out of the city the same way I did when the Hoyt took control last year: through the sewers. It doesn't smell all that pleasant, but it will get us out undetected. I don't think we should risk passing through the gates again, especially Ola. We can avoid large cities until we reach Oreanna and figure out what to do about Idanox and the Hoyt. At least now we know where he is. Now that he's in power, he won't go running and hiding again. He would never be able to redeem himself in the eyes of the fools who follow him if he did. It simplifies matters. Let's go to Oreanna and kill the bastard," Alsea said.

It's not a bad plan, Adel thought. Once again, Alsea had proven herself invaluable, not only with her reasoning but with her uplifting spirit. If it were not for her spirit, this news might have crushed Adel. Instead, she had filled him with a renewed sense of hope. The three of them could not be seen out in the streets again, but they could likely make it into the sewers undetected after nightfall. General McLeod would soon become a target as well. Idanox would not want a man with McLeod's influence running free and conspiring against him. The general had not spoken yet; he seemed to be contemplating Alsea's suggestion. At last, he came to a decision.

"I do not have a better plan than the one Alsea has presented. If we try to move a large force out through the city gates, Idanox will know immediately. We can slip the men into the sewers in small groups and join forces near the river. It will be a small force, but it's better to remain undetected. The three of you cannot be seen at all; this is vital. If you are spotted here in Kolig, Idanox will know we are working together again and move against us. I can have everything prepared by tomorrow night, but I suggest the three of you remain here in this shop. It has been abandoned for some time and is likely the safest place for you to hide. I wish you could come to the barracks; you would be more comfortable there. Unfortunately, I don't know which of my men I can trust and which might be tempted by Idanox's promise of riches. That's what I am going to spend the next day trying to determine."

Adel was not keen on spending the next day in this dusty old shop, but he agreed it was better than being dead or a prisoner of the Hoyt.

The three companions agreed to wait in the shop until the following night. General McLeod would return for them when it was time to make their escape from the city. He departed shortly after that, and there was nothing more for them to do but wait. Adel found sitting and waiting was not a pleasant pastime, especially considering the news they had just received. He wanted to get out of this shop and back into the fight against the Hoyt before they could inflict even more harm upon the people of Thornata.

General McLeod had said they would march to Oreanna but had been vague regarding his plans once they reached the capital city. Adel supposed this was because the general's plan was still forming. Seizing control of the capital would be challenging enough even if they did not have to contend with Thornatan solders who had changed sides. He did not envy the choices the general would face once they reached Oreanna. The prospect of possibly having to fight and kill his own men must've weighed heavily on him.

"If it's true Idanox has convinced Thornatan commanders to pledge to him, we have quite the challenge ahead of us," Alsea said, echoing Adel's thoughts. "If they have rallied enough men to their side, it may very well mean we cannot defeat the Hoyt in a battle." This was true, though Adel much preferred the more optimistic tone she had taken earlier.

"If that does prove to be the case, we will likely need to undertake a different type of mission," Ola said.

"What type of mission?" Adel asked.

"The type which involves us slipping into the city and palace unseen and killing Idanox before they know we are there. If the army is siding with the Hoyt, our best chance is to cut the head off the snake. We have to hope the body dies with it. Idanox is the brain and heart of the Hoyt, and there is no other who would be able to lead them effectively in his absence. Most of the Hoyt were not recruited for their intelligence; they were recruited for their willingness to follow Idanox blindly. None of them would be able to step into his shoes adequately. I am sure virtually all of the Thornatan soldiers would immediately turn against them as soon as Idanox is dead," Ola explained.

He was right. Getting to Idanox and killing him without being detected would be a challenge, but it was perhaps their best hope for victory. After overcoming the relentless beast that had pursued them across the province, Adel was confident that together they could overcome any challenge in their path. Even if there were some Hoyt who kept fighting after Idanox was dead, they would lack leadership and would likely be dispatched without much difficulty. It was a more likely means of achieving the victory than meeting the combined forces of the Hoyt and the army in a battle they had little hope of winning. It was somewhat comforting to know they had options, but Adel still struggled with the reality of their current situation.

The following day passed as swiftly as molasses running down a tree trunk in the dead of winter. The trio was eager to get underway, and the endless waiting was taking its toll on them. They knew General McLeod would return after dark, and there was not much to do in the meantime besides wait. They discussed the challenges ahead of them ad nauseum, but they knew developing an elaborate strategy at this point was a useless endeavor. Any plans they could form were nothing but dreams and fantasies until they reached Oreanna and saw the situation for themselves. Adel wished they could train with the sword, but they could not risk the noise drawing unwanted attention to the abandoned shop. Even conversation was kept to a bare minimum during the afternoon, when countless people milled past the shop, going about their days.

True to his word, the general returned shortly after dusk, accompanied by four of his men. They were a welcome sight to the three who had whiled away most of the day in tense silence. He closed the door behind him and ordered one man to listen for any disturbances outside. After satisfying himself with a furtive glance around the room to ensure their safe house had not been discovered, he began to speak in hushed tones.

"We will wait here for another hour or two. I don't want to be out in the streets until the night is as dark as it can get. Ola is too easy to spot, and I am too easily recognized. The men at the barracks are growing restless; word arrived from Oreanna that Idanox has placed a bounty on me as well. I don't like to think any man in my army would be tempted to claim it, but it's a risk I'm not willing to take. I hope we weren't followed here, but I didn't feel it was safe to stay at the barracks any longer. This mission will only involve those whom I trust beyond all doubt. I did not inform anyone else about our plan."

"How many men do you trust beyond all doubt?" Ola asked.

"I've made arrangements for fifty men to join us on this journey. All of them will slip out of the city through the sewers tonight and meet us near the Kival River south of the city before dawn." General McLeod sighed, his voice betraying the fact that he was quite aware fifty men would not be enough.

"If fifty is what we have to work with, then fifty will have to be enough," replied Alsea, reinforcing the confidence the trio had spent the last day building in one another. Adel wondered if she and Ola were indeed as confident as they sounded or if deep down they were flooded with the same uncertainty that plagued him. If they were, he knew they would never show it, and he hoped they could not see it in him.

Before any of them could reply, there came a sharp knock at the door of the shop. Everyone inside jumped in shock, General McLeod glaring furiously at the man who had been assigned to warn them of anybody approaching. The man peeked through the window nearest the door, then hurried over for a brief whispered conversation with the general, who at last nodded that the man could open the door. Adel tensed up as the door opened, and he noted that Ola and Alsea had placed their hands near their weapons. Following their lead, he let his hand drift close to the pommel of his sword.

The man who entered was a familiar and rather unwelcome sight. General Bern looked as ill-tempered as he had at their first meeting, his two massive bodyguards flanking him as he entered the shop. The memories of General Bern's treatment of his friends after the Battle of Kolig had done nothing to soften Adel's attitude toward the man in the months since. It appeared little had changed in the man's attitude as he shot them a brief dismissive glance before approaching General McLeod.

"What are you doing here, Bern? I told you to ready Kolig's defenses against a possible attack by the Hoyt. That was two hours ago. I cannot imagine all preparations have been made," General McLeod said, sounding none too pleased at the other man's failure to follow orders.

"Apologies, Randall. I was not aware you were leaving the barracks tonight. I looked for you in your office and then in your quarters, but you were nowhere to be found. I was worried you had abandoned us."

Adel was shocked to hear General Bern address his superior in the same sneering tone he had previously used with them.

"You dare to suggest I would abandon my men while the Hoyt are in control of the province? I am here on a sensitive mission, a mission which you are jeopardizing by following me!" Adel had never heard General Randall McLeod so angry. "Explain yourself at once!"

"Again, I do apologize, Supreme General McLeod. I meant not to interfere. I was merely trying to bring you urgent news." General Bern's eyes darted toward Adel and his friends as he spoke, sending a tingle up Adel's spine. Whatever Bern's purpose in coming here, Adel doubted it was a good thing for them. His hand inched slightly closer to the pommel of his sword.

"What news?" General McLeod asked.

"I'm sorry if this news is redundant; it appears you may have already been aware. Word came into the barracks that the Rawl wielder and his friends were spotted here in Kolig yesterday. Idanox has put a rather large bounty on them, and I was coming to ask you what we should do about it."

Adel did not dare turn his eyes away from Bern, but he could feel Ola and Alsea tensing up behind him. If

Bern had come here looking for trouble, he would not leave this shop alive. Any qualms Adel felt about fighting Thornatan soldiers did not apply to Bern. He would be all too happy to put his sword through the arrogant man's chest.

"What do you think we should do, General Bern? Should we hand them over to the man who has repeatedly brutalized and murdered our people?" General McLeod's face was livid.

"I thought we might as well hand you over as well, Supreme General," Bern announced, drawing his sword with his bodyguards following suit. "You see, I have been doing some thinking, Randall. I have found your leadership has grown rather ineffective of late. After all, what type of Supreme General allows an enemy force to seize control of his province? And less than a year after losing control of another major city no less? Perhaps if I am the one who brings the four of you to Idanox, he will see my potential as the new Supreme General. Your time is past, old man; you cannot save Thornata. You will lead us all to our deaths trying to resist the Hoyt. At this point, all we can do is adapt to our new reality. That has always been your weakness; you have never been able to recognize when you have been defeated. Lay down your weapons, all of you. I have this building surrounded. If you try to fight or escape, over three hundred men will be on top of you before you can blink. Too many even for you, magic boy," he finished with a last disdainful look at Adel.

For a moment, nobody spoke or moved. Inside the building, Bern was outnumbered eight against three. But if he was telling the truth that three hundred men were waiting nearby, the odds were severely stacked against them. Adel, Ola, Alsea, and General McLeod all exchanged glances, none of them confident enough to make the first move, all fearful of getting the others killed. It was Ola who finally acted, springing forward in one graceful leap, driving his shoulder into the nearest bodyguard and sending him crashing into his comrade so they both tumbled to the floor.

General Bern screamed out in rage, swinging his sword wildly at Ola, who seized him by the throat and flung him viciously against the far wall. Bern fell prone to the floor, his only movement a few slight twitches. The bodyguards were struggling to find their feet, but McLeod's men were on them at once, cutting them down as they tried to rise to their feet. One of them was turning to finish Bern as well when the front door of the shop was blasted from its hinges, and Thornatan soldiers came flooding into the building. There were too many for Adel to count and definitely too many for them to try to fight.

"This way!" Ola cried out without hesitation. He charged toward the far wall, slamming into the wood panels with as much force as his massive frame could muster. The wall gave way to the ogre's power, a gigantic hole splitting open and allowing the others to follow him out into the streets of Kolig.

Chapter Seventeen

The moment Adel burst from the shop and out onto the city street, it became apparent just how dire their situation was. They had emerged from the shop into a narrow side street, finding the night that would usually be silent as a crypt erupting all around them with shouting and the clanging of weapons and armor. Perhaps a half dozen soldiers were already advancing on them from each end of the street. Ola ripped his greatsword free of its sheath and was turning to engage one group while General McLeod screamed for the other to drop their weapons, all to no avail. The soldiers continued to advance, ignoring the commands of their Supreme General. General

Bern had somehow persuaded a significant number of Thornatan soldiers to betray them.

Looking desperately in every direction as more soldiers spilled toward them, Adel could see Bern had not exaggerated while gloating about how badly they were outnumbered. They needed to break free immediately, or they would never escape. More soldiers were spilling into the street on both sides, and Adel doubted even Ola would be able to fight his way through them. Fighting these men hand to hand would not end well for them; they would be overwhelmed in seconds. They were eight against a seemingly endless stream of men. He had to find another way to break them free.

"Everybody, drop to your knees!" Adel cried out, his plan still forming as the words left his mouth.

His companions did as he'd instructed, none of them questioning him for even a second. They were in a nearly impossible predicament, and they all understood trusting him was their best hope for survival. He was already summoning the power of the Rawl as they dropped, sending wind gusts rushing over their heads from each end of the narrow alley. The first two gusts knocked the advancing soldiers off-balance. The two blasts met in the middle of the street, right above their heads, and Adel worked quickly, forming the colliding winds into a miniature cyclone. Elim had told him of monstrous storms in the southern provinces that developed in this way. In some cases, they were powerful enough to level entire cities. This was the same idea on a much smaller scale. He had never used this technique in an attack before; he could only hope it would work. The cyclone fully formed, he sent it straight into the closer of the two groups of soldiers.

The cyclone struck the soldiers with shocking force, shattering their formation and sending the men careening in every direction. Some of them were merely knocked to the ground. Those less fortunate were thrown with stunning force into the wooden walls of nearby buildings. The path was momentarily clear, and Adel did not hesitate, charging forward, crying for his friends to follow him. They would have a matter of seconds before the soldiers reformed their blockade; they had to move fast if they were going to escape. He did not know where he was going, as he was unfamiliar with this part of Kolig. He only knew that staying where they were would not have a happy ending for them. If they were going to survive the night, they had to find a way out of the city. To make things more challenging, they had to do so while being pursued by the Thornatan army.

Adel reached the first intersection of the alleyway and glanced left and right rapidly, dismayed to find more soldiers approaching from each end. Unable to turn in either direction, Adel continued straight, his eyes scanning for any foes who might appear in front of him. He had the power of the Rawl readied at his fingertips, prepared to unleash another attack at the first sign of a threat. He did not slow down to look back. He could feel Ola's enormous presence directly behind him, but he dared not look back to check on the others. He knew even a moment's hesitation could be the difference between life and death for all of them. One stumble could spell disaster; he had to maintain his focus on finding a path of escape.

They were nearing the far end of the alleyway when their path was blocked again, more men appearing at the intersection ahead of them. The glow of their torches reflected off the blades of their weapons, and Adel struck once more. This time he targeted the torches of their attackers, sending the flames lashing out wildly at the men holding them. The men cried out in pain as the fire burned their faces and hands, dropping the torches and stumbling away from the entrance to the alleyway, allowing Adel and his friends to burst out into the main street uncontested.

If he had hoped their situation would be better out here, he was sorely mistaken. Men were already gathering in every direction; they were obviously trying to surround the entrance to the alleyway from which the group was emerging. General Bern, bloviating fool that he may be, had planned an effective ambush, Adel had to admit. He spun in every direction, searching for a possible escape route. The Kival River ran along the southern edge of Kolig; it was their best hope of escape.

"Alsea, which way is the river?" he cried out, praying she was still with them.

"Left!" came the response, affording him the briefest moment of relief. At least they were still together. Adel had feared they would be separated in the chaos of the ambush.

If they could reach the river, he would have far more options for using his power, and he believed it could help them escape. The army was forming up in the street to their left, blocking off the path entirely. There was no room to run around them, and dipping into another side street was a gamble. They could just as easily find themselves surrounded in a narrow place again if they tried to find a way around. Their best option was to go right through the blockade.

The street was far broader than the alleyway they had just fled through. Another cyclone might work, but in such a large area, the attack was not a sure thing. He needed a new attack, and he needed it fast. Struggling to calm himself, he let the power of the Rawl take over. He needed a way through the soldiers, and he would allow his power to find the way. Just as when he had first struggled to move the water from the jug to the goblet in the temple, he felt the power begin to take control. He let it guide him, not trying to exert his will over it, trusting it to know what was needed.

The power responded in a manner he would never have dreamed of employing on his own. Instead of directly attacking the soldiers themselves, the power of Rawl struck out at the earth beneath their feet. Not at the cobblestone of the streets, but at the ground far beneath them, turning the hard soil instantly into the softest mud. The cobblestones began to shift right under the soldiers' feet, sinking deep into the wet earth, causing the soldiers to lurch and fall in every direction. Adel sent a gust of wind tearing through their ranks as well, exacerbating the problems the men were having staying on their feet.

"Let's move!" he shouted, leading the way once more.

He raced through the gaggle of confused soldiers, weaving to avoid passing closer to any of them than was necessary. One of them grabbed at him, seizing his arm in a vicelike grip. One second and a sharp cry later, the grip released. Ola had taken the man's hand clean off before Adel could even turn to face his attacker.

Adel raced on, giving no thought to the soldier who had grabbed him. Once they were through the soldiers, he continued along the main street, running as fast as he could. As he did so, he hoped he could keep his pace up and that his continued use of the Rawl would not deplete him at the wrong moment. Collapsing from exhaustion now would be the end of him and likely his friends along with him. He had been running for several minutes when he began to worry he was heading the wrong way. It felt as though they should have reached the river by now.

"Alsea, how much farther is the river?" he asked, still not daring to slow enough to look behind him.

There was no response. Adel repeated the question, louder this time, but still nothing. For the first time, he allowed himself a glance over his shoulder. There was

Ola, right at his back as always. But looking past the ogre, his heart dropped like a stone falling into a pond; the others were gone! There was no sign of immediate pursuit, so he brought them to a halt, his eyes scanning desperately for any sign of Alsea or General McLeod.

"Ola, they're gone! Alsea, General McLeod, and his men are all gone. When was the last time you saw them?" he asked, his eyes sweeping the street desperately, searching for any sign of their missing companions. The panic was already setting in. He had not lost Alsea; he could not have!

"They were right behind me as we broke through the soldiers' blockade. Something must have happened to them after that. This is my fault. I was listening for them behind me, but my concentration was broken when that soldier grabbed your arm," Ola replied, his ordinarily steady voice frantic in a way Adel had never heard it before. "I should have noticed they were gone. I just wanted to make sure you got out of there! They can't be far away."

"We have to go back and find them, Ola. Let's hurry!" Adel said, starting back the way they had come only to find the ogre's large hand fastened on his shoulder.

"We can't do that, Adel. There are too many soldiers back there. We must trust in their ability to escape on their own. If we go back, we will be captured or killed, and then we will be of no use to anybody," Ola said, his voice calm once more, his panic already under control.

Apparently, seeing Adel go reckless had snapped him back to his senses.

At that moment, Adel had no patience for Ola's calm reasoning. All that mattered was finding Alsea. It did not matter how many Thornatan soldiers stood in his path. Any man standing between him and Alsea would not live long enough to regret their mistake. He immediately began trying to shake free of Ola's iron grip.

"Ola, we are not leaving them behind. Let go of me right now. If you don't want to come, I will go myself. We don't have time to waste standing here arguing. Let go of me, or I will make you let go of me," Adel warned, calling up his power, ready to use it on his friend if he refused to release him. Ola did not back down and did not loosen his grip in the slightest, his eyes fierce as they locked into Adel's.

"Listen to me, Adel! I don't want to leave them behind. You know me well enough to understand this. I am not suggesting that. But it is too dangerous to go back right now, and we must escape this city immediately. If they escaped, they will be waiting for us by the Kival River, like we had planned. We should go there first, and if they do not meet us there, then we will figure out our next move. But getting ourselves killed right now is not the answer; you are smarter than that. We are no use to them or anybody else if we are dead. We cannot stay here, Adel. The soldiers will be on top of us again in moments. You are the one they want more than anyone else. Just breathe for a moment. You know I am right."

As badly as Adel hated to admit it, he was right. If their friends had escaped, they could be anywhere in the city by now, and as resourceful as Alsea was, their chances of finding her were none too promising. Their best bet was to get away themselves and then find their friends later. No sooner had he furiously conceded this to himself than a cry split the night behind them.

"There they are! The boy and the ogre are over there! Take them alive if you can, but kill them if you must! They must not escape! Send for General Bern!"

The argument forgotten in an instant, they were off running again, continuing in the direction Alsea had directed them to travel in to reach the river. Just as Adel was ready to acknowledge that Alsea had perhaps been mistaken, there it was in front of them. He reached out toward the water with the power of the Rawl. He drew some from the river and released it onto the ground behind them. No sooner had the water touched the ground than he was working his power on it again, turning it instantly to ice.

Hoping his ice sheet would slow down any pursuit, he slowed his pace at last, leading Ola down to the riverbank. He was familiar with their location now. Almost all his time in Kolig had been spent near this short stretch of the Kival River. The planned rendezvous was meant to take place south of the city along the banks of the river. But the river passed right beneath the walls of the city, and if they attempted to walk, they would be spotted easily from above. Archers would cut them down if they came within sight of the walls. If they somehow eluded the archer fire, they would still be seen, and patrols would be sent after them. Adel knew from his time on the barge that the docks were a bit east of the spot they were standing, maybe half a mile. Perhaps they could find a boat there and use it to get free of the city. Ola could crouch low in the craft, hopefully disguising himself sufficiently. It was their best chance to conceal their identities as they passed beneath the walls and out into the plains outside of Kolig.

"Ola, we have to get to the docks, but if we walk, we will be fully exposed to anybody watching from the shore," he explained, hoping his friend would have an answer to the dilemma.

Ola may have had an answer, but he cried out a warning instead. More soldiers had found them and were advancing quickly. They were trapped again, their backs against the river, soldiers in front of them. Adel had not felt so frustrated since the endless pursuit of the mindless beast.

Wait. He stopped himself. *That's the answer!*

"Ola, pick me up and jump into the river right now!" he shouted. There was no time for explanations, and Ola did not argue. Grabbing Adel in his impossibly powerful arms, he sprung into the river without hesitation. They hit the water and began to sink, the water sucking them down toward the floor of the river. Adel had managed to draw in a breath as they struck the water, but he knew it would not last long. He had to work fast, or they would be forced to surface and expose themselves to the soldiers.

Adel was already using his power, working to form a platform of ice beneath them. But he knew this would not be enough; they would still be exposed to archers on the walls or the riverbanks. It took him no more than a second to form a pocket of air around them so they could breathe, but the rest of his plan would require precise work that he would have to complete rapidly. Adel worked as quickly as he could, pulling water up from the river beneath them and freezing it around them, forming a wholly enclosed ice capsule. Once or twice he thought he heard an arrow glance off the ice around him, but he could not be sure. He could only hope he had made the makeshift shelter thick enough to deflect any attack and prevent the water from breaking in and drowning them.

Once the ice was surrounding them completely, shielding them from any attack, Adel put his power to work one last time. This time he focused on the river itself, reversing and hastening its current, sending them east at a speed no boat would be capable of matching. They had to move fast; he knew there was not enough air inside the small capsule to keep them alive for more than a few minutes.

He could not see through the ice he had formed around them. All he could do was trust the instincts of his power would not allow them to collide with any objects in the river. Reversing the flow of a river was a practice Elim would no doubt discourage, but Adel had been left with few other options. He had to assume the old man would understand the gravity of the situation.

They could not see through the walls of the strange ice capsule that Adel had formed so hastily. He had been forced to make the walls completely solid in order to fully protect them from any arrows that might come their way. They had to hope the soldiers could not keep up with the rapid current.

At last, the pursuit fell behind them, and the tiny capsule of ice made its way east through the city unharmed, though its occupants were far from reassured. As they drifted upriver, Adel felt a shiver run the length of his body that had nothing to do with being submerged in a capsule of pure ice. They were cut off from Alsea, General McLeod, and his men, and they understood that reuniting would be no simple task.

Chapter Eighteen

lsea chanced a lightning glance out into the street, her eyes darting in every direction for any sign of the soldiers pursuing them. While she was pleased to see no indication of their pursuit, there was also no sign of her friends. They had become separated from Adel and Ola while racing through the blockade the Thornatan Army had formed to capture them. The shifting cobblestones had not been easy to run across while maintaining footing, even for one as sure of foot as Alsea. Two of General McLeod's men had gone down, slain by their former comrades as they tried to shield their general. The rest of them had broken through the soldiers at last, forced to kill a few in a frenzied fight to make their way out. By the time they had done so, Ola and Adel were out of sight.

The pair must not have realized their companions had not kept up, Alsea assumed. They must not have had the same issues navigating the blockade. Adel's power likely assisted him with moving through the shifting cobblestones, and Ola was as agile as anybody she had ever met despite his gargantuan size. Alsea knew her friends would never leave her behind intentionally. Perhaps it was a good thing her friends had not noticed her falling behind. They would have come back for her, which would have led to a more prolonged battle. If Adel and Ola had stopped to stand and fight, they would likely all be dead right now.

Alsea had been forced to improvise, leading them down a series of side streets, drawing on the knowledge of the various streets she had acquired during her considerable time in Kolig. She was hoping to escape but also to draw the pursuit off the trail of her friends. Putting distance between themselves and their pursuers proved to be far more difficult without Adel's powers to aid them. Alsea had spent a lot of time in Kolig and knew its streets and alleyways well, but the men pursuing them were highly motivated and were not about to allow them to slip away easily. They had wound and weaved their way through a maze of streets and alleys for what had felt like hours, attempting to break free of the pursuit. Twice they were forced to stand and fight with small groups of soldiers who blocked their path. Twice they had all been fortunate enough to escape with their lives.

When it seemed they had at last put some distance between themselves and their pursuers, Alsea had led them into a street lined with shops. Within moments, she had successfully picked the lock on the nearest shop door, and the four of them had slipped inside to hide. The shop specialized in selling leather boots, and it would be several hours before the shopkeeper would turn up, or so they hoped. General McLeod was hopeful the soldiers would not take the time to check inside each building. The army would assume they would be trying to escape the city, not hunker down inside of it.

They had remained inside the shop for several hours, hoping the soldiers would eventually give up their search. Alsea was eager for the moment she could slip out of the city and find Adel and Ola. Thus far, they had heard several patrols pass down the street outside of the shop, but none had come inside. But they would not be able to remain in place much longer. As dawn drew ever nearer, Alsea knew they would need to move soon to avoid discovery. They could not gamble on hoping the shopkeeper would be sympathetic to their plight. One look at General McLeod and the thought of collecting the bounty on his head could prove to be too tempting for a simple cobbler. One shout could alert the army to their whereabouts, and that would be the end of them.

"Is there anyone out there?" General McLeod whispered from the shadows in the corner of the shop where he crouched with his two remaining men.

"I don't see any soldiers on this street, but that doesn't mean there aren't any nearby. I think we should wait a little while longer," Alsea replied, moving back to the corner to join them. She was reluctant to do so, but better to be discovered by a boot seller than a platoon of soldiers. "I don't want the owner of this shop to find us hiding here, but I think the longer we can hold out, the more the soldiers will have dispersed to search for us elsewhere in the city."

None of them had been badly hurt in the escape, though this was more a result of luck than skill.

Not to mention Ola and Adel's fast thinking, Alsea thought to herself. The ogre had broken them free of the abandoned shop, and Adel had used his power with tremendous skill during their flight. Had the two of them not been there, the chase would have likely not had a happy ending for the rest of them. That still might've been the case if they did not find a way out of Kolig soon, and this time they would not have Adel and Ola there to save them. This only reinforced Alsea's conviction that they needed to locate her friends as soon as possible. Without the two of them, the rest of them were vulnerable. Even if they managed to join up with General McLeod's fifty men, there was not much they could hope to accomplish without Adel.

"There is a sewer entry not too far from here. It's only a few streets away. We could be there in a few minutes. When we do decide to leave, I think we should make straight for it. Adel and Ola will stick to the plan and meet us by the river. I'm sure of that much. Adel might want to come after us here in the city, but Ola is more calm and calculating. He will talk Adel out of whatever rescue mission he cooks up. We should not keep them waiting too long. I don't want them thinking we were caught and doing something reckless." It wasn't a request, and she did not want to phrase it as a question. It was what she would do regardless of whether McLeod and his men agreed with her.

"I'm not so sure that's the best move we can make, Alsea. If they've been captured, the Hoyt may have interrogated them already. If so, they likely know about our plan to meet by the river. If they do, they could be laying a trap for us by the river as we speak," General McLeod said, skeptical of her plan as she had feared he would be. But the suggestion that Adel or Ola would betray them shifted her reaction instantly from exasperation to anger.

"They haven't been captured, and even if they were, they would never sell us out!" Alsea snapped back at the general's insinuation. "How can you even think they would after everything they have done to help you fight the Hoyt?"

"Please don't take this as an insult, Alsea. I do not doubt for a second they would resist as long as possible.

But you have no way of knowing how a man will respond to the type of savagery the Hoyt are capable of inflicting. Adel is still a boy, and if you think a talented interrogator could not break him, you are sorely mistaken." The general was refusing to look her in the eye as he spoke, his gaze locked firmly on the wall. His refusal to look at her incensed her further.

"Broken? Is that the excuse you will use for the men in your army who have betrayed us to the Hoyt time and time again? What about the man who told you Idanox was in that warehouse where we would have all died if not for Adel? Was he just broken? What about the men who were chasing us through the streets a few hours ago? Were they just broken? My friends will never betray me, which is a lot more than you can say about your men, General McLeod. I will find them with or without your help, so if you do not want to come with me, it's your choice. Please don't take this as an insult, Supreme General McLeod."

She was trying to speak with as much respect as possible and falling utterly short. She knew she should not have taken that last little jab at him. General McLeod was not a bad man, and he was only saying what he thought to be true. Alsea understood he had suffered a terrible betrayal. Such a thing could not be easy for a man like McLeod to bear. He had invested his entire life in the Thornatan army, and he truly cared for the well-being of his men. To pour so much of himself into the military only for them to turn on him in the name of claiming a bounty must've felt like a dagger to the heart. He had treated Alsea with kindness and respect, but if he was not going to help her find her friends, she would not hesitate to leave him behind.

"Listen to me, Alsea, please. I meant no disrespect to Adel or Ola. I owe them my life several times over, and I have not forgotten it. But you must understand, I need to regain control of the army in this city. I cannot allow Bern to run the garrison as an extension of the Hoyt. If we retake control of the troops, I can send out search parties all across the region to find Adel and Ola. That is the right move for us to make."

Supreme General Randall McLeod was an intelligent man, which made it all the more shocking to Alsea how dimwitted he was being. She could understand his desire to take back what had been taken from him, but he must've seen what a foolhardy idea this was. He wanted to believe the bulk of his men would prove loyal when he had just received a demonstration to definitively show him otherwise. The allure of gold could make men do terrible things. She had to make him understand this. She was frustrated with him, but the last thing she wanted to see was McLeod's stubborn pride get him killed.

"General, if any of us go anywhere near the barracks, we will be killed on the spot, and that's if we are lucky. If we're less lucky, we will be dragged off to Idanox, and then we will be killed in a far slower, far more unpleasant manner. You have to understand that your men are operating out of fear right now. They fear Idanox and the Hoyt more than they fear anything you can do to them. A court-martial is not quite as intimidating as what the Hoyt will do to them and their families if they refuse to follow orders. The only way to fix this is to deal with Idanox. The only way to do it is to get out of Kolig as soon as we possibly can."

He did not respond right away, so she plowed forward. She would talk for however long it took to make him seem the truth of things.

"You sent fifty of your own men to meet us by the river, correct? If they are all as loyal as you suspect, that is the most sizeable force you will be able to muster here. It isn't enough to retake the garrison of Kolig, but if we can get to Oreanna, we may be able to make a difference there. With Adel's help, we will have a real chance of getting to Idanox. It's the only thing that's going to end this nightmare. Please, General McLeod, just stop and think for a moment. You will see I'm right. Getting yourself killed here will not do the people of Thornata any good. They need you to be the leader you have been for decades. Being a leader means accepting defeat in a battle in the name of winning a war. It's a hard choice to make; that's why it requires a strong man such as yourself to make it."

General McLeod was silent for a few moments, still refusing to make eye contact with Alsea. Her frustration aside, she could not help but feel sympathy for the man. He had spent his life in service to his army, trying to lead his men with wisdom and empathy. Every decision he had made throughout his career had been made with the well-being of his men in his heart. Now those same men had turned on him in the blink of an eye. They were trying to capture or kill him while he was forced to hide in the corner of this dark shop. She could not imagine a more painful betrayal for the career soldier.

"You are right, Alsea, as usual. We have to cut the head off the snake if we want to defeat the Hoyt, and doing that would be a tall task without Adel and Ola. Even with them, it will be an immense challenge, but one we have to undertake nonetheless. We will go to the river, as they will expect. There is one complication. I have men making their way to the river as well, just as you have said, men whom I trust. But the fact is if even one of them has turned to the Hoyt, there could be trouble waiting for us."

Alsea felt a surge of respect for General McLeod; he had needed to swallow a great deal of pride to admit that. The shop was dark, but in the shadows, McLeod's face appeared as though it had aged a decade in the year they had known each other. She had thought critically of some of the man's decision-making over that time but had never once doubted his character. He loved the people of Thornata and wanted them to be safe, and she could not fault him for that. Still, she wished he had been more care-ful when selecting which of his men could be trusted with his most sensitive secrets. This was not the first time they had been placed in a precarious position because he had put his trust in the wrong people.

"If there is trouble waiting for us, so be it. Hopefully more of those men are loyal to you than aren't. We don't have any other choice but to trust in your judgment of the men you have chosen for this mission. There is nothing the four of us can do to put an end to the Hoyt. We need help. If there is a trap waiting for us, we will fight back with everything we have. Maybe we will win, maybe we will lose, but we have to try. We owe that much to our friends. We owe it to the people who are under the thumb of the Hoyt," Alsea exclaimed, pleased to see the general nodding in agreement.

They waited for another hour before attempting to slip out of the shop. The street outside was empty, but it would not stay that way for long. With the first hint of sunlight beginning to break the eastern horizon, Alsea knew it would only be a matter of time before it filled with merchants and citizens starting their day. General McLeod was a well-known man, and he would be recognized immediately if they were spotted. They had to move swiftly, or this would be a brief escape attempt.

Alsea led them through backstreets and alleyways as much as possible, winding toward the nearest sewer entry that she knew. Twice they were forced to dart into side streets as patrols passed by, each time holding their breath in anticipation of being forced to fight. Twice they were fortunate, as the patrols passed by without noticing them.

Once they were forced to dart across a major thoroughfare, fearing the cry of a patrol that never came. Alsea breathed a sigh of relief each time but wondered how long they could expect this luck to last.

As they neared the sewer entrance, Alsea motioned for the general and his men to hide behind an abandoned building while she checked to see if the coast was clear. She confirmed their path to the sewer was clear before side-tracking back to a larger thoroughfare. There was one last thing she needed to do before leaving Kolig. She soon found what she was looking for: a small group of soldiers standing in the street conversing amongst themselves. She cautiously made her way toward them, trying to get close enough to make out what they were saying without drawing attention to herself. There was no bounty on her; she could only assume the Hoyt were not aware of her. But she had been seen the night before fleeing with the others, and if she was recognized, they would not hesitate to kill her.

"From the sounds of it, there's still no sign of any of them. The two we killed on the street last night are the only ones we've gotten," one of the men was saying. "If we haven't found them by now, odds are they're already out of the city and long gone. What a fiasco."

"You can thank Bern for that, the blubbering oaf. Say what you will about McLeod, but he's not dumb enough to reveal himself to his enemy before launching what should be a surprise assault. None of the lads can figure out why the damn fool went into the shop last night," another replied.

"He went into that shop because he's an arrogant twat who wanted to taunt his prey before he ate it. He's always been jealous of McLeod. He's always wanted that kind of respect from the soldiers, but he never wanted to go to the trouble of earning it. How did it work out for him? I don't envy him if the Hoyt find out why McLeod and that boy escaped. Idanox isn't known for his mercy no matter how hard you try to lick his boots," the first man said.

That was all Alsea needed to hear. Adel and Ola had not been found. Breathing easier than she had all night, she made her way back to the general and his men. They were still waiting in the alleyway where she had left them. She had believed they would not be found there and was relieved to discover she had been correct. She motioned for them to huddle in close so she could speak in a lower tone.

"Our path to the sewer is clear. I heard some good news on my way back. They have not found Adel and Ola. Also, General, you may be happy to hear the foot soldiers patrolling the city do not have a high opinion of General Bern at the moment."

The brief smirk that flashed across McLeod's face was unmistakable; the news was welcome to him indeed. But Bern's issues with his men were not their concern. They needed to get out of Kolig and were not likely to get a better opportunity. Not wanting to waste any more time, Alsea led the way once more, and they reached the entrance to the sewer without incident. She cast one last look around to ensure they were not seen before motioning the general and his men into the opening.

"This is not going to smell particularly pleasant," she cautioned as she led the way down into the damp tunnels. It was not a journey she looked forward to, but on she pressed, relieved to know her friends would be waiting for her at the end of it.

Chapter Nineteen

My dear friends, I have gathered you here to express my deepest gratitude for everything you have accomplished. I understand these past few weeks have been a challenge for all of you. But you have shown true intelligence and grit by joining forces with us, and the people of Thornata are better off for it," Idanox said, pouring it on rather thick. For this particular audience, he felt he needed to. "The common people of this province thank you for the sacrifices you are making on their behalf every day. History will remember you as the heroes who saved this province from endless war and death."

Idanox had gathered the Thornatan Army commanders who had joined the Hoyt at the duke's palace and was lavishing them with praise. He needed them to believe him, needed them to understand what they were doing was essential to the safety of their countrymen. He needed some of them to undertake a rather dangerous task on his behalf, and he preferred volunteers. He suspected they would perform more effectively than men who were being forced into their actions, or at least being forced more than they already were. Thus far, their assignments had been safe and relatively menial, simple tests of their cooperation. This mission would be a different story. He would be asking these men to put their lives on the line for a mission which did not make much sense on the surface.

"I am afraid I must ask a favor of you, my friends. As I am sure you are all aware, the Imperial Army has several fortresses manned along the southern and eastern borders of this province. This aggressive presence by the Empire is an overreach, an intrusion on the sovereignty of our great province. As we speak, the Empire could be using one of these bases to muster a force to attack this city. They would love nothing more than to seize back control of Thornata for the cowards who have forced it to bleed so profusely for so many years. We cannot allow this to happen," Idanox said, ignoring the expressions of shock on the faces of his lieutenants.

He had not told them of his plan before this meeting, had not wanted to be bothered with their questions.

Their opinions were irrelevant to him. His wishes were all that mattered—a fact they should have understood by now. They were there to see to his grunt work, nothing more. He saw the glances they exchanged with one another out of the corner of his eye.

The fools should know better than to question my judgment by now, he thought.

"Are you asking us to launch assaults on Imperial fortresses?" one soldier asked, a lone eyebrow arched nearly to his hairline. The skepticism was to be expected; Idanox had been aware of this coming in. What he was asking them to do was not logical. It made no sense, not even for the Hoyt. The Imperials had shown no interest in the conflict between the Hoyt and the Thornatans. Their policy had long been one of nonintervention when it came to the internal conflicts of the provinces. But he had made a deal, and it was time to uphold his end of the bargain.

"I'm afraid we have no choice, my friend. If the Imperials attack this city, it is the common people who will be hurt the most. I understand this is a terrible thing to ask of you, but would you rather ask the people of this city to bear the consequences of our lack of action? Your own families and loved ones could very well be the ones to pay the price for such a mistake. Is this something you are will-ing to ask of them?"

Idanox knew the best way to win these men over was to play to their sympathy for the ordinary people. And fear for the safety of their families, of course. He had not threatened them directly; he did not need to. They had all seen firsthand what he was willing to do when they defied him. He knew the mere mention of their families would be enough to win them over. None of them wanted a repeat of what had happened in the prison.

There was a long moment of silence, their uncertainty palpable. Idanox knew he could convince them; it was just a matter of finding the right words. One of the benefits of always being the smartest person in the room was that he could win any argument if given the opportunity. It had served him well in business and would serve him well again tonight as the duke of Thornata. These soldiers were more intelligent than the average Hoyt fighter, but it would not be enough. Idanox was always smarter, and he always had a superior argument. Clearing his throat, he launched into a final monologue that he knew would seal the deal.

"I know none of you have any love in your hearts for me, brave soldiers. There is no need to deny it. I understand the truth. Honestly, I cannot fault you for feeling this way. You did not join this cause willingly; I forced you to do so. I regret that things needed to happen the way they did. The fact is, I needed you on my side to protect the people under my rule. You may think of me as an evil man, but if I were truly evil, would I not have merely killed any who dared to revolt against me? Instead, I sought you out, seeking your help in controlling the populace, knowing all the while that you could betray me at any time. But you have not betrayed me. You have served me well, and I am truly grateful for it. More important than serving me, you have served your people well. I need five volunteers. Who here has the courage to continue defending the people who need him most?"

Idanox knew as soon as he finished speaking that he had succeeded. Their uncertainty remained, but it was apparent they were weighing their options and realizing there was no better alternative. If they did not cooperate, Idanox might have their families brought in again, and another brutal lesson would be inevitable. None of them were eager for this to happen. Better to accept the fate that would be forced upon them anyway. One man finally stepped forward, nodding his consent. It did not take long for four of his comrades to join him. Pleased, Idanox set about explaining what he needed from them.

"There are five fortresses along the border with the province of Verizia. Each of you will be responsible for evicting the Imperial Army from one of them. Gather at least a hundred men each, men who will not hesitate to do what must be done. I will assign some of my own Hoyt fighters to accompany you as well." He did not fail to notice the frustrated glances a few of them exchanged. Perhaps they had thought they would be allowed to operate without oversight. If so, they were fools. Did they really expect him to turn them loose with a hundred men each under their command?

"You may offer the Imperial soldiers the opportunity to vacate the province of their own free will if you wish. In fact, I would suggest it better to resolve this matter without violence if possible. But if they refuse, you are to do whatever is necessary to seize control of your assigned fort. I know you will not fail me. More importantly, I know you will not fail your people. Long live Thornata."

Idanox dismissed the men to gather their soldiers and make their plans. He was putting a lot of trust in men who would have been delighted to put a sword through his heart not so long ago. Actually, they would all still be just as excited to do so tonight if given the opportunity. He had to have faith that the threat of what would happen to their loved ones would keep them in line. Fear was a powerful weapon, but would it be enough to control men once they were out from under his watch? Idanox did not have enough Hoyt fighters to send on such missions while also maintaining control of the capital. Twenty men each was all he had to spare. He had considered sending smaller Hoyt forces along with one of his beasts for each group, but his creatures were of more value here in Oreanna, controlling the populace and, most importantly, keeping him safe.

"Sir, you know I would never question your decisions, but do you honestly think it is wise to launch assaults on the Imperial Army at this time? We have heard no rumors they plan to move against us. Attacking them may provoke them to strike before we are prepared to counter them. Most of the cities have still not sent any troops to bolster our defenses. We may even have to send men to put down rebellions. Historically, the Empire has preferred to remain out of internal conflicts within the provinces," one of his commanders said, some chubby fool whose name he could not recall. So many had come and gone that he struggled more than ever to keep them straight.

"I find it odd that you say you would never question me and then proceed to do so in your next breath," Idanox snapped. He had no patience for these fools. Did they not realize by now that the thinking was best left to him?

"My apologies, sir. I was merely hoping you could explain your thinking." The man had gone pale at the criticism, but it had not been enough to shut his mouth effectively.

Idanox gave a moment's consideration to having one of his monstrous bodyguards silence the fool permanently. Still, he did not have so many men that he could afford such a display for so trivial a reason. He longed for the day when he could afford to have such imbeciles killed without a second thought. Taking a deep breath, he spoke to the man with as much respect as he could muster.

"We have no men inside the Imperial Army, and we have no idea what they are thinking. We have no way of knowing if or when they intend to move against us. By forcing them out of these fortresses, we remove a foothold they could use to muster a large force inside our borders.

If we take control of the fortresses, we will then have a position of strength from which to defend against any invasion. They may stay out of our affairs; this is true. Do you suggest we leave a large well-trained military force inside our borders and just hope this will be the case? We cannot afford to assume they will not intervene. You do not wait until the wolf is at your door. You need to go out into the woods and kill it before it can pose a threat to you," Idanox explained, hoping this would be the end of the matter. His patience had its limits, and this fool was perilously close to discovering them.

"Yes, of course, sir." The man still seemed uncertain but unwilling to press the matter further. Maybe he was smarter than Idanox had suspected.

"Select our most trusted men to accompany the soldiers on these missions. Any hint of betrayal is to be dealt with swiftly and brutally. I don't think any of them will be bold enough to try it, but we can't be too careful. I want twenty of our men men assigned to each group. That should be enough to keep the soldiers in line. Now, leave me." Idanox dismissed his commanders, and he was alone at last, except for the two beasts that now flanked him everywhere he went.

Idanox retreated to the duke's private quarters, desperate for an evening of reprieve from the stress of managing the incompetent fools under his command. As soon as he had closed the door behind him, he knew it was not to be, as a shadowy figure detached itself from the wall in the darkest corner of his parlor. The chill that ran down Idanox's spine had nothing to do with the temperature of the room. He knew without a closer look precisely who it was that had come to see him. Nobody else would've dared enter his private chambers unannounced—not even the arrogant mage Srenpe.

He would have immediately ordered the death of any man for making such a bold move. But this was not a man—not in the traditional manner of speaking, at least. It was too large to be a man, large enough to be mistaken for an ogre at a distance. But as it moved closer, its features becoming more visible in the candlelight, it became clearer that this was a creature unlike any other that roamed the Empire. Idanox forced himself to look it in the eyes as its face came into the light.

The color of the skin was difficult to identify. It seemed to shift depending on where the creature was standing. The angle in which the light reflected off it also seemed to cause changes. One moment it appeared white as the purest winter snow. The next it had the yellow shade of a mountain sunflower in the spring. As the candles flickered in a different direction, the creature appeared to be more of a greenish hue. Its facial structure was mostly human, though the eyes were distinctly feline, resembling a mountain lion more than a man, cold and calculating. There was no discernible facial expression, and there had never been in any of his encounters with this creature.

The garb was also unlike any Idanox had seen elsewhere. It was incredibly minimalist in nature, clinging snugly to the creature's tall, wiry frame. It was made from a material Idanox could not identify. Black as night, it seemed to move with the flexibility of the softest silk yet also appeared to be as hard as an iron breastplate. It carried a weapon as well, the six-foot handle carved from some type of wood Idanox could not identify, ending at the top in a massive blade made of an also unidentifiable black metal. It was pointed like a spear yet also had razor-sharp edges on both sides, allowing it to be used for both slashing and thrusting effectively. Idanox eyed the blade of this weapon apprehensively as the creature advanced on him, coming to a stop within a foot of him. He would never permit any man to stand so close to him, but on this night, he dared not speak a word of protest.

The creature stared at him, unmoving, unspeaking. This was not like any other man Idanox had ever met, but this creature was not a man at all. This was a Thrawll emissary. He had wondered when this meeting would happen, knowing the Thrawll could not be happy with his failure to deliver what he had promised. While his interactions with them had been few, the Thrawll had never given him the impression of being a forgiving people. Stealing a quick glance to reassure himself that his two monstrous bodyguards were firmly in place behind him, he spoke.

"Welcome, my friend. I was not expecting to receive you this evening, but it is a pleasure to see you again.

May I offer you a cup of wine or ale?" Idanox asked in his best diplomat's voice, as though he were welcoming the duke of a neighboring province into his home. If this formality impressed the Thrawll in any way, it did not show it. He had met this particular Thrawll several times, and not once had he witnessed a change of expression cross its face. Not once had a word of kindness left its mouth. It saw Idanox and all things human as inferior to itself, a disdain it made no effort to mask.

"We can dispense with the pleasantries, Idanox. You know why I am here," the Thrawll replied, its voice scratching and guttural, as though the common language was foreign to its tongue. The Hoyt leader had once heard this creature speaking with another Thrawll in their own language. It had been nothing but a series of harsh scraping noises, and Idanox had been unable to decipher even a single word.

"I assume you are referring to our agreement, emissary? I am pleased to inform you I have just given the order for each of the Imperial fortresses along the Thornatan border to be assaulted. My men should be departing within the next few days to make it so. Everything you were promised shall soon be complete," Idanox said.

"You know perfectly well this was not our agreement, and do not dare to pretend otherwise, Idanox. You may be a fool, but you cannot plead ignorance on this matter. You agreed to launch assaults on the fortresses immediately upon coming to power. You have been in control of this city for weeks, yet your forces have not even departed. This is not to mention the fact that you assured us Oreanna would be yours by the end of last fall. Yet another broken promise. You have many pretty words at your disposal, human. You are skilled at spewing false promises. It is one of the reasons we agreed to work with you. We felt you would inspire love and devotion among your countrymen with such a talent. But a partner who does not deliver on his word to us is not a partner we will have much use for going forward. Have you anything to say in your defense, or should I cut your throat and be done with it?"

Idanox did not mistake the threat at the end of the statement as mere bluster. The Thrawll did not make idle threats. This creature would be all too happy to end his life at the slightest provocation. The Thrawll had not changed its tone or done anything to be more intimidating than it already was. Such actions were unnecessary. It was true; he had made a deal with the Thrawll. It was also true that he had failed to meet the terms that had been set. Still, they had expressed no displeasure until this moment. He had heard no word from them at all in over a year. They were aloof creatures who would no doubt prefer never to exchange words with him at all.

"Please forgive me, my friend," Idanox began before the Thrawll emissary immediately cut him off.

"We are not friends, you simpering fool. You sought out a deal with us, not the other way around, or need I remind you of that? You wanted to rule this province out of a need to satisfy your overblown ego. But you knew perfectly well you would not be able to hold it against any Imperial forces who came to reclaim it, so you came to us for help. I told the king he should have killed you for having the audacity to contact us in the first place. I told him you were a weak fool, every bit as simpleminded and blind as those you seek to rule. I suspect he is beginning to agree with me," the emissary hissed.

"With all due respect, emissary, the deal I presented to your king is mutually beneficial. Yes, I get control of Thornata, but your people get the opportunity to assault an empire at war with itself. You have the benefit of knowing one of its largest provinces will not attempt to fight against you," Idanox retorted. His failures aside, the Thrawll needed to realize the value he could still provide them. This line of reasoning was swiftly cut short.

"Do you honestly believe we need anything from you, you arrogant fool? We have business to conduct in your empire. This is true. But if you think we are not perfectly capable of doing this without your assistance, then you are an even greater fool than I assumed. We agreed we would leave this stain you call a province alone when the time for our invasion comes. But this was only if you drew the Imperial Army into mustering a force to march against you. This would allow us to conduct our business in the Empire without their immediate interference. In turn, they would have to turn their forces around to engage us before they could reach you. By the time they realized what was happening, it would be too late. We would have destroyed them before they could even understand what was happening. You have failed to deliver on this agreement. How do you intend to atone for this?" The Thrawll emissary was not one to mince words, blunt and to the point as always.

Idanox was not a man who allowed himself to be insulted, and his anger was at risk of overwhelming his fear. He stole a glance at his two bodyguards, reassuring himself that the monstrous beasts would be a match for the Thrawll if it came to a fight. The Thrawll was an intimidating presence, but it was alone in this room. The Thrawll seemed to read his mind, emitting a harsh crackling sound that Idanox could only presume was a laugh. The grating sound drew an involuntary flinch from Idanox despite his best efforts to hide it.

"Do you honestly believe I am the least bit threatened by your pets, Idanox? Attempting to unleash them against me would be the last blunder of a life that has been full of them, let me assure you of that. You are a proud man; your legacy matters to you, does it not? Know that after I kill you, every Hoyt you have tricked into following you will be shown exactly what you are: a bumbling moron incapable of carrying out the simplest of tasks. Then we will kill all of them too. They will die knowing they were taken for fools by nothing more than a cowardly con artist, one no smarter than they, who was only above them due to being born into a wealthy family. Imagine that, Idanox. This image of yourself that you have strained so hard to cultivate for so many years will be destroyed by an act of your own foolishness."

Idanox had heard stories about the Thrawll, tales of the things they were capable of doing. They possessed the power of the Rawl at the least. That alone made this a dangerous potential enemy. He had seen firsthand the damage even a single Rawl wielder could inflict, and these creatures were more powerful than that boy could ever dream of being. Another glance at the menacing weapon in its hand reminded Idanox that the Rawl might not have been the sole tool at their disposal. Setting aside his thoughts of lashing out, he decided to return to a more diplomatic approach.

"You are correct, of course, my dear emissary. I have failed to deliver on our agreement in a timely manner, and you have my sincerest apologies. Perhaps I can offer you a token of my appreciation of your unending patience with me, one which will make your patience worth your while. After all, I have wronged you, and your people deserve compensation in payment for this failure."

"We have no use for apologies, and our patience is far from everlasting, human. What type of token do you think you have to offer us? I hope for your sake that it is worth our time. Think carefully before you offer me something of no value."

"Surely a mighty Rawl wielder such as yourself has heard of the Children of the Rawl, the same group that strives to prevent your own people from finding a home here in our fine empire. You noted we have been delayed; this is true. This is largely because a young man under their tutelage has been working against us, using his powers to disrupt our ability to take control of Thornata successfully. I am sure you would very much like to see such a group eliminated. After all, I imagine they would have objections toward an empire ruled by the Thrawll. The Imperial Army may not be able to stand against you, but a group who possesses such power could be a different matter," Idanox said, hoping this would work. If it didn't, he was not likely to live to see another sunrise.

"What exactly are you offering other than excuses?" the emissary asked. If the offer interested him at all, he didn't show it. Come to think it, Idanox was not sure if the emissary was a male at all. He had met a few Thrawll, but all of them were nearly identical. Were there women among them? Did they even have sexes like a typical species, or were they all the same? He had many questions about these people he had entered an alliance with, but he doubted the emissary would be inclined to answer any of them. Forcing his curiosities from his mind, he continued.

"Allow me to continue my work here in Thornata, and I can give you this group of terrorists. The Temple of the Rawl is located in this province. I already know the region in which it lies. Give me more time, and I can give you its precise location. You and your people are welcome to eliminate them at your leisure. You and I both know the only true threat to the Thrawll is the Children of the Rawl.

Let us work together to rid you of that threat." Idanox knew as soon as the emissary allowed him to finish without interruption that he had succeeded. He tried his best to refrain from letting out a visible sigh of relief.

"Very well, Idanox. I will take your proposal back to our king, and I believe he will find this arrangement acceptable. But if you fail to draw out the Imperial Army as you have promised, or if you fail to provide us with the exact location of the Temple of the Rawl, that will be the end of our partnership. I believe you know what the consequences of this would be for you. This is the only warning you will receive. Farewell, human."

The Thrawll emissary walked around him, opening the door and vanishing into the corridor without another word. Idanox collapsed into a chair, relieved the encounter was over. He hoped none of his men would spot the emissary, though in his experience, the Thrawll had no issues with coming and going undetected. He had sought the Thrawll out years ago, using all of his wealth and resources to attempt to locate them. He had found them deep within the Thrawll Desert, but they had been far from what he had expected.

Men he could deal with. Men were predictable. But these creatures were an enigma that he had thus far failed to unravel. Enough coin could buy any man, but the Thrawll had no interest in such things. He had sought their help in helping him take control of Thornata. Instead, they'd offered merely to not wipe him out along with the rest of the Empire when the time came.

The agreement had been simple enough. Once Idanox came to power, the Hoyt were to attack the Imperial fortresses inside of Thornata. This would elicit a strong Imperial response, and the emperor would send a sizeable force to remove him from power. While the army was marching, the Thrawll would make their move. By the time the attack force turned around, it would be too late; the Thrawll would have already won. Their intentions were no secret. The Empire would effectively cease to exist, though their motives were a mystery to him. At the time, it seemed a small price to pay for the power he had always craved. It was a partnership he regretted every day, but there was no going back on it now. The emissary had said their relationship would end if he failed them again. He harbored no delusions about precisely what that meant. He would succeed, or he would die for his failure.

Chapter Twenty

It looks like we chose the right place to wait the day out. I don't think anybody is going to come up here," Adel said. His voice was barely a whisper, not confident enough in that fact to speak any louder.

They had taken refuge in a small relatively empty room on the upper floor of one of the many warehouses that lined the docks of the city of Kolig. It had taken them longer than he had hoped to elude the army pursuit the night before. By the time they reached the city docks, the morning hustle and bustle had already begun. Any hopes of procuring a boat discreetly had vanished, and they had scrambled to find a place to wait out the day. They had little choice but to take cover before somebody spotted them again. Ola stood out like a sore thumb in Kolig—or anywhere else in Thornata for that matter. Now they crouched in the shadows, hoping to avoid discovery until nightfall. This warehouse had seemed less packed full of stores than the others, and Adel had hoped it would see little traffic. Thus far, it appeared he had been correct.

The waiting was unbearable, as he wanted nothing more than to get out of the city and reunite with Alsea. This, of course, was assuming she had escaped the night before as well. If she hadn't, they could only hope she had been captured alive. If that was the case, they would immediately set about rescuing her. Adel would not allow himself to entertain thoughts that she was not alive for even a second. She had proven herself as capable as anyone he had ever met, and he was confident she had survived the flight from the army. She could survive anything.

Throughout the morning, they had heard several army patrols sweep through the docks below, asking if any of the workers had seen any sign of them. Thus far, the door of their tiny room had not flown open, so Adel assumed they had managed to slip into the warehouse without being noticed. Still, his sword lay unsheathed at his side, ready to be seized at the first sign of trouble. If the army found them again, they would fight tooth and nail until they broke free.

Adel and Ola had agreed that they would wait until nightfall when the docks were deserted once more. Once the docks were sufficiently clear, they would quietly make their way back outside and steal a small boat, as they had planned the night before. Hopefully Alsea and General McLeod would be able to wait near their planned rendezvous point south of the city. Adel would give anything to depart right away, but he knew it was not the smart move. Better to reunite with the others late than never at all. Once they were reunited, they could get back to the task of liberating Thornata from the control of the Hoyt. It was a challenge that seemed all the more daunting now that the bulk of the army had turned against them. But still, Adel knew they had little choice but to try. Allowing Idanox to remain in power was not an option he was willing to consider.

"You should try to sleep for a few hours, Adel. We still have a long time until the sun sets," Ola said.

"I don't think I could if I tried," Adel replied, knowing it would be for the best if he could. The thoughts of Alsea running through his head would never allow him to fall asleep.

He had used his powers a lot the night previously, and if he did not rest properly, he knew they might not respond when he needed them most. The prospect of running into an army patrol and having his powers fail him was not a pleasant one to consider. His sword skills alone would not be enough to get him through a situation like the one they had faced the night before. Had it not been for the Rawl, all of them would have been cut down as soon as they set foot outside of that shop.

"It's been several hours since I heard a patrol come through. Hopefully the army has concluded that if we were here at the docks last night, we are long gone by now. If so, we should have an easy enough time slipping out of here tonight," Ola said, shifting the topic.

"I hope you're right about that. If you are, it should be a relatively simple matter for us to get out of the city and down to the rendezvous point tonight. They probably think we are miles from Kolig by now, and if that's the case, they will expand their search outward and not be worried about boats leaving the docks. Of course, where we are concerned, things rarely go as smoothly as we expect."

It occurred to him that he had not given much thought to what would come after they were out of the city. They had discussed it at length while waiting in the abandoned shop the day prior, but that felt like a lifetime ago. They had assumed they would be able to travel to Oreanna with little resistance, a prospect which seemed unlikely now. General Bern seemed intent on capturing or killing them, and even if they did escape Kolig, he would not allow them to make their way to the capital without being harassed. He would bring every resource at his disposal against them. Of course, these issues were only relevant if Alsea and General McLeod had escaped the pursuit last night as well. If he and Ola were alone, their chances of being able to stop the Hoyt were virtually nonexistent.

"I keep thinking about Alsea and General McLeod. I wish we hadn't gotten separated. Do you think they escaped?" he asked Ola, unable to keep the question to himself any longer. It was a question he had avoided asking outright. Ola had a knack for brutal honesty, and Adel was not sure if he could bear to hear his honest and unfiltered thoughts.

"Alsea is quite resourceful, as is General McLeod. I have faith in their ability to escape. I also believe if they had been captured or killed, the army would likely have come through shouting it for us to hear. They would try to enrage us and draw us out of hiding. That is the type of strategy General Bern would employ, trying to bait us into a reckless reaction."

That was a good point. If the army had captured Alsea and paraded her through the streets to draw him out, it likely would have worked. He would not have been able to sit by and do nothing, and he would likely have gotten himself killed trying to save her. Still, not knowing for sure pained him more than he ever would have thought possible. There was a part of him that regretted not telling Alsea how he felt about her even though he had decided adamantly against it. He could not help but wonder if he would ever have another opportunity. If he had known how the past few days would play out, would he have made the same decision? He liked to think so, but he had his doubts.

"When you see her again, maybe you should just tell her already."

Adel jumped in shock. It was as though Ola had been reading his mind.

"Tell her what?" he asked, trying and utterly failing to appear genuinely confused. Ola could not possibly know about his feelings for Alsea, could he?

"Oh, come on now, Adel. She isn't stupid; you know that. In case you haven't noticed, Alsea can be quite perceptive. If I can see it, I guarantee you that she can," Ola replied, a sly smirk splitting his face. "Don't look so surprised. I've grown somewhat capable of reading human expressions over the years, and you are far from skilled at concealing yours. To be honest, you have been good practice for me. Your feelings for Alsea are constantly engraved on your face. I see it every time she smiles at you, every time you are looking at her when you think nobody is watching."

"If you were right—and to be clear, I'm not even admitting you are—it's not something I would be able to share," Adel said, making sure he hedged every word.

"Why not? No, wait, don't answer. Let me take a guess and see how well I've gotten to know you. As I said, it's good practice for me. Knowing what men are thinking behind their words is a useful skill for me to possess. It's because you feel that being with her would cloud your judgment, isn't it? You feel like you wouldn't be able to make intelligent decisions where she is concerned. How close am I?"

Adel had rarely seen Ola smirk so broadly, and he could not decide if the gesture amused or angered him.

"What is so bad if that is the case? Is wanting my decision-making to be based on sound reasoning instead of emotion such a bad thing?" Adel shot back, giving Ola a cocky smirk of his own. He was confident the smug ogre would have no retort to his reasoning, but all it did was elicit a chuckle.

"The problem with your line of thinking is that you are the one making all of the decisions in this relationship. You are not giving Alsea a chance to decide for herself what she is or is not comfortable with as far as these feelings are concerned. You have a protective nature about you, Adel. It's nothing to be ashamed of; in fact, it is one of your better qualities. But you have to understand that Alsea is not somebody who needs or wants your protection. She is more than capable of handling herself. You owe it to her, and to yourself, to be upfront and honest about the way you feel. It will be uncomfortable—I don't doubt that—but sometimes real leaders need to suck it up and do uncomfortable things," Ola replied, his sly smirk replaced by a more genuine smile. "Besides, you can try to shove your feelings aside all you want, but it won't work. When you ran after her in that burning warehouse after she was wounded, were you using sound judgment?"

Despite all the time they had spent together, Adel was still caught off guard by the fact that Ola had been able to decipher his feelings so easily. He privately wondered if

Ola had spent as much time trying to gain a grip on Adel's emotions as Adel had Ola's. Was he as much of a mystery to the ogre as Ola had been to him in the early days of their friendship? It had never occurred to him that humans might've been as big of a mystery for ogres as ogres were for humans. Perhaps Ola was right; his line of thinking in this matter might have been flawed. If nothing else, Alsea was his friend, a friend who had risked her life on his behalf time and time again. If he could not be upfront and honest with her, then what type of a friend was he to her?

"Thank you for your advice, Ola. I promise I will consider what you have said. Maybe I do need to be up-front with Alsea about the way I feel. She does deserve that much," Adel said. "But if I may change the subject, dusk will be upon us within hours. How do you feel about our escape?"

"I will admit I know next to nothing about boats," Ola said. "If we are going to escape on a boat, the act of sailing it is going to fall almost entirely on you. I will follow any instructions you have for me, but be warned that I may not be the best deckhand. Your Captain Boyd would probably decline to pay me much for the level of service I will be able to provide."

Adel chuckled at the thought of Ola as a deckhand. At least he would be physically strong enough to make loading and unloading the ship a speedy process. Fighting back the laughable image of Ola sweeping the deck of a shipping barge, Adel forced himself to get serious.

"We don't need to steal a particularly large craft; in fact, we will probably be more likely to go unnoticed if we take a smaller one. Large craft tend to be stopped for inspections on their way out of the cities more frequently, and that's the last thing we need tonight. At a distance, nobody will be able to tell you are an ogre, but I don't think you're fooling anybody up close. I feel bad about it, but we will leave the boat in good condition downriver. Hopefully the owner will find it after we are long gone. If the Hoyt are allowed to rule Thornata unchallenged, a stolen boat may be the least of their worries," Adel said, trying to justify his reasoning to himself as much as Ola. He was no thief, but desperate times called for extreme measures.

There was not much more to discuss; their plan was relatively straightforward. Without anything left to say, they fell back into silence, making the wait for nightfall all the more insufferable. Adel's mind was racing, thoughts of Alsea, the Hoyt, their escape, and the war ahead of them refusing to allow him even a moment of calm reflection. He found himself glancing out the window every few minutes as though expecting nightfall to sneak up on them suddenly. Their lack of a backup plan was not comforting to him, but he knew there was no other option available to him. Neither he nor Ola were familiar with Kolig's sewer system, the route Alsea would have used to lead them to safety. The city gates were no doubt being watched day and night. Using a boat was the only alternative either of them had been able to produce.

After hours that had each felt like an eternity, nightfall came at last. Ola confirmed his sharp ogre ears had still heard no hint they had been discovered, so the pair gathered their few belongings and made their way back down through the warehouse. A few hours prior, this warehouse floor had been filled with the noise of nearby docks, but now it was silent as a crypt as the two crept through the massive facility.

Adel's eyes darted in every direction as they exited the warehouse and made their way out onto Kolig's main docks. There was no sign of any soldiers—or anybody for that matter.

This is a bit unusual, he thought. There would usually be at least a few men on the docks at this hour, cleaning up for the following morning. Perhaps the patrols earlier in the day had scared the workers away. Setting aside his misgivings, he headed toward the southern end of the docks, where he knew the smaller craft were housed from his many trips to these docks with Captain Boyd.

They encountered nobody as they neared the south end of the docks, much to Adel's relief. Ola was trying his best to hunch over and appear inconspicuous, but Adel did not think the disguise sufficient to fool a soldier who knew he was looking for an ogre. The sooner they got aboard a boat, the better. With every step they took unchallenged, he breathed a bit easier. They would have a boat and be out of Kolig within minutes; everything was going according to plan. They were slipping past one of the last warehouses, the small watercraft coming into sight at last, when the silence of the night was disturbed not by soldiers or passersby, but by none other than Ola himself.

"Adel! Watch out!" he cried, followed by the noise of his greatsword being ripped from its sheath.

Adel spun to face his friend just in time to see to the shaft of an iron spear collide with the side of the ogre's head. The blow sent Ola crumpling to the ground before his sword had been fully drawn. Panic flooding him, Adel drew his own sword, spinning instinctively, knowing an attack must be coming from the other direction as well. A similar strike was coming for him. His sword came up just in time to catch the spear, an act of pure instinct. The crash of colliding metal split the night like the roar of thunder over a deserted prairie.

Behind him, he heard another distinct thud followed by the sound of a massive object crashing to the ground. It sounded as though Ola had tried to rise and been struck down again. He lashed out with his sword, trying to cut down the man attacking him. He glanced around, desperately searching for a way to utilize his power, thinking of a way to draw water from the river and redirect it into an attack. If he could scatter their attackers, they might be able to escape. No sooner had the thought crossed his mind than a voice cried out.

"Stop! Cease your attack; we want him alive!"

Adel spun toward the source of the voice, enraged to find the despicable General Bern coming toward him.

He quickly became aware of how badly the odds had been stacked against them. He had been caught completely off guard, so focused on his own attacker that he had not been aware of the two dozen men that had encircled them with spears leveled toward him. They must have hidden in one of the warehouses and somehow remained hidden until the very last moment. He didn't think anyone could sneak up on Ola, so how had they done it? Looking at his attackers, he saw that instead of their usual iron boots, they were wearing soft leather shoes, their chain mail swapped out for black cotton garb.

Clever. They managed to make themselves too quiet for even Ola to hear them until it was too late.

Ola was prone on the ground, a slight trickle of blood pooling near his head. He had managed to get his sword free of his scabbard but had been dropped before he could mount any sort of attack. Turning in every direction, Adel spotted archers positioned on the roof of the nearest warehouse. Bern did not come too close, halting with several men between himself and Adel.

Coward, Adel thought in disgust. He tightened his grip on his sword. If this was going to be a fight, he was going to take as many of these traitors with him as he could.

"Enough, Adel. You have led us on a merry chase, but it is over now, boy. Lay down your sword and surrender at once. If you attack my men again, or if they suspect you are even thinking about using your power, they will finish off your pet ogre here and now. If you surrender, maybe we will take him alive. Are you truly prepared to watch him die right in front of you?" General Bern called out to him.

He was surrounded; there was no way out—or no way that would not result in Ola being killed, assuming he was still alive at all. Adel looked down, and he thought he saw a trace of movement in Ola's neck. If there was even the slightest chance that Ola was still alive, he could not attack. Ola would never abandon him, and he knew he would never be able to live with himself if he did something to get his friend killed. A Thornatan soldier stood over Ola's prone body with the blade of a spear held menacingly a few inches from his neck.

Adel took a deep breath, struggling to fight down the sense of despair and failure that was flooding him from head to toe.

This wasn't happening; this couldn't be happening. He wanted to scream out in frustration but did not want to give his foes the satisfaction of hearing it. He dropped his head in shame, refusing to meet Bern's eyes, knowing the sneer that would be waiting for him would send him into a rage he wouldn't be able to contain. How had he been bested by such a despicable man?

With no other option available to him, Adel opened his hand and let his sword tumble to the ground in defeat.

This story will conclude in the final installment of the Rawl Wielder trilogy!

Acknowledgments

Wow, is it already time to sit down and do this again? When I released *The Path of the Rawl Wielder* in September of 2021, I could hardly believe the warm and generous response it received. Sitting here now, it is still difficult to wrap my mind around. So, another book has been completed, and once again, it is a journey I could never have completed on my own.

First, as always, my wife Mercedes, for seeing me through the chaos of releasing my first book and encouraging me to go through the madness again. If you have enjoyed my work in any way, you have her to thank for it! I can safely say that you would never have read a single word of my work if not for her love and support.

My editor, Natalia Leigh of Enchanted Ink Publishing, once again managed to turn my manuscript into something coherent (and hopefully, enjoyable to read). I suspect she will soon be far too big and in-demand to want to work with me anymore, but every bit of her success is earned and well-deserved. Natalia, your knowledge and feedback are always invaluable! Thank you so much!

How about the cover on this thing? Did Joseph Gruber knock it out of the park, or what? Joe, I don't know how you manage to keep outdoing yourself, but I'm immeasurably grateful for the hard work you have put into turning my books into works of art. If I have it my way, your incredible work will be on the cover of every book I ever write.

I must also mention the contributions of my many friends and family, who have supported me throughout this journey. I swear, it seemed as if they were trying harder to sell my book than I was! I appreciate every single one of you.

Last but certainly not least, I have to thank every person reading this right now. I hope you have enjoyed this story, and please know that the conclusion to this trilogy will be arriving soon! Thank you all for your support. It means the world to me!

~Pete Biehl

About the Author

Pete Biehl, the author of the Thrawll Saga, has been an aspiring author for as long as he can remember. This is his debut novel. When not writing, he enjoys reading and traveling. He lives in Idaho with his wife, dog, and way too many cats that she keeps bringing home, but that he wouldn't trade for anything.

Please visit:

www.petebiehl.com

www.instagram.com/petebiehlauthor

www.facebook.com/petebiehlauthor

If you enjoyed this book, please consider
writing a review!